CLASS
Clown

ALLAN EVANS

Immortal Works LLC
1505 Glenrose Drive
Salt Lake City, Utah 84104
Tel: (385) 202-0116

© 2022 Allan Evans
evanswriter.com

Cover Art by Ashley Literski
strangedevotion.wixsite.com/strangedesigns

ISBN 978-1-953491-33-6 (Paperback)
ASIN B09S6MSKJW (Kindle Edition)

This book is dedicated to my family, as well as the real life U17 soccer team that Abbey's team is based on, and to Jen. Without you, this wouldn't have been possible.

A GATHERING OF CLOWNS

THE IMPROBABLE AND THE EXOTIC AND THE SPECTACULAR OF the traveling circus became something entirely different with the departure of the young kids and daylight. Twilight moved in as the circus switched to night mode and the last show of the day began. The bright red of the soaring big tent took on a bloody hue with the arriving shadows, while the entertainers looked glamorous in an old-Hollywood way.

Yes, I was at the circus. Not what I wanted to be doing, but there I was.

Most of our day had been exactly what I expected: little kids, silly clowns, elephants and Bengal tigers, trapeze acts, jugglers, peanuts and hotdogs. We sat through three shows, my mom and I following my dad to fresh vantage points for each one, my father committed to thoroughness in his research.

This wasn't how I had expected to spend my last day before starting high school, but my father had other plans. We were having Sunday breakfast when my mother mentioned that my dad had a surprise.

"What is it?" I said eagerly through a mouthful of Cinnamon Toast Crunch. I know I sounded like a kid on Christmas, but I've always liked surprises.

"We're going to the circus today," my father said with a smile.

I didn't like that surprise, though. Did he think I was ten years old?

"Have fun," I replied. "Let me know how many clowns they fit into that little car."

"You don't want to come with us?" My father asked, a wounded expression coloring his face. Guilt began its familiar trip to join the always-present anxiety and sarcasm in my frontal lobe. "I thought it would be fun to go as a family," he said. "With school starting, we won't have many opportunities to hang out together, especially if you get on the soccer team. And, it would look more natural if all three of us went."

Wait, what? Natural?

"So, Dad, there wouldn't be more to the story here, would there?" Clearly, he wasn't being forthright with me, so I fixed my unyielding gaze on him. Believe me, I could be quite a force of nature when I put my mind to it.

As my father looked back at me with his seemingly infinite patience, I understood where my stubbornness came from.

"Constantine," my mother, ever the peace maker, murmured behind her journal.

My father sighed. "It's for an article I'm writing."

Aha, I knew there was more to the story.

"Clowns International is the oldest clown society in the world. Dating back to the mid-1940s, they've managed to keep the clowning tradition alive, while hiding some of their unsavory aspects. I'm writing a feature on their origins, as well as the bizarre history of clowns."

My father was a magazine writer who wrote investigative pieces on the mysteries of our times. He's written articles on UFOs and the Roswell crash, Bigfoot, Stonehenge, the Bermuda Triangle and my father's favorite, the Mackenzie Poltergeist. A number of people exploring the Black Mausoleum—where Sir George Mackenzie lies—on the City of the Dead tour in Edinburgh had experienced bruises, scratches and fainting spells. My father returned with a great story as well as scratches across the back of his neck. Though I didn't make that trip, I've been on many of his trips as my father's unofficial research assistant. I was no stranger to helping with his stories in some capacity.

"So, we have to be your cover while you explore the circus." I groaned. "But clowns, really?"

"Are you afraid of clowns?" my father asked. "It's okay, many people are."

Was he serious? After all, I was the girl in those scary movies who insisted on being the first to enter the haunted house. I was the girl who regularly faced down paranormal intruders. I was the ghost girl, after all, even signing yearbooks as *Abnormally, Abbey*.

I tried to read his expression as my mother studied me over her journal while she waited for my response.

"Hardly," I replied. "I've never cared for clowns, but I'm definitely not afraid of them. When you've seen what I've seen..." I let my words hang there as both parents nodded in understanding. They knew some—but by no means all—of the paranormal freak show I've had to face. But if I was being honest with myself, deep down, there was something about clowns that brought out my anxiety.

"So, you'll join us?" My father's face was almost childlike in his eagerness. How could I refuse him?

"I'm in," I answered, not realizing the chain of events that those words would instigate.

So, there I was at the circus, my rear end tired of the wooden benches after sitting through three shows. The fourth show of the day was ready to begin, and "Here I Go Again" by Whitesnake popped into my head. The Eighties was the soundtrack of my life, but not in a good way this time. While the kid in me had enjoyed the comedy of the clowns and the daring high wire acrobatics, the teenager in me had grown bored with seeing it multiple times. I excused myself, telling my parents I needed to find a bathroom before the show began.

Outside the big tent, jugglers and a hobo clown entertained the late arriving stragglers. The hobo clown gracefully slid in-between a middle-aged couple and grabbed hold of the unsuspecting wife's hand. She hadn't yet realized her husband had given up his trailing position to the clown. She was still oblivious as they disappeared out of sight into the tent. I would have paid money to see her reaction when she finally turned around.

The sprawling circus held a big tent surrounded by a sea of smaller ones housing the animals and various performers. It was organized to herd the crowd into predetermined areas, keeping them with the performers and merchants, and away from the backstage area. All the restricted areas were clearly marked with yellow corded rope, making it easy for me to find the way into trouble. I wasn't concerned about possible consequences—it was just a circus after all —so I ducked under the rope and stepped into another world, leaving behind the familiar circus noise and smells.

The backstage area was a series of corridors between the tents and trailers, an obstacle course of ropes and cords, twists and turns. The noise level dropped off considerably as I followed the well-worn path. Behind the big tent, I passed the performer entrance where women in sequined costumes, looking glamorous in a years-gone-by sort of way, crowded next to four men in tights. Obviously brothers, these men were rippling with muscle as they gyrated through some last minute stretches. A petite, but muscled Asian woman was doing the splits in the center of the group. Behind them, an older clown towered over the group. He faced in my direction and caught me staring. It was a long moment as he held my gaze while I held my breath. He continued to watch me as I stepped closer to the edge of the tent, not wanting to be discovered.

Boisterous voices grew louder as another group of men moved into view. Judging by their clothing, rough hands and rougher language, these men were roustabouts—circus laborers, in other words. I knew these men would not appreciate my transgression into their inner sanctum. And I'd rather not find out the hard way what they do with trespassers. Looking for a way out, I glanced back at the august clown, his grandfatherly features evident under his makeup. He gave me a wink and nodded to the left. Just ahead, I saw where he wanted me to go. There was a break between tents, a corridor branching away from the crowd. I gave the older clown a thumbs up and darted to safety, relieved to be putting distance between me and the laborers.

Picking up speed, I took a right, then a left, and another right, feeling like a hamster running through a maze of tunnels. When I reached the end of the corridor, I stood in awe of the marvel in front of me; brightly painted trailers and tents, looking to be the residences of the circus people, filled the large, open space. The trailers were mobile billboards advertising the performers: The Flying Cortes Brothers, Marco the Magnificent, Mystic Harmony French, Christina the Contortionist, Weary Willie, the hobo clown, and Mademoiselle Octavie LaTour. Her trailer was subtly billed as the Sensation of All Sensations, fitting for the circus' main attraction. A few people moved about the trailers, but no one seemed to care I was there. Finding myself drawn to the elegant redheaded woman sitting outside the Harmony French trailer, I moved in her direction.

A small white dog repeatedly jumped as it tried to reach an offered treat, held tantalizingly out of reach. The woman laughed and cajoled the dog to continue its efforts. With the sun setting, the nearby bonfire cast a warm light over the woman's features. Looking to be in her late twenties, her hair was a rich shade of copper, flowing in waves to embellish her glowing, cream-colored skin. Her eyes were emerald green and brightened the world around her. With a straight nose and full lips, she looked the picture of grace and perfection. She glanced up at me and smiled. "Join us," she said as she relinquished the treat to her happy dog.

Taking a seat next to her, I felt self-conscious being in the exotic woman's presence. She studied me for a long moment, her appraising eyes taking in my bright pink Pine Ridge High School top, jean shorts and flip flops. Her eyes lingered on my face as a wrinkle appeared between her eyebrows.

"There's something unusual about you, isn't there?" She said this observationally, not in a judgy sort of way. I don't like being around judgy people. Judgy people need to go away. Far away.

I shrugged in reply, unwilling to give away any of my secrets. Sharing them hasn't always worked out well for me in the past.

The redheaded woman leaned forward in her chair, her penetrating eyes looking into me. "My name is Harmony French," she said in a voice that was slightly louder than a whisper, that yet carried an air of importance. I found myself leaning in closer. "Gifted with the ability to see past the outside, I am a mystic," she continued. "Whether through intuition, instinct or insight, I can often see what others cannot." She reached out for my hand and held it with both of hers. She had a hint of a smile; the sort of smile that seemed to speak volumes about the wisdom gained from a life of seeing into others. "We have much in common, it appears."

How could I possibly have anything in common with a woman like her? My head spinning, I had zero idea what to say.

"What is your name, dear girl?"

"Abbey."

"The joy of the father." Harmony smiled again, recognizing my confusion. "Your name. Abbey means the joy of the father. You must make your father quite happy."

I shrugged. "Yeah, but I think I scare him, too."

"He's stronger than you think," Harmony insisted. "Trust him. He can be just what you need."

I found myself nodding. "I'll try to include him more often instead of keeping everything in my life to myself. But it hasn't always been easy for me to make new friends."

"We all have a desire to connect with others. It works best if you open up and be vulnerable, and then you allow people in."

"About that...I don't really let anyone in. I'm kind of a private person." Unable to stop my smile, I paused, finding myself willing to open up to her. "Well, there might be one exception."

Harmony's eyes danced as she smiled. "There is a boy, I see."

"There is always a boy," I said, looking at my nails, attempting to sound flippant.

Harmony wagged a finger at me. "But this one is special. He gets you, and accepts you for all that you are, and yet, still adores you for each fresh thing that you utter. Teenage love," she murmured.

Teenage love, I thought. *Going to the mall, wandering around hand in hand, with a silence that's comfortable. Walking around at night, for no reason at all; his chest, her head, looking at the stars. Uncertain of how long it will last, a risk you're both willing to take, even if it means having a broken heart. It's not yet true love—not like, not lust, nor infatuation. It's teenage love, here to stay, here to play with our hearts, and never go away.* Maybe a song I heard, possibly something a friend shared, but it fit.

"What's his name?" she asked.

"Turner," I replied, a warm feeling spreading across my cheeks. "We met over the summer." Turner was at camp with me, and I'd been instantly attracted to his smile and bad-boy looks.

Harmony nodded in that knowing sort of way. "Yet I sense you have an unusually strong bond. It must have been quite the summer."

That was putting it mildly. Turner and I had almost died together, trapped in a burning building at camp. We'd relied on each other, finding shared strength, as we overcame every obstacle placed in our path to safety. It was because of each other that we survived at all.

"We shared a near-death experience. That sort of thing brings people together."

He was also my first kiss.

"I see you like to downplay things." She held my gaze, her warm eyes lighting up her face. "But we both know there was more to the story than you're willing to let on." After a long moment, she looked away at something unseen in the distance. Harmony squeezed my hand as her smile faded.

"There are more challenges ahead. Larger ones. Events are escalating, and many will be drawn into the coming chaos. It won't be you alone facing the darkness. But, remember, a swirling storm must have something at its center." She paused, waiting for me.

Okay, I'll play. "And..." I offered with a wave.

"You, my young lady, will be at the storm's center. Much is riding on your shoulders. Be strong, be courageous and be decisive." She held my gaze for a moment, not saying another word. She didn't have to, as her eyes conveyed the magnitude of her message. Harmony abruptly stood and headed for her trailer, her dog trailing a few feet behind. I found myself rooted to the spot as I thought about her warning. Life sure gets complicated.

"Ahem."

A boy stood there looking at me. Wearing jeans, cowboy boots and a white t-shirt—at least, it had been white a very long time ago—with the words, *Life is a Circus* stenciled on the front. Tattoos colored his arms, working well with his tan and the grime. He wore his brown hair long and hanging into his eyes. His brown eyes. And he was smiling at me.

"Hi," I replied, feeling self-conscious as he eyed me, a smirk replacing the smile.

"It's easy to get lost around here. I can see why you may have taken a wrong turn. Let's get you back." With that, he walked away before pausing and turning. "Aren't you coming?" he asked, waving me forward, mock impatience in his body language. "I have other jobs to do around here, I can't hang out with you all night."

I hurried to catch up. He walked like he had someplace to go, making me work to keep up with him. We moved into the maze, taking seemingly random turns. After a few moments, he slowed down, allowing me to walk alongside him. "Hey," I asked, "what's your name?"

"Jake."

"Okay, Jake, what's it like working in a circus? I bet it's fun."

He slowed down a bit more and shook his head. "On stage, the performers get all the attention, but backstage, you live packed into a small space with a lot of people and a lot of smells to go along with the hard work, so the stars get knocked out of your eyes in a hurry. It's no great lifestyle. It's like living the life of a rat that is constantly moving from one place to another. You'll be underpaid and you will lose all contact with time and reality."

"So, you're in it for the glamor?"

His laugh, a loud barking sound, caught me off guard. It took a moment for him to compose himself as we made another turn. "Hardly. I grew up here. My father is the operations manager of the circus. It's all I know."

We walked in silence for a moment before Jake spoke again. "You know, I've never seen Miss French talk with anyone like she did with you. Other than her husband, she only talks during her performances. To say she is a private person isn't saying it strongly enough. I've spoken with her once in all the time she's been here. And that was after two years. Consider yourself lucky."

Unsure what to do with the information, I simply nodded. We turned another corner, to the right this time, and unexpectedly, my travel guide held out an arm, stopping me in my tracks. He put a firm hand on my bicep, pulling me back into the shadows.

A group was gathered outside a tent. Silhouetted by the overhead lights, I couldn't see who made up the group, but there were over a dozen of them. Loud voices suggested an argument was taking place. Jake's grip tightened on my arm, and he pulled me closer. I could smell his sweat, but it wasn't altogether an unpleasant scent, either. Catching my eye, Jake held a finger to his lips, making it clear he wanted my silence. No problem, as I was straining to hear what was going on, catching only bits and pieces.

"He creeps me out. And that's saying something."

"How can we trust him?"

"What if he does? What if he hurts someone? What then?"

"He's not one of us. Rellik never was."

"Have you seen the way he watches her? It's not right."

"We need to say something. We need to come forward."

Something about those words set the crowd off, and tempers overflowed. Several of the men converged on one of the smaller men, pushing him. A man jabbed a finger into the smaller man's chest. "That's not what we do. We stick together," the man spat.

The argument looked likely to become a brawl at any moment. Just when it appeared the first punch was going to be thrown, everything changed.

The strident voices hushed, and the men separated—yet the tension was more palpable than ever. The flap to the tent pushed open, and a man emerged. He paused, looking around the group without comment. The light from the tent illuminated the scene before us, and I gasped.

The man, made up in full clown makeup, was exactly what scared people about clowns. Wearing dark shades of crimson and black, his eyes were sunken pools of fury. The expression on his face —meant to be a painted smile—was a grimace of hate. His body was coiled, seemingly ready to lash out at anyone that got in his way. The other men parted and moved away, looking to put space between them and the dark performer. As the men stepped into the light, I recognized them for who they were. Despite the variety of appearances, they all had one thing in common. They were clowns. The most terrified group of clowns I'd ever witnessed.

The crimson clown left the entrance after a moment and stomped in our direction. Jake's hand squeezed my arm so hard I let out a small cry of pain.

The clown stopped in mid-stride and looked right at me, an arm's length away. Nothing was said as he studied me, my goosebumps rising as his eyes bored into me. At that moment I feared for my safety. Jake must have felt it too, because he pushed me away from the tent's shadow. "Go," he hissed, "get out of here." There was definitely an edge of fear in his voice.

Moving away from Jake and the clown, I was anxious to be anywhere else. I took the first turn and broke into a run, not stopping until I found the yellow rope and the safety of the crowd.

CAPTAIN OBVIOUS

My classes were done, and I'd survived the first day of school. Well, almost.

I'd decided that joining the school's soccer team would be a good way to make friends at my new school, and so I waited to meet with the coach. Leaning on the wall outside her office, I waited while the coach talked animatedly on her phone. She caught my eye and waved me in, pointing to an empty chair across from her as she continued with her conversation. "It looks like we're going to have a good team this season, but we're missing a strong central defender. If I get that, no way you're beating me again this year. Yeah, you too. Got to go."

The tall, blonde coach smiled and reached across her desk, offering her hand. "I'm Coach Johnson. How can I help you?"

Trying to mirror her confidence, I gave her a firm handshake in return. "My name is Abbey Hill, and I'm here to join the team. We moved to this school district over the summer." After all the physical training I endured at summer camp, I didn't want to waste my newfound level of fitness. So, if I got on the soccer team, I'd keep in shape and hopefully make some friends—a win-win. All I needed to do was convince the coach.

Coach Johnson studied me for a moment. Still attempting to mirror her confident manner, I held her gaze. I've played soccer exactly three times in my life, but she didn't have to know that. *How difficult could it be? It was just kicking a ball, right?* After a moment, she sighed and replied, "The problem is, Abbey, we've been practicing together for several weeks already. I don't know if I can throw you into the mix. I'm sorry."

It was my turn to sigh.

"Thanks for considering it, though." Feeling my opportunity slipping away, I felt my resolve grow and decided I wasn't going to give up without a fight. I stood and made to leave before turning back with a dramatic pause. "You probably have too many players in my position, anyway."

Coach Johnson hesitated before biting my hook. "What's your position?"

"Defense. Central defense." I folded my arms as I said this, clearly one tough chick.

After a long moment, Coach Johnson relaxed and smiled. "Get your gear on, then. Practice starts in five minutes." She waved me out the door as she picked up her phone again.

As soon as I was around the corner, I let loose, jumping up and down. Yes! I was in! Hopefully, my fake-it-until-you-make-it strategy would work on the soccer field.

WALKING out to the practice field, I felt self-conscious as the other girls studied me. Looking down, I knew my brand-new cleats would give me away as a complete newbie and tried to scuff them as we stepped onto the field. Instead, I ended up bumping into one of the girls.

"Walk much?" she asked, as we headed for the benches.

I glanced at her, trying to get a read on her. Sarcasm or anger? Her face betrayed little, though. What did was her hair. It was multicolored, with varying shades of red, purple, and blue. Not your typical soccer look. You know: blonde hair pulled into a ponytail. Anyone that was trying so hard to look different was someone who may be willing to accept someone who actually was different.

"Sorry, I'm new to the whole walking thing. My name is Abbey."

"Hey," she offered as a reply. After a moment, she asked, "Why are you starting now? Where have you been the last two weeks?"

"I was at camp. I only got home a few days ago."

"You look a little old for girl scout camp, but I'm not one to judge. To each their own." There was a definite twinkle in her eye.

"I wish. It was a boot camp for troubled teens. Camp ToughLove."

That did it. She stopped in her tracks, mouth hanging open. "Really?"

I nodded as she studied me for a long moment, before her impassive face broke into a great big grin. "Sweet. I'm Savannah." Perfect. Instant street cred.

DURING THE CONDITIONING and drills that Coach Johnson ran, I stayed near my new friend and followed her lead. Savannah was aggressive and physical as she competed against her teammates. The entire time, she offered me pointers to make the drills easier. If she could tell I didn't know what I was doing, she didn't spill the beans. As the practice went on, it felt like the other girls accepted me, and I was going to pull off the perfect tryout. That was, until the coach announced it was time to scrimmage.

"Okay, ladies, we only have a few minutes left, and it's time to see what you got. I want two teams, so get yourselves arranged. But I have two requests: Abbey needs to anchor the defense on one team, and I want Kelly playing against her on the other."

Coach Johnson's last comment brought a lot of buzz, and Savannah elbowed me. "You're in for it now," she whispered.

"What do you mean?" I asked her.

Pulling on a pair of goalie gloves, she said, "Hey, I don't like facing her either. I'm glad we're on the same team—except for our practices."

"Explain." But not sure I wanted to know.

"Kelly scores goals. A lot. But, being on the same team means I have to play against her in practice. If the coach puts you on opposite teams, then you are in for one tough afternoon. I'd say good luck," she added with a wry smile, "but I don't think that's going to help you, either."

"Sledgehammer," the Eighties horn driven dance-rock, blue eyed soul and funk classic from Peter Gabriel came to mind. That's what I needed to be out there on the field: a sledgehammer. I'm not talking the heavy, slow-moving kind of large hammer here, but a quick strike kind of sledgehammer that created chaos and carnage among the attackers who had the nerve to get near my goal with the ball.

But as I walked onto the field for the scrimmage, I was convinced it was going to be a short tryout. With zero idea of what to do out there, other than the obvious: a central defender played in the middle of the defense. Savannah stood in goal behind me. "So, what do I do?" I asked her, nodding toward Kelly.

"Don't let her score."

When the scrimmage game started, it was obvious right away that Kelly was going to be a challenge. Blonde and ponytailed, Kelly was the definition of confidence, as she demanded the ball. The redheaded girl with the ball immediately sent a hard pass to Kelly's feet. Her first touch put her around my defensive teammate, and just like that, it was the two of us.

Sledgehammer.

I got into a defensive stance the way the others had during our drills. Kelly paused and looked up at me, giving me the sort of smile I'd imagine a wolf might give a lamb.

"Don't let her score," Savannah called out to remind me. Thanks, Captain Obvious.

Studying Kelly, her body tensed as she leaned to her left. Okay, that meant she was likely going to the right. I lunged in that direction.

Sledgehammer.

She did go right, and we slammed shoulders as we fought for the ball. Kelly pushed back fiercely, not willing to give even a single inch. We both ran shoulder-to-shoulder towards the goal.

Putting more of my weight into our duel, I leaned hard into Kelly, thinking I could guide her away from the goal to the corner. Glancing down at the ball, my plan was to poke it away the next time she pushed it out in front of her. Savannah cheered me on. "Yeah, Abbey! You got her!"

Sledgehammer!

A life lesson I learned several years back taught me that as much as you need, want, or expect something to go a certain way, it often doesn't. This was one of those times.

Just as I made my move for the ball, it was no longer there. Kelly had pulled the ball back and cut in toward the goal. My lunge left me laying on the ground, embarrassed beyond belief. Kelly laughed as the ball rolled into the net.

My head dropped back to the ground, the song fading away. My sledgehammer days likely over. Oh well, it was a good soccer career while it lasted.

We were walking back to the locker room when a surprising thing happened. Coach Johnson came over and put an arm around my shoulder. I glanced up at her, expecting the worst. Please be gentle with me.

"Nice job out there. No one else has been able to keep up with Kelly. Welcome to the team."

She patted me on the back and moved on.

Wait. I was on the team? Unbelievable! Nothing could surprise me as much as that news. Or so I thought.

Sʜᴏᴡᴇʀᴇᴅ ᴀɴᴅ ᴄʜᴀɴɢᴇᴅ, I headed down a deserted hallway to grab my backpack from my school locker. Long shadows filled the halls of Pine Ridge High School, the last of the day's light fading away. Humming to myself as I thought about Coach Johnson's announcement, I looked forward to sharing the news with my parents. Who would have thought I'd ever be excited by organized sports?

Turning a corner, I paused at the strange sight in front of me.

A lone figure stood silhouetted at the far end of the hall. The hairs on the back of my neck jumped up and waved their little hands to get my attention. It was a lot like in class when the smarty-pants who always sat in the first row couldn't wait to answer the teacher. These hairs of mine were well trained and could recognize danger whenever it reared its ugly head.

Taking a step closer, I studied the silhouetted figure. Obviously a man, he looked large compared to the nearby lockers. But there was something odd about his appearance. Needing to get a better look, I took another step—and froze.

No way I was seeing what I was seeing.

Startled, I glanced behind to see if anyone else saw what I saw, but I was the only person there. Turning back, the solitary man was gone. Shaking my head, it didn't make any sense.

The silhouetted figure had been a clown.

JUST THE USUAL—AND CLOWNS

DAY TWO BEGAN MUCH THE WAY DAY ONE ENDED: WITH confusion. I got that I was a new student at a new school, but Pine Ridge had to be like any other high school. It should have the same general rules, same general goals, and same general type of students. Which would mean no clowns, right?

And yet, there had been a clown in my school.

The clown had to have been a ghost. I get that it may be quite the leap to be so confident it was a ghost, but this wasn't my first rodeo.

Some people attract love, others attract money or winning lottery tickets. Not me, I attract ghosts. Yep, I'm a spook magnet.

Dead people—ghosts, if you will—have been coming to me all my life. Whenever they Intrude, I interact and communicate with them best I can. Though the communication happens in a primal way, as words are rarely used.

Ghosts have appeared in our home, at church, and in hospitals. I've seen them on the bus, in a field, and on the road. But with apologies to Dr. Seuss, I have not seen them in a boat with a goat.

Ghost girl problems: it wasn't always obvious when someone is from the spirit world. Some dead people looked surprisingly alive. But, given enough time, I could usually make the distinction between a ghost and a real live person.

In this case, common sense told me the clown was a spirit, as it made no sense for a live clown to be in our school. And since I didn't believe in coincidences, logic would point to a dead clown from the circus having attached itself to me. But why?

The random clown sighting played through my mind most of the morning, severely distracting me from the teacher's lecture—though I was reasonably sure my life wouldn't be hanging in the balance due to lack of understanding the nuances of exterior angles of triangles. But to be on the safe side, I planned on being more focused on school tomorrow. However, a text from Turner pulled what little attention I had away from the teacher. My phone was in my lap to hide my no-texting-in-class rule-breaking.

Turner: How R U?

Abbey: Good. U?

Turner: Miss U. How's the new school?

Abbey: Like it. Joined the soccer team.

Turner: Wait...what? You?

Abbey: I know! It's fun though. After summer camp I didn't want to revert back 2 nerd girl couch potato

Turner: I see

Turner: Any spooky things happening?

Abbey: Just the usual. And clowns.

Turner: Wouldn't expect anything less

Abbey: Gotta go. In class.

MINE WAS the first lunch period, and I headed to the commons area where lunch was served. The hallways were full as I maneuvered through the passing crowds, looking for a familiar face from the team. I paused at the corner, unsure which direction to go, when I felt a hand on my back. The touch became a shove before I could turn around. Caught off balance, I was propelled into a group of boys, falling at their feet. The embarrassment kept me from glancing up in their direction, but my anger had me searching for the person responsible.

Only one group was close enough, and all of them were staring at me. Of the four girls, I recognized the one closest to me—the one most likely to have pushed me. It was Kelly. She had a grin on her face, as she stood there with folded arms, looking down at me. "How Will I Know" by Whitney Houston, a classic eighties song popped into my head. While I didn't want to believe it was my teammate, I didn't know who else it could have been.

A hand appeared in front of my face. "Let me help you," the boy offered. I placed my hand in his, and with a firm grip, he pulled me up. Now face to face with him, I noticed his brown eyes, blondish-brown hair and broad chest.

"Hey, you're the new girl. Where did you come from?" he asked.

Really? People have heard about me? The benefit of Pine Ridge being a small school. Woodbury was so large, there was no way you'd ever know everyone there.

"I transferred from Woodbury."

"Well, nice to meet you, Woodbury." He smiled. A very nice smile.

"Most people call me Abbey."

"Everyone calls me Max. Except for my little brother, who insists on calling me Maximilian," he added with a grin.

I glanced over at Kelly, who flipped her hair and moved away with her group. "Did you see who pushed me?" I asked Max. "Someone gave me a shove."

Max looked after Kelly and her friends. "No, but you can never trust those soccer girls. They're a sneaky bunch."

"Good to know," I said. However, what I didn't say was that I'd committed to being with the sneaky bunch of soccer girls every day. I hoped I hadn't made a huge mistake.

✦

"As you know, our first game is tomorrow," Coach Johnson said as we got to the practice field, "and we're playing Hill." Our gathered team buzzed with discussion, as Hill was a nearby private school—and you should read private as rich-kid school—and a longtime rival. "I don't need to remind you that Hill beat us last time we played them. Let's make sure it doesn't happen again."

Looking around the group, our coach continued. "Some people may say that we should be realistic, that we can't beat that wealthy team with the expensive equipment. When someone tells you to be realistic, they're trying to protect your feelings in case you don't achieve your goals. But they're missing the important part. When you dream big, you begin to take little steps to achieve those goals. You create habits and learn new things that help you grow. Even if you don't achieve those big goals, you've made tremendous strides. There's a saying that if you reach for the moon and fall short, you're still among the stars. You'll have had an amazing experience and have learned a lot of amazing things along the way. Team, let's not limit ourselves. We can beat the rich kids."

"They have the nicest uniforms in our conference," a tall blonde whispered to me. "Let's get them really filthy." Looking up at her smiling face, dotted with freckles, I couldn't help but like her immediately.

"So, let's make sure we beat them," I said to the blonde as the coach directed us to our spots for the drill.

"It's not just beating them, it's playing them so hard they never want to face us again. I'd like to leave a lasting impression. On their shins," the blonde said with a grin.

Sticking out my hand, I said, "I'm Abbey."

"Lexi." She shook my hand firmly. "I split goalie time with Savannah. She plays goal in the first half, while I play forward. At halftime, we switch."

Another girl, a tall brunette with light eyes, joined us. "What are you guys doing?"

"This is Ryan. She plays defensive midfield right in front of you."

Ryan smiled and gave a little wave. "Hi. It's my job to stop the ball before it gets to you."

"I'm Abbey. And I appreciate you making me look good."

"But, don't forget, defense is on the field to make us goalies look good," Lexi said, "Don't let them shoot the ball."

"Got it."

"We're a team." Ryan put her arm around my shoulder as we moved in front of the goal. "We play for each other. If we can make each other look good, no one can stop us."

Ryan had been drinking the coach's Kool-Aid, but I was fine with that. I liked being part of a team.

The drill had the attacking girls coming at us defending girls. Lexi's words ran through my head each time they attacked, "Don't let them shoot." I made it my mission to chase down the ball like my neighbor's terrier. Murphy's dog followed the ball every inch and never gave up. So, that was what I did every time the ball went to the central attacker. My pressure seemed to work as the player had to either pass the ball away or lose it to me.

Look at me, winning at soccer.

Everything was great until Kelly moved in from the left side. There was steel in her eye as she came at me. She changed directions at least three times as I stayed with her. Just as I realized what Kelly was doing—pulling me out of position—she rolled the ball to another player who had moved into the space she'd vacated. *Boom.* Back of the net. And there was that laugh of hers again.

EVEN THOUGH I knew I was tempting fate, I went back to the same hallway after practice, wanting to know if yesterday's clown sighting was a onetime thing. The hallway was darker today, as the sky outside was overcast. I lingered as long as I could, but nothing appeared. Not a clown in sight.

"Sure, you decide to hide today. Stupid chicken clown." My voice carried down the empty hallway. Deciding to head for home—and a mountain of homework—I turned to leave. That's when I heard something and froze.

The sound became louder as it echoed down the long and empty hallway. It was unmistakable as it got closer and closer—it was the sound of shuffling feet. The thing was, there wasn't anyone in sight.

The shuffling grew in volume as whatever it was moved right up to me. For some reason, I got the sense that it was another clown. I decided right there I wasn't going to back down, determined to stand my ground—no matter what. If something wanted to scare me, well, bring it on. I've had tougher things come after me than some circus clown.

Easier said than done. It was so close I could feel it breathing on me. The sickly sour smell was absolutely rancid, and it took every ounce of willpower I could summon to keep still. Even while I held my breath, I fully realized my answer was a short-term solution.

The hair rose on the back of my neck and I shivered when the invisible thing let out another foul-smelling breath. Wherever it came from, regular dental hygiene was not a priority.

My heart rate shot up as my fight-or-flight response kicked in. However, my body knew I wasn't going anywhere. I was only fourteen, but I was a fighter and I'd had enough. "Time for you to take your sorry clown—"

The attack came both quickly and viciously. Grabbed by the throat, I was thrown back against the lockers, my feet no longer touching the ground. Lightheaded, I likely had only moments before I lost consciousness. The stranglehold was unrelenting as I flailed my arms, attempting to dislodge my attacker's grip. The problem was obvious as I couldn't see anyone strangling me.

Have. To. Focus.

Closing my eyes, I visualized the arms holding me. I knew it was my last chance. Swallowing my panic, I focused everything on my hands and reached for where his hands should be. The second I made contact, my attacker faded, and I slid down the lockers to the ground.

Rubbing my neck, I fought to get oxygen through my raw windpipe as I processed what just happened. *It was a ghost. And an angry one at that. At my school.*

The ghosts who've come to me have been a mixed bag. Some were lost, some were angry, some had messages and some were too stupid to know they were dead. It was the angry ones that I needed to watch out for.

But the ones trying to deliver a message were frustrating. It was like they were using a blunt instrument to communicate—all subtlety gone from their communication skills.

The way it looked, I was either the recipient of a blunt instrument or I'd met up with one of the angry ones. This one could have killed me if I hadn't fought back. Sadly, I could expect more interactions like that to add a little spice to my life. Sigh.

Dear today, I wasn't born with enough middle fingers to properly tell you how I feel about you.

A SCREAM IN THE NIGHT

IT WAS MORNING, AND THE LINE TO GRAB COFFEE FROM THE Just Java stand at our school commons was long. I wasn't the only one thinking caffeine before class, as there was a line both in front of and behind me. I recognized some familiar red, purple and blue hair directly in front of me. "Morning Savannah," I offered as I tapped her on the shoulder. She turned and gave me a sleepy face, not saying anything, but not really needing to either. "I'm guessing you're not a morning person either," I pointed out.

"Mornings suck," she replied and turned back to the girl in front of her. "Sometimes people want to have a deep conversation when you first wake up in the morning," Savannah grumbled to her friend. "It's okay to hurt those people."

While I wasn't a morning person—and I seriously doubt I'd ever be—Savannah took it to a new level. Her morning demeanor, plotted on a scale, would be far closer to an angry wolverine than to a well-adjusted high school student. Clearly, she never woke up to the Wham! song, "Wake Me Up Before You Go-Go." As Eighties music goes, it was one that would get you up and dancing as you ate your morning waffles.

But you can't reason with crazy—or the caffeine deprived, so I let it go. For the moment.

IN MY SOCIAL DYNAMICS CLASS, I grabbed a seat next to Christina, the redhead from our team. She smiled at me; her bright eyes making me feel welcome. "Good morning," she said, glancing at my coffee. "That should keep you awake for the class. I'm already on my second cup of tea," she said holding up her own cup.

"Some people need the jump start more than others. I ran into Savannah this morning at the java stand. She almost bit my head off."

Christina laughed and leaned in. "I wouldn't exactly call her a morning person."

"After this morning, I wasn't convinced she's even a person. The first thing out of her mouth was telling me that mornings suck. And that was the most positive thing she said. I don't know her very well, but I'm pretty sure she's not a happy person."

Christina nodded as our teacher, Mrs. Ashby, closed her computer and pulled out a stack of paper from her briefcase. Christina leaned in closer. "Here's the thing: Something about everything sucks. The people who choose to live their lives miserably are the ones who find it. I chose not to go looking for the bad in things and I've been happier for it. It's a choice we all make." Her eyes searched mine. "How about you? What are you looking for?"

I shrugged as Mrs. Ashby moved to the front of the classroom. "I don't go looking for it, but trouble sure seems to have a way of looking for me."

Mrs. Ashby cleared her throat. "Good morning, everyone. The fundamental assumption of Social Dynamics is that individuals are influenced by one another's behavior. For example, let's say you want to fit in with a group of strangers at an event. You don't know anyone there, but you're looking to join a group to get close to a particularly high-value target."

A girl in the front row raised her hand. "A high-value target?"

Mrs. Ashby nodded. "A high-value target is someone you're very interested in. Depending on the circumstances, if you're with the CIA, it could be a member of a foreign intelligence community you're trying to connect with. If you're a highly motivated job seeker seeking another way into the company, it might be a group of Google employees. It just might be an extremely attractive man or woman you want to impress." Her last statement broke up the room with laughter.

Mrs. Ashby, a woman of that interminable age my parents were a part of, had a twinkle in her eye, and I liked her right away. She scanned the room, a subtle grin on her face. As she moved down the aisle, her eyes landed on Max, the boy who picked me up off the floor earlier. She stepped up to him, beckoning with her finger. "Max, I could use your assistance with our little experiment." He shrugged and stood up.

"Class, while I brief Max on his assignment, I'll need you to form yourselves into three different groups."

Mrs. Ashby pointed at the front of the room. "The first three rows, you'll be the honor society members. Fresh off from receiving near-perfect SAT scores, you're looking forward to making brilliant discoveries in only the nicest state-of-the-art laboratories at the most prestigious universities around the world. As you look around the room, you know that the other groups will end up working for you someday."

Walking up the aisle, she paused. "Rows four through six, you'll be members of the school's concert band, the band picked to lead the Rose Bowl Parade after winning the America's Top Band reality show. Gifted with the soul of an artist, the music you make has touched many a person's heart. When you're on stage, the audience members either want to be you or be with you." As I was in that group, I glanced around to see who else was included. Christina's was the only face I recognized.

"The last group is our student athlete group. Best of the best, these multi-sport athletes are busy sorting through the many scholarship offers they've received. Truly the stud muffins of the school, they are used to fending off the advances of the opposite sex."

Mrs. Ashby gestured for Max to step out into the hall. Pausing at the doorway, she continued, "Go ahead and move around the room, gathering into groups of your peers. I want you acting the role of a group member as you see fit. Pretend you're at a reception put on by the Governor honoring Pine Ridge's best and brightest. Have fun and get into your part. I'll be back in a moment." She followed Max out into the hall and closed the door.

There was a moment of hesitation as the class awkwardly looked around. But then everyone got out of their seats. Christina smiled and announced, "I sure like playing the saxophone." I cracked up along with some of the other students.

A boy said, "Can't get enough sax." His remark was followed by both snickers and groans.

"That's because you've never been near a saxophone—and you probably won't," a girl behind me said. Burn.

"I sure love being smart, don't you?" said one of the of honor society girls.

"It is absolutely fantastic to have such a gifted brain."

"I totally agree," a third girl chimed in. "If there were only a way to share it with those...less fortunate," she said hooking a thumb toward the student athlete group.

Max entered the room and promptly shook hands with the first guy he met. Smiling big, he confidently moved to clap the back of the boy standing near him. "Good to see you," Max said and moved across the room, high-fiving everyone he passed. Moving in our direction, Max approached us with the grin of a politician entering his home district.

"Ladies," he said, "How are we doing?" He looked me up and down. "I like your nails, they almost look real."

"Hey, wait," I said, but he'd already moved on to another group. Max sauntered around the room like he owned the place. He was smiling, laughing, shaking hands and high-fiving nearly everyone. If I didn't know better, I'd think he was running for mayor.

"Hey, Max, over here," one of the student athletes called out, as he waved to Max. Within a moment, the guy had his arm around

Max's shoulder, while another gave him a fist bump. Max comfortably interacted with everyone in the group.

Mrs. Ashby cleared her throat. "All right, everyone. Please take your seat. Nice job, Max, by the way." Max smiled and nodded to the class.

Mrs. Ashby walked to the front, hands on her hips. "My instructions were for Max to do the mayor walk, which is basically bringing energy and value to each group he encounters. Did you notice how Max's successful interactions with one group brought him success with other groups? With his confidence and positive energy, Max influenced members of a group, and in turn, the group dynamic spread to individuals around the room. Ahh, the wonders of social dynamics. Read chapter three for tomorrow."

The bell rang, and we were out the door.

PLAYING under the lights was an amazing experience. The atmosphere was crazy as we took the field. Everyone was high-fiving us as we walked out into the cool night air.

I was nervous as we crowded around the bench. Hill was Pine Ridge's nemesis since the beginning of time according to our coach. And judging by the stands full of rabid fans, it could well be the biggest game of the season. It was a minute before kickoff and everyone prepared in their own way. Savannah paced back and forth, muttering to herself as she got ready to play goal. Kelly, Lexi and Ryan looked relaxed as they joked around. Christina was hanging with Sophie, a tall blonde girl who played defense with me. Julia tightened the laces on her cleats while Haily texted on her phone. Jasmine, Bri and Fran were quiet, while Lyndsay and Greta were laughing and talking about music. Mary stretched and leaned on Jessica as they talked. Coach Johnson diagrammed on her clipboard, her forehead wrinkled with concentration. There was a definite feeling of pressure as the scoreboard clock ticked down to the opening whistle.

With less than a minute left, the coach called us into a huddle and looked each of us in the eye. "Are you girls ready to play? Hill is going to come out strong and try to run the ball right at us. They play a direct style, not much for creativity. But don't underestimate them, they are tough as nails."

Savannah looked in my direction and said, "But we're tougher," and kicked me in the shin. Hard. I gave her my best "*WTF*" look as Coach Johnson sent us out onto the field. Glancing over at Savannah, she gave me a big grin.

"Get tough."

"When the going gets tough, the tough get going." Sometimes a song title is all you need.

I got a fist bump for that one. "But don't let them score," Savannah said again. The girl was more than a little intense. If I could survive her, the game should be relatively easy.

It wasn't.

The first half featured wave after wave of attack. Hill's strategy was to play through one girl. And I was using the term *girl* loosely there. Hill's center forward more resembled bigfoot, to be honest. She was as tall and thick and as elusive as any bigfoot.

The first time the ball was passed up the middle, I knew it was headed for Balbricker, as her jersey read. I pushed up tight on her to discourage her teammates from passing to her. At the very least, she wouldn't be able to turn and face the goal. I was so close I could smell her, and I wondered if bigfoot also had a personal freshness problem. The next thing I knew, she elbowed me in the spleen and darted toward the ball, receiving and turning in one fluid motion. I was able to get a leg out and barely tipped her shot wide.

"I said don't let them score."

On my back after my less than graceful landing, I looked back at

Savannah, who—from my current position—looked upside down. "I did, didn't I? I stopped her."

"It shouldn't be that close," Savannah said with a frown. "Be a little more aggressive next time."

Getting back to my feet to defend the ensuing corner kick, I shook my head. Defense sure could be a thankless job.

The first turning point in the game came when Balbricker received the ball late in the first half. She was sprinting with the ball glued to her foot. I was right alongside her, shoulder to shoulder, trying to nudge her away from the goal. Suddenly, she yelled, "Hey," and flopped to the ground. Right away, she was up and in my face. The referee was quick to join us.

"But I didn't trip her," I protested. The referee didn't listen and blew his whistle, pointing to the penalty spot. Balbricker winked at me and picked up the ball. *Not fair, she took a dive to draw the penalty.*

Savannah was on her line in the goal, waiting for the ref to blow his whistle. For penalty kicks, it's one versus one. Goalkeepers must keep their feet on the goal line and not move until the ball was kicked. As Balbricker ran up to the ball, Savannah guessed and dove to her right. Unfortunately, the ball went into the opposite corner of the goal. As Hill celebrated, the ref blew his whistle signaling halftime.

"Next time, don't be so aggressive," Savannah said as she walked by.

Really?

The game was back and forth for most of the second half, neither team getting an advantage over the other. That was until the next turning point with ten minutes left in the game. Ryan had the ball, and after stepping around a Hill player, sent a nice pass to Greta on the outside. Sprinting forward, Greta hit the ball to our central midfielder, Haily. With a simple one-touch pass, Haily sent it to Julia who was running on the other wing. Julia took a few steps with the ball and shot at the far corner of the goal. The ball looked to be going wide of the goal until Kelly launched herself forward and redirected the ball past the diving Hill goalkeeper.

The home crowd went wild, and we had a tie game.

After Kelly's heroics, the game was back and forth with plenty of chances as both teams played for the win. The clock showed less than a minute left in the game and Hill had the ball. Predictably, they were driving it straight up the middle. Behind me, Lexi was in goal and I heard her calling out, "Don't let them score." Must be a goalie thing, I thought as I put a hand on Balbricker's back. No way was I going to let her elbow me again.

A Hill player had the ball twenty yards away as Christina pressured her, blocking her forward progress. She looked up, and I knew this was the moment they were going to pass the ball to my nemesis. Stepping around Balbricker as her elbow pistoned back, I sprinted forward to intercept the ball. Magically, the ball ended up at my feet, with Balbricker safely behind me. Since no one was in front of me, I kept moving up the field.

I looked anxiously for someone to pass the ball to, but everyone seemed to have a Hill player glued to their hip. With me being so far out of position, I didn't want to lose the ball, so my only option was to continue my forward run.

Julia was tied up by a Hill player roughly twice her size, so I continued.

The crowd counted down the seconds, "Ten, nine, eight."

Haily had two Hill girls surrounding her. I had to keep running.

"Seven, six, five."

An enormous Hill defender had Kelly tied up with an arm around her waist and her jersey clenched in a fist out of sight from the referee. Kelly looked pissed. I couldn't pass the ball to her, either.

"Four, three."

There was only one option left, and I took it. I hit the ball as hard as I could.

"Two, one."

The ball soared over the goalie's outstretched hands and dipped below the crossbar into the back of the net.

Wait, I did that?

The referee blew the final whistle to end the game, and I stood in front of the goal in shock as my teammates mobbed me.

I did that!

I'd never scored a goal before and had zero idea of what to do. Giving into the moment, I hugged the girls back as tears ran down my cheeks. Some teammates were shouting with excitement, some had tears of joy, but all of us were celebrating a rare win against the rich kids. It felt wonderful to be alive right then.

Savannah put an arm around me as we walked off the field. "Way to go, rookie. Nice game." She left me with a hard punch to the bicep, but my smile lived on. Life was sweet, I thought as I headed for the locker room, singing an eighties favorite of mine, "Walking on Sunshine." If there was ever a bounce in my step, it was right then.

A PHONE CALL to my out-of-town parents followed by a long relaxing shower meant I was one of the last out of the school. Since I was supposed to catch a ride home with Christina, I hurried out to find her. The nearby stadium lights winked off as I stepped outside on the moonless night. Beautiful by day, our school was built in a valley surrounded by a ridge of Pine trees—hence the name. Not much gets past me. However, the surrounding woods gave it a decidedly spooky feel after dark. Zipping my jacket, I headed for the parking lot, looking for Christina's car. And that was when I heard a scream.

It was a girl, and she sounded terrified as she screamed, "No, no." Her panic tore at my heart.

The scream abruptly ended as the sound echoed on the brick of the school building. I couldn't tell where the scream came from and I was frantic as I looked around, not seeing anyone. There were maybe twenty cars spread around the lot, but absolutely no one around to help. *How could I be the only person out here?* My phone was in my hand, unsure if I should call 911 before I knew what's going on. One thing was for sure though; someone needed my help.

Heading toward a cluster of vehicles in the shadows, I wasn't sure what I expected to find, but I needed to look. The sound of the girl's screams still echoed in my mind.

Glancing over my shoulder, I saw a pair of girls walking down the sidewalk from school. As they passed a light, I recognized Kelly and Sophie. I wanted to call out, but what would I say? I was worried about the girl, but what if there was someone else out here besides her? What if there was someone who caused the scream? I didn't want to endanger anyone else if I could avoid it and decided to keep quiet for the moment.

Approaching the closest car, I knelt down to look under the car, figuring I could spot someone trying to hide. The pavement was cool against my cheek as I scanned the area, but there wasn't anyone there.

After breathing a welcome sigh of relief, I grabbed hold of the door handle to pull myself up. But then...

A face showed across the glass of the car. But it wasn't a regular face. No, it was a clown face. While the face was completely white with blood red around the eyes, the mouth was the most terrifying part. Pulled back into a deathly grimace, the teeth were insanely sharp and looked capable of tearing flesh from bone. His eyes told me he was more than capable—he'd savor the opportunity to get ahold of me.

Screaming, I fell away from the car, desperate to get away. I tried to get to my feet knowing the clown was behind me, but my body wasn't cooperating. Every limb was trying to move in a different direction, which wasn't getting me anywhere.

Willing myself to take a breath, I got to my feet and ran to Kelly and Sophie. I know I mentioned earlier I wasn't scared of clowns. *Really*. But there comes a time when retreat is necessary. And I'm well aware this explanation didn't exactly cover my scream.

"Abbey, what's up?" Sophie asked with concern.

I was trying to speak, but I was winded and panicked, and my words weren't working. Kelly looked at me with concern. "Are you alright? Are you having a stroke?"

I paused, taken aback by her sarcasm. "Really?" I spat out, but I needed her help.

Grabbing her by the sleeve, I didn't give her an option, and we moved toward the car—and the clown. "Come with me, someone's in trouble."

"What happened?" Sophie asked.

"I heard a scream from this direction. It was a girl. And when I went to investigate, I saw..." I paused, unsure how to explain what I saw.

"What did you see?" Kelly asked. "Did you find her?"

"No, I saw a man's face. Through the window of a car," I paused thinking of that horrible clown face. "I was worried he may have hurt her."

The three of us approached the car and moved around to the rear. Hesitantly, I ventured a peek around the corner. There wasn't anyone waiting there. No clown, no girl. Should I be relieved or frustrated at not finding anyone? Frankly, I leaned toward being relieved.

The next vehicle was a larger SUV, a Tahoe. As before, we moved along the rear bumper and peered around the corner of the passenger side. There was nothing there, either.

The last vehicle was a silver minivan. Parked at the end of the row, it was right at the edge of the woods that bordered the school grounds. The dense woods offered too many places to hide—and that made me nervous.

"Should we call someone?" Sophie asked. "This may not be safe." *Just what I was thinking.*

Kelly pushed past us both. "No way. What are you going to say? We heard something and now we're afraid to peek around a minivan. For God's sake, we're soccer players. We are tougher than that. Way tougher." Kelly stepped around the side of the minivan and I held my breath as we followed her.

And again, there wasn't anyone there when we looked.

"I know I saw someone," I said.

"What did the man look like?" Kelly asked. "Did you recognize him?"

"No, I caught a glimpse through the windows and then I was moving fast in the opposite direction." I shrugged.

"I see," Sophie said. "You turned tail and ran."

"Well...yeah." I shrugged again.

"Hey, no judgment here. Simply keeping the facts straight."

Kelly had her cell phone out and turned on the flashlight app. "Turn yours on too. Let's see if we missed anything."

"Kelly wants to be a cop when she grows up," Sophie whispered.

We separated and headed in different directions to check the area where I saw the clown. Moving to the front of the minivan, I headed for the first car, a Mini Cooper. The flashlight helped, but didn't offer near enough light to see beyond a five-foot radius. I swung the cell phone around to make sure I wasn't missing anything—or anyone—when something grabbed my leg and I went down.

Landing hard, I rolled over frantic to shine the light on what had grabbed me. Relief flooded over me as I saw it was only a backpack. Clumsy as ever, leave it to me to trip over the only backpack in the entire parking lot. *But why was there a backpack here?*

"Hey, guys. Over here," I called.

When Kelly and Sophie arrived, I asked them the same question. "Why is there a backpack here?" In the light of our flashlights, we recognized the name stitched across the front: Christina.

Could that have been Christina I heard screaming? Lord, I hope not. If it was, I was worried about her life. "Keep looking," I said. "We have to find her."

But Christina was nowhere to be found. However in short order, we found: the Mini's passenger window a spider web of shattered glass. A cell phone underneath the Mini. And most disturbing, a smear of fresh blood running down the side of the car.

There was no longer a question of what to do. I punched in three numbers on my cell. 911.

"Police. What is your emergency?"

DREAM A LITTLE DREAM

I WAS DREAMING.

At least, I think I was. I'd laid in bed staring at the ceiling for what felt like forever. It had been difficult to get to sleep after Christina's disappearance, yet here I was walking down a hallway at school with no memory of how I got there. The sun shone unnaturally bright through the windows. People were everywhere in the halls, but no one noticed me as I padded down the hall in jeans, my school hoodie and bare feet. Everyone moved sloth-like, giving a surreal feel to the scene. Their voices sounded distant as if they were far down a tunnel. I took note of how people moved out of my way.

Turning a corner into the commons area, things were different. The daylight was gone and everyone stared at me. No one moved, they just stood in their clusters watching me. Hundreds of eyes were on me, but I didn't care. Nothing was spoken, nothing was heard. Only unnatural silence.

As I approached the gym, the crowd closed in and everyone reached out, touching me. Hands on my arms, my shoulders, my back, my hair. The touches got rougher, no longer gentle, no longer nice. I was struggling to get through, swatting at the hands, pushing back, and I slipped through and turned the corner.

The gym hallway was empty, all signs of life forgotten. The dim lights flickered. At the end of the hall, a single bulb burned unnaturally bright as it hung from the ceiling. I moved toward it, the flickering lights winking out as I passed.

There was faint music dead ahead. Soft at first, the music reached a crescendo as I made my way down the deserted hall. The music evoked feelings of the first circus I saw as a wide-eyed first grader, and I felt the dream-like nature of being a child again. But it didn't bring any of the expected joy. The music evolved from the carnival and circus-like atmosphere and melody into something wrong, something bad. It became twisted and nightmarishly evil, as the maniacal image of an evil killer clown manifested in my head.

A clown picked that moment to step into the light at the end of the hall. But he wasn't your average circus clown. No, this clown was a grotesque parody of his big-top cousins, hiding hideous malformed teeth behind terrifying circus makeup. Dark eyes burned with equal portions of hatred and madness. His hands at his side clenched and unclenched.

Dream or no dream, I couldn't take another step forward. But I didn't have to as he lurched towards me. My need to scream grew, and I hoped it'd be enough to wake me from the nightmare. I desperately wanted to hear myself scream, but instead, it was music that invaded my auditory senses.

I was rooted in place as he came for me.

The scene unexpectedly shifted, and I was outside—now thoroughly convinced I was dreaming, but unable to do anything to prevent the impending terrors. The night was bitterly cold, a strong wind whipping up the dead leaves around me. A feeling of dread washed over me, as I knew something was after me. I had to get away.

"In the Air Tonight," Phil Collins' classic atmospheric eighties song was in the background as I raced through the forest. The tree branches scratched at me like a ravenous predator. It was nearly impossible to get through the underbrush surrounding the massive oaks shooting up into the pitch of the night sky. But I couldn't stop running even if I'd wanted to—because I knew there was something right behind me. Panic took hold of my senses and shut them down. All I could do was run.

My body took a beating as the razor-like branches cut at me, but I had to get away.

Without warning or transition, the outside vanished. Instead, I found myself enclosed in a dark space.

My hands slid along the rough wood of the walls. They were close on every side, the only open area above me. I tried to move, knocking my knees against the wall. Though I couldn't see it, I felt a wall mere inches from my face. I raised my arms like the jumping jacks I hated in gym class, reaching my hands up to see if I could grab onto something. Something I could use to pull myself out of there. But there was only open space. My predicament became clear: I was confined.

Claustrophobia had never been an issue for me. But then, I'd never been stuck inside a wall before with not even enough room to sit or turn around.

My heart raced, threatening to pound a hole through my chest. Panic was coming fast, and I couldn't let that happen. Because of my bizarre life, I'd learned meditation to take control of my thoughts. When you're able to see dead people and experience the dark and gritty side of the afterlife, a little calming meditation can be a good thing.

Taking a large, slow breath, I held it momentarily, before letting it out. Again. Again. And again as I willed my heart to slow down. The accelerated rhythm slowed as it returned to normal. The calm soothed and relaxed me as I gained focus. To figure out how to escape my wood prison, I needed that focus.

The quiet had one disturbing side effect, however. I heard everything. He was so horrifyingly close I could hear his breathing. Without a doubt, I knew it was the clown. Gradually, I realized he was whispering, too. It was the same two syllables over and over. Frustrated, I strained to understand what he was saying. He was so close I should have been able to hear it.

Positioning my ear against the wall, I understood what he was saying. And my blood ran cold.

"Ab-bey." He was drawing out each syllable. "Ab-bey."

The psychopathic clown knew my name.

"Abbey." Louder this time.

"Abbey." Louder still.

Pulling my ear away from the wall, I needed to get away.

"Abbey."

His voice got louder with each syllable.

Boom. The wall shuddered from a blow—right where my ear had been moments before.

"ABBEY," he shouted.

Boom. Another blow, heavier this time, rocked the wall.

"ABBEY."

His voice, a savage growl, was the enraged fury of a Kodiak bear furious at being shot by a hunter with a death wish.

Boom. The third blow was enough to splinter the boards. Light entered my space for the first time since finding myself trapped.

"ABBEY."

His voice had lost its human quality as he screamed my name, drawing out each syllable. He tore at the wall, demolishing the structure and exposing me more and more of me with each second. Dust and debris filled the air as my unveiling fueled his intensity.

At last, the horrible mockery of a clown stood in front of me, surveying his prize. His hands clenched and unclenched with the rhythm of his panting. He took a step closer. There was evil in his voice as he smugly whispered my name one last time, "Abbey."

Paralyzed before his fury, I screamed as he reached for me.

ROUND AND ROUND

D*ON'T-TALK-ABOUT-IT,* D*ON'T-EVEN-THINK-ABOUT-IT,* NO-*seriously-stop-thinking-about-it.*

Trying to get last night's nightmare out of my head, the images were so strongly imprinted, I didn't know if they'd ever fade. The scream woke me up from the horrible nightmare that wouldn't end. Have you ever had one of those dreams that were so ultra-vivid you had to believe you were genuinely there?

Shaking, sweating and close to throwing up, I ran to the bathroom, but was able to hold things down. It was only when I splashed cold water on my face that I noticed my arms. They were full of scratches and dried blood.

Wearing a long sleeve top to school, I didn't think anyone would believe I hadn't been cutting—not that I'd be the only girl here with souvenirs of bad coping skills. I wasn't going to judge anyone, though. Sometimes life could throw more things at you than you could handle.

However, it was death that was throwing things my way these days.

First, it was the clowns, and now Christina was missing, and I was the only one who knew what was going on. My father had taught me that with knowledge, great responsibility was expected as well. Which meant it was up to me to get her back.

When the police had arrived, I told them about the man I saw through the car's window, but not the fact that he was a clown. Ghost clowns might not be a description they could work with. The police said the backpack and cell phone belonged to Christina. Though it was too early for the blood test results to come back, everyone knew whose blood it was.

Better it was unspoken, because if we said it, our worst fears might come true.

Though I'd seen plenty of dead people—or more accurately, people who were dead—I've never known anyone that had died. Except for my grandparents, but when you get to be a certain age, those things happen. Sure, I was sad, but you weren't shocked when someone passed away of old age. But having one of your friends die would be the worst thing imaginable. There's nothing I wouldn't do to save Christina.

*

Surprisingly, one of my favorite classes was an engineering class, "How to make almost anything." Class was in the Fab Lab, which stood for fabrication laboratory. The lab was a cool place where we actually got to build things. It may be something we designed digitally and created out of wood, paper, metal, even plastic with the help of a 3D printer.

We watched a video on the digital design equipment being used at MIT.

The room was dark, and not surprisingly, my mind wandered. I heard the video's voices but didn't follow what was being said. Looking around, I wasn't the only one being inattentive. Several girls were on their phones, hiding them under the table. The two guys behind me were kicking each other and trying not to laugh. A stern glance from Mr. Ahmret quieted the giggling, but didn't quite stop the kicking. Boys will be immature boys.

The shadows from the video caught my eye as they danced on the walls of the lab. It was odd enough that it gained my full attention.

The shadows were moving.

Surreal, the shadows revolved around the room and moved up and down as they went around and around. There was a pattern to what I was seeing; it wasn't random movement. It took a few moments as I whipped my head around while I tracked the shadows. But then I recognized it, and my jaw dropped. It was a carousel.

The horse was what gave it away. I recognized the riderless horses as they moved up and down and was marginally surprised there wasn't music to complete the circus merry-go-round experience. Incredulously, no one else seemed to notice. How could my classmates not see what was going on?

The video credits were on screen, which meant the lights would be on in a moment. Wanting someone else to notice it before it went away, I tugged on Max's sleeve, one of the boys that were kicking each other. "Max," I hissed, pulling him closer. "Do you see that?"

He looked around and then back at me. "See what?" His face had that distracted, *why are you bothering me* look.

The classroom lights came on at that moment, the video over. "Never mind. Just thought I saw something in the background."

The bell rang, and everyone headed for the door, hurrying to get to the next thing. I hung back, looking around.

"You Spin Me Round (Like A Record)" was a hit from my favorite decade and it fit with the phantom merry-go-round and how these strange experiences were making me feel. I was confused by why this was happening and what I should do about it.

But something was definitely happening, and there was some sort of message being sent. And, as it often happened, I was the only one who saw the message.

I hate it when that happens.

MIRROR, MIRROR ON THE WALL

"YOU USE A MIRROR TO SEE YOUR FACE; YOU USE WORKS OF ART TO see your soul."

The quote—not coincidentally—was posted on the mirror in the girl's bathroom outside my art class. We had some clever people at Pine Ridge High School.

My reflected eyes looked tired as I tucked a strand of auburn hair behind an ear. Last night wasn't a good night for sleep. Hopefully, tonight would be more restful. Maybe instead of a nightmare featuring an evil clown, I'd just have Freddie Krueger chasing me down Elm Street. It would have to be an improvement.

I decided that I needed to have a change of attitude, and the only way that would happen was if I started dancing. One of my favorite songs for this was the classic, "Blue Monday" by New Order. The drum machine programming and ramped-up synthesizers anchored by the irresistible bass line made it the perfect song to get me moving on my bathroom dance floor.

I realize that not everyone gets pumped up the same way, but for me, it was moving and grooving to the eighties. Even if I was in a school bathroom.

Closing my eyes, I could hear the music soaring through my mind. I knew every beat of the song and swayed to the beat. This was one of my mom's favorites for us to dance to. My hands raised on their own as I was swept up, losing myself to the rhythm. I found myself dancing in complete abandon of worries, fears and societal norms. My body was gloriously alive.

After I felt wonderfully energized and happy, I opened my eyes and looked at the amazing person reflected back at me from the mirror.

Unexpectedly, there was movement in the corner of the mirror. Not realizing there was anyone else here in the bathroom, I glanced behind me. No, I was alone. I had stepped out of my drawing class five minutes early, so there shouldn't be anyone coming in for a few minutes. Turning back to the mirror, it was there again.

Something moved along the edge of the mirror. A glance back confirmed my earlier observation. I was alone in the bathroom.

Taking a step closer, I bent down to see what might be causing the movement. As I got close, a face slid into view, scaring the crap out of me. And just like that, the face slid back out of view. But it wasn't my face like I'd expect to see reflected in a mirror. Of course, it had to be a clown.

What was happening here?

My mind raced. Two things struck me right away: It wasn't the same terrifying clown from the parking lot. And this clown was actually in the mirror. He wasn't a reflection—it was more like he was looking through a window at me. But he didn't feel like any sort of threat, and I relaxed. I was almost disappointed he wasn't currently in the mirror.

I tried waving a hand in front of the mirror, but still no clown. Getting an idea, I placed my palm against the mirror. Tentatively, a white-gloved hand entered the mirror and was placed underneath mine. *So cool.*

Sliding my hand up, the hand followed mine. Moving my hand slowly in a circle, the reflected hand moved along with mine. This was becoming fun.

I put my other hand on the mirror. He followed my lead and added his other hand. Another idea came, and I moved to the middle of the mirror. The clown moved to the center as well.

We studied each other for a long moment. He was a hobo-style clown. Wearing a beat-up floppy hat, he smiled at me with warm eyes. He had white clown makeup, with exaggerated eyebrows drawn in, a red bulb nose, and a black sketched-in beard. A fluffy red bowtie completed his clown ensemble. I couldn't help but smile back at him.

Moving my right hand up and then down, I watched him do the same. When he moved his other hand up and down, I did my best to mirror him. I laughed as he squirted water from a flower on his lapel and rotated his hand as if he was cleaning the glass. Minus the squirting water, I copied his motions.

He followed it up with a little dance with zigzagging arms. He had a sweet, childlike combination of shyness and eagerness.

Lowering my hands, I looked at him. He looked back out at me.

"Why are you here?" I asked after a moment. He cocked his head and raised an eyebrow.

"Are you with the other clown?" I asked him. And to clarify, I added, "The scary one." He shook his head vigorously. Something changed in his eyes, the bright twinkle dimming.

"I think the scary clown took my friend. But I'm going to get her back." I folded my arms and tried to look tougher than I felt. My father was the one who originally told me about faking it until you make it. It was a method he used when he would go undercover for an investigative journalism piece. He said if you act a certain way, people will start believing you in that role, and your subconscious gives you the necessary tools to make it a success. Sort of like the power of positive thinking on steroids.

The clown renewed his head shaking, getting more violent as he continued. He was moving his head so fast, he'd be visiting the chiropractor for whiplash first thing in the morning if he were human.

Holding my palms up, I mouthed the word, "What?"

Waving his arms, he was trying to convey something. He was shaking his head again. Didn't he want me to get Christina back?

The clown was agitated, and I decided it'd be best to end our chat, especially before someone else came into the restroom. I gave him a little wave and said, "Gotta go."

He stared back with his sad clown eyes.

I'd almost made it to the door when I heard something behind me. It sounded like a fist hitting the glass. When I turned to see, the clown stood with fists on his hip. He was the picture of defiance. He didn't say or do anything, so again I turned to leave.

Bam. He punched the glass again. I stopped and turned to face him. His eyes were dark as he stared at me.

Bam, he hit the glass, while I watched him. Incredulous, I took several steps toward him and raised a finger warily at him. *Please stop* I mouthed at him.

His eyes had more than a spark of madness. Concerned with what he may do next, I stared at him. He moved closer to his side of the glass. He had clearly boarded the crazy train and had lost most of his ability to communicate. Leave it to my ongoing soundtrack to start playing Prince's "Let's Go Crazy" in my head. But this was not a good kind of crazy.

Not at all.

Bam, he hit the glass. *Bam. Bam. Bam.* The mirror cracked with his last blow. But he didn't let up and punched it again. And again and again.

Now, the glass was cracked all around the middle and his gloves were red with blood. The sweet hobo clown I'd first encountered was no longer recognizable. His face contorted with fury as he let loose with a string of punches using both fists. The glass bowed into the restroom, out into our world. Pieces of glass fell into the sink and shattered.

"What the hell?" a voice behind me said. I turned to find Kelly standing with her mouth open. With zero idea what to say to her, I said nothing. We simply held each other's gaze.

I turned back to the mirror as a large piece of broken glass fell into the sink, blood running down the mirror's glass, my distorted reflection staring back out at us. Of course, there wasn't anyone else in the mirror now that a witness had arrived. Ladies and gentlemen, the clown had left the building.

"Abbey?" Kelly whispered in a strained voice.

My emotions got the better of me and I couldn't help but break down and cry. Dashing out of the ruined restroom, I left behind a very confused Kelly.

STERILIZING FROGS FROM 50 FEET

"I'D LIKE TO GIVE A SHOUT OUT TO ALL THOSE SELF-SACRIFICING people without smartphones. Someone has to honk when the light turns green," Lexi announced. Queen of the random comments, Lexi could be surprisingly funny. We had talked about Christina and decided that joining the team for ice cream would help us all process our feelings about our missing friend.

The clowns were a mystery and a huge source of frustration for me. I knew they were responsible, yet they continued to show themselves. If I could get my hands on one of the clowns, I would beat it with its own oversize shoe until he begged for mercy and told me where Christina was being held. And then for good measure, I would tip over his stupid little clown car. I hate clowns. Especially dead ones.

"Hey, stay in your own damn lane," Lexi called out at the woman in the blue Toyota minivan and punctuated her displeasure with her horn. I put both hands on the dashboard to protect myself in case things got out of hand. Glancing in my direction, Lexi shrugged. "Hey, if you're not cussing at others while you're driving, you're not paying enough attention to the road."

"True," I offered. "I can't wait to get my license. You make driving look so fun," I said as Lexi took a hard turn onto a country road. She looked at me like she wasn't sure if I'd been teasing or not. We rode in silence for a few minutes, both of us in our own thoughts. After a moment, Lexi turned on the radio and hummed along with an over-played song on the local hits station.

As shotgun—the person riding in the front passenger seat—it was my God-given right to be in charge of the radio. And after hearing the same song for the hundredth time over the last three days, I changed the station. Lexi looked over at me, shocked. "Hey, I was listening to that. That was my jam."

"Really? That station plays it every ten minutes, so you'll hear it again soon enough." I folded my arms smugly.

"Well, not if we're listening to *your* station," she said and hit the tuner button, bringing it back to the hits station. There was a hint of a smile playing on her face.

"You need a little more variety in your life," I suggested and pushed a tuner button at random. Country music filled the cab of her Escape. "The boys 'round here like their music country, thank you very much," I added, making a reference to the Blake Shelton song on the radio.

"Ugh. Not country." Lexi stabbed her finger at the button.

"Hey, it's your car, your presets. How was I supposed to know you'd program your radio to stations playing the kind of music you don't like?" I paused, my finger hovering over the buttons. "That would be a very blonde thing to do."

Lexi—who was blonde—laughed and held up a finger. "How do you know my hair is naturally blonde?"

Laughing, I replied, "Oh, I know. As does anyone who meets you." And then I pushed another preset button. The music was now classical. "I had no idea you were so sophisticated, Lexi. You surprise me."

"I am a woman of culture. Elegant, classy and stylish. So deal with it." Lexi cranked up the volume, and we rode without speaking for a while, as I pretended to conduct the orchestra. The music swelled and an opera-singing woman joined in. But not an amazing fat lady singing at the end of the opera kind of singing. No. It was more like a drunk woman jumping rope while singing opera through some sort of reverse auto-tune device that made things even more out of tune than they already were.

I glanced over at Lexi, and she looked ready to crack up. As the woman built toward the song's climax, I decided we needed to hear more and cranked it up even louder. The opera singer's enthusiasm didn't redeem her lack of any real talent, and the two terrified screams at the end were less at home in the concert hall than they would be in a maternity ward.

I couldn't take it anymore and switched back to the country station. "Holy crap. That woman could sterilize frogs from 50 feet. This is so much better."

Lexi smiled as she changed the radio back to the hits station. "Even better now," she said.

Laughing, I changed it back.

Without a moment's hesitation, Lexi jabbed a finger, and the radio played hits again. She was laughing, too.

And then we were laughing, jabbing fingers and pushing the other's hands away from the buttons, trying to take control of the radio.

"Oh shit," Lexi yelled and jammed the brake pedal to the floor, putting the Escape into a skid. I glanced up to see a man standing in the middle of the road with our SUV headed right at him.

It all happened so fast. We both screamed. Lexi fought furiously with the wheel, attempting to get the car back under control. We slid sideways as we headed directly at the man in the road. Oddly, the man wasn't moving at all, making no effort to get out of the way. And it was my side of the vehicle that was going to hit him. This wouldn't end well, I thought.

Surprisingly, it did.

We came to a screeching stop a foot away from the man, our vehicle sideways in the road. We'd missed him!

I glanced over at Lexi, and she was going green, possibly seconds away from throwing up. Poor thing. But I needed to get out and check on the man; he had to have wet himself out of fear. Opening the door, I looked up and froze.

"No way. No effing way." It wasn't a man in the road. It was a clown.

Whether it was ghosts, clowns, or mean people, I always stood up for myself. My mom told me about a rock anthem. "We're Not Gonna Take It," by Twisted Sister. She said people the world over embraced the song and used it for a rallying call against injustice. Like much of Eighties music, the words came to me when I needed them the most.

"We're not gonna take it," I snarled and was out of the car in a heartbeat, frustration igniting my fury as I confronted the clown. Seeing him, however, gave me a moment's pause. The clown was tall, going on seven feet. Thin as a goalpost and hunched over, he was dressed like a tramp with a well-worn hat, black coat and tails. He had the red nose and drawn in beard, but no white face. The important thing was, he was a clown—and I'd had enough.

"Leave us alone," I screamed at him. "Whatever you think you're doing here, it's wrong and has to stop." The tall clown looked down at me, his dark eyes emotionless. Taking a step closer, I watched his eyes track me. So far, that was his only sign of movement. Having no idea if he understood me, it only added to my mounting frustration. I was going to have to try a bit harder to get his attention.

Going in swinging, there was a problem with my plan, such as it was. I couldn't connect at all. He was less solid than he looked and he faded further by the moment. We could see right through him to the cornfields lining the side of the highway.

My brain started to catch up with my emotions and I realized I could use the clown to find out about Christina.

The clown continued to fade away from view, as his lower body below the knees was almost completely out of sight. Taking a step closer, I reached out with a hand, focused on making contact with him. Cold seeped into my hand, but I wasn't having much success other than that. Desperate times made me try something I normally wouldn't ever consider. I pulled Lexi from the Escape.

Judging by the vomit smell, Lexi was okay with leaving the Ford. "I need your help," I told her. "We have to hurry."

We moved to the front of the vehicle as the first approaching car came to a stop behind us. Time was running out on all sides.

The clown was still there, but looking more like a reflection on a window than a real, physical person. "What's happening?" Lexi asked, her confusion quite obvious.

"I need you to hold my hand," I told her. Hand in hand, we moved closer to the fading clown. "Reach out with your other hand and picture yourself touching this clown. Focus on your hand making contact with him."

Trying to clear all thoughts from my mind, I slowed down my breathing and focused everything on making contact as I touched the clown. My left hand was cold, and going colder by the second. The iciness seeped up my arm as my fingers latched onto his coat. The cold moved down my right arm and most likely into Lexi as well. She trembled and whimpered, which I took note of, but didn't dwell on. My mind focused on the ghost clown, now appearing significantly more substantial.

Contact made, I mentally pictured Christina while I whispered her name. "Christina. Christina. Christina."

Much like a dam bursting at the height of spring thaw, my mind flooded with images, impressions, feelings, sounds, smells, pain, color, darkness and fear. The mental onslaught overwhelmed me, making it near impossible to think. Lexi's hand squeezed mine, and I knew it hurt, but the pain wasn't registering. The freight train running through my mind engulfed me, and I would be lost forever if I didn't break free soon.

As I searched for strength, a bald eagle soared overhead. My mind wasn't my own, but I was able to follow the majestic eagle as it floated on air currents. Turning on a tight pivot, the eagle performed a breathtaking dive, absolutely screaming toward the earth. A second later it had a little creature in its talons and headed for the tall pines in the distance.

Something about the strength of that bird of prey struck me, giving me exactly what I needed, and I was able to pull away from the shadow clown. Lexi still had her hand on the clown, and I needed to break the connection. I yanked her away. Of course, the clown didn't go quietly into the night. No, there was a vortex of wind and a roaring sound before he was gone out of our lives. Ahh, freedom, I thought as we crumpled to the pavement.

IN BED LATER, I dwelled on the clown event. It may have been a mistake pulling Lexi into my world, but I didn't feel like I had any other option. The tall clown was fading away and so were my opportunities to get answers to Christina's disappearance. And so I rocked Lexi's world.

When we hit the pavement after the tall clown left our plane of existence, we both lay there stunned and drained until someone came running and helped us to our feet. Still not acknowledging the weirdness that had invaded her life, Lexi grabbed an old sweatshirt from her soccer bag and wiped up her vomit. Done, she tossed it in the backseat and climbed into the Escape—moving it to the shoulder to let traffic get by. Taking one last glance around, I joined Lexi. She held my gaze for a long moment, sighed, and headed us back in the direction we'd come from. All she had said was, "Ice cream doesn't feel right anymore." I had to agree.

UNDER THE BUS

"I GUESS ANYTHING IS POCKET SIZED IF YOUR BUTT IS BIG enough..."

Another girl answered, "I'm not saying I hate her, but I would unplug her life support to charge my phone."

Sitting in American History class, waiting for the teacher to make her appearance, I listened to the snarky conversation going on behind me. Some girls could be amazingly cruel when talking about other girls. It's kill or be killed when you're hanging with the popular crowd. Maybe it was how you existed and survived when you sat on top of the school food chain. Me, I'll take my chances eking out a lower profile existence.

Mrs. Sparrow came bustling into the classroom, and as usual, a cloud of chaos was her constant companion. I love her, but she was so unorganized and her unintended consequences always made me smile. "I have your homework to return to you," she said, and tossed a pile of papers onto the edge of her desk. They promptly fell off the edge and landed in the wastebasket below. Peering over her desk, Mrs. Sparrow frowned and said, "Oops. Sorry about that."

A minute later she wrote a timeline of the American Revolution on the chalkboard. She finished and backed up, studying it. She shook her head and wiped away the middle third with an eraser. Turning around, she made a beeline to her oversized bag. She had that *I'm going to sneeze* look and grabbed a tissue just in time. "Excuse me," she said through the tissue and proceeded to give a loud honk as she blew her nose. After tossing it into the wastebasket, she paused. "Oh, dear. Be careful when you get your homework." Like I said, unintended consequences.

Lexi sat two seats across from me, close to the door. She nodded and smiled at me when she came in, but we hadn't talked since the clown fiasco. It has been my experience that some people, when faced with the impossible, simply put it out of their head. They don't want to deal with it, talk about it, or even think about it. If it violates their view of how the world should be, they shut it away. I hadn't imagined Lexi as being closed minded, but you never know.

Movement caught my eye as someone passed by outside the closed door. Because the glass was frosted, I couldn't see who it was, just their outline. It wasn't unusual to see an occasional passerby, but not one so freakishly tall. After yesterday, I was more than a little wary of tall people. Especially tall people wearing hats. And definitely tall people wearing hats who were clowns.

The thing was, I could've sworn the tall passerby had been wearing a hat.

I tried catching Lexi's eye, but she was focused on Mrs. Sparrow's lecture—the lecture I hadn't caught a single word of. My bad. How I was going to pass any of my classes with all that had been going on, well, that was going to take a miracle.

Another someone moved past the door headed in the same direction. Relief coursed through me as I took in the relatively short and stocky stature of the passerby. My relief was short lived, however. Another person went by with some unusually shaped hair. A very tall person—who was definitely wearing a hat—followed that one.

Fidgeting, I was beside myself sitting in my chair, stuck in class. And I was the only one who saw what was going on outside the door. Of course, Lexi wouldn't look in my direction, and it drove me nuts.

Trying to not be obvious, I shifted in my chair to get a better view. Holy guacamole, what I watched through the window pane was ridiculous. There was absolutely no doubt they were clowns. It was one after another, all shapes and sizes. There had to be a parade out there. Two shorter clowns followed the tall one, with a heavy-set one and three more progressively taller figures coming next. Unbelievably, the tall one with the hat went by again. The parade was non-stop now, and the clowns followed each other closer and closer. There was the tall one again!

I coughed, hoping Lexi would look in my direction. She did not. I coughed again, louder this time. Grace, who sat between us, glanced in my direction and sniffed. But Lexi was still occupied with the teacher's lecture, which might be about the American Revolution. I'd have to get Lexi's notes to know for sure.

It looked to be a crowd passing our classroom door now. Coughing again, I tried to make it even louder. Andrew, who was sitting behind me, tapped me on the shoulder and handed me a cough drop, "Maybe you should quit smoking—or at least switch to a filtered cigarette."

Several comebacks came to mind, but I let it go. He may not realize it, but Andrew had helped after all. I reach out a hand and tapped Grace's arm. Gesturing for her to lean back, I threw the cough drop right past Grace and hit Lexi with it. She was startled and jumped, but thankfully looked in my direction. Finally.

Nodding toward the door, Lexi tensed up instantly when she saw the freak parade going on in the hall. She whipped her head back around, confusion and fear coloring her expression. I turned up my palms, gesturing that I had no idea what it meant or what we should do about it. Grace looked toward the door as well.

The bell rang, and everyone headed towards the door, but Bri was there first. Holding my breath as she pulled the door open, I expected her to scream. But the only people out in the hall were students. Not a single clown in sight.

WALKING AMONG MY CLASSMATES, I felt like I was living in a different world. The ironic thing was, the different world had come to invade ours, not the other way around. The question was why?

What brought them here? There had to be a reason—there always was.

As I processed the afternoon's strangeness, I felt a bump. "Hey," Kelly said as I glanced in her direction.

Not sure what to say, I replied with, "Hey."

She held my gaze for a moment, until we turned a corner, headed for our English class. "What was that about in the bathroom yesterday? Not gonna lie, it was pretty out-there."

I took a deep breath and looked at Kelly. She was the kind of girl most of us want to be. She's beautiful, with a figure that was quite capable of stopping traffic, athletic, confident, outgoing, and popular. If that wasn't enough, she had a mental toughness that wouldn't settle for anything less than getting exactly what she wanted. I asked her the question that ate at me. "Did you tell anyone?"

She shook her head. "It's not my place to say anything. Besides, what would I tell them? Abbey went all She-Hulk on the girl's restroom? No, it's just between us."

I nodded. "Thank you."

Outside our English classroom, Kelly paused and gave me a determined look that told me she wasn't going to let me off so easily. "So, what happened?"

The bell rang, saving me. "We'll talk later," I said quickly, and we entered the classroom and took our seats. Saved by the bell.

We were discussing *To Kill a Mockingbird*, one of those novels everyone had to read during their high school years. My father said it's been a staple in every school for the last 40 years. There was a picture of Atticus Finch addressing the jury from the movie adaptation projected on the smart board at the front of the class. And on the left chalkboard, written in fancy lettering, was the book's title. Mr. Karp expounded on the book's exploration of the moral nature of human beings.

"The moral voice of To Kill a Mockingbird is embodied by Atticus Finch, who is virtually unique in the novel in that he experiences and understands evil without losing his faith in the human capacity for goodness. Atticus understands that rather than being simply creatures of good or creatures of evil, most people have both good and bad qualities." Mr. Karp walked down the center aisle and cleaned his glasses with a cloth pulled from his back pocket. He paused and looked at our faces, one by one, before stopping at Kelly. "The important thing is to appreciate the good qualities and understand the bad qualities by treating others with sympathy and trying to see life from their perspective."

Putting his glasses back on, he smiled and asked a question of Kelly. "Why do you suppose he—Atticus Finch—teaches this ultimate moral lesson to Scout and Jem?"

Kelly nodded, looking up at our teacher. Mr. Karp was well liked, because of his easy-going manner. He was never confrontational and always supportive. "I suppose," she began, "To show them that it's possible to live with a conscience without losing hope or becoming cynical."

"Perfect answer, Ms. Nelson. High five." He held up a hand, and she gave it a satisfying slap. Mr. Karp walked back up the aisle, turning off several of the lights, leaving a single spot shining down on the desk. He leaned against his desk and reached behind him, pulling out a dog-eared copy of the book. The light shone directly on him, fittingly like an actor on the stage. Finding his page, Mr. Karp sets aside his bookmark and looked up. "During his closing remarks, Atticus seems to hold out hope for the town of Maycomb—significantly, his eloquent closing argument is devoid of despair. Rather, he speaks to the jury with confidence and dignity, urging them to find the same confidence and dignity within themselves."

Mr. Karp cleared his throat and began reading. "*We looked down again. Atticus was speaking easily, with the kind of detachment he used when he dictated a letter. He walked slowly up and down in front of the jury, and the jury seemed to be attentive: their heads were up, and they followed Atticus's route with what seemed to be appreciation. I guess it was because Atticus wasn't a thunderer.*"

There was a noise behind Mr. Karp and I strained to hear it between his words.

"Atticus paused, then he did something he didn't ordinarily do. He unhitched his watch and chain and placed them on the table, saying, 'With the court's permission.'"

The sound got louder. When I got that spine-tingling, hair-raising reaction that only nails on a chalkboard could bring, I recognized it. Our classroom had one of the electronic whiteboards on the right and an old-fashioned chalkboard on the left, which was totally obscured in shadow. That was where the sounds came from.

But there wasn't anyone back by the board.

"Judge Taylor nodded, and then Atticus did something I never saw him do before or since, in public or in private: he unbuttoned his vest, unbuttoned his collar, loosened his tie, and took off his coat. He never loosened a scrap of his clothing until he undressed at bedtime, and to Jem and me, this was the equivalent of him standing before us stark naked. We exchanged horrified glances."

More and more of the class peered toward the dark corner. Mr. Karp didn't seem to be aware of the sounds behind him as he continued his reading.

"Atticus put his hands in his pockets, and as he returned to the jury, I saw his gold collar button and the tips of his pen and pencil winking in the light."

The horrible sounds of the fingernails had stopped—only to be replaced by the unmistakable sound of chalk on the chalkboard. Kelly gave me a little kick and nodded to the front, a questioning look on her face. Curiosity gripped the class as they squirmed in their seats trying to see what was happening. Mr. Karp, still oblivious, continued.

"'Gentlemen,' he said. Jem and I again looked at each other: Atticus might have said, 'Scout.' His voice had lost its aridity, its detachment, and he was talking to the jury as if they were folks on the post office corner."

The screech of chalk was distinctive. Somebody was up there, in the dark, writing on the chalkboard. Almost everyone in the class focused on the corner rather than on Mr. Karp's dramatic reading.

"'Gentlemen,' he was saying, 'I shall be brief, but I would like to use my remaining time with you to remind you that this case wasn't a difficult one, it requires no minute sifting of complicated facts, but it does require you to be sure beyond all reasonable doubt as to the guilt of the defendant. To begin with, this case should never have come to trial. This case is as simple as black and white.'"

Mr. Karp lowered the book and returned the bookmark to its original place. He looked up. The screech of the chalk had stopped, but many eyes were still focused on the corner. "When something is black and white, it means that there is a plain right and wrong answer. In addition, stating that a thing is black and white might indicate that the meaning or the answer is clear. In his closing arguments, Atticus Finch stresses the simplicity of the evidence and shows that the facts point toward Tom's innocence. However, in this case—pun intended—Harper Lee shows us that it indeed does come down to black and white. Meaning the whole case revolves around racism, and in that time of our country's history, white always won."

Mr. Karp pushed himself up from the desk with a groan and walked over to the bank of light switches. I was sure I wasn't the only one holding their breath as he hesitated, fingers tantalizing inches from the switches. "Thanks for letting me shed some light on this great novel." And he flipped the switches, lighting up the front of the room. There was a collective gasp as everyone looked at the single word written on the chalkboard during Mr. Karp's reading: *Abbey.*

All eyes were now on me as everyone turned and stared at me with shock written all over their faces. Leave it to those damn clowns to throw me under the bus.

WE HAVE TO TALK

IF SOMEONE ASKED ME HOW I WAS DOING AND I GAVE MY HONEST response, they'd definitely never ask again. Yeah, it was that kind of day.

It was Kelly that cornered me, as she pushed me into an empty classroom. Her face said she was all business and her words backed it up. "Sit your butt down, we have to talk." There was fire in her eyes.

Fine. I've got enough fire for three people. I took a seat and leaned back, folded my arms and held her gaze. "So, let's talk."

She studied me for a long moment. The pause didn't appear to have a calming effect, as she looked even angrier—if that was possible.

"What was that all about back there? We all heard the fingernails on the chalkboard. We all heard the screech of the chalk. And we all saw your name appear on the board." Kelly took a step closer. "There was no way someone could have been up there. And yet your name appeared on the board." Another step forward. "Sure, it was dark, but there wasn't a place for anyone to hide." She took another step and leaned right into my space. "And yet, your name appeared on the board. How?"

I've faced this kind of moments before. Moments where I had no choice but to confide in someone about my abilities. Based on my history, this probably wouldn't go well. I've lost friends over the years when I've had to talk about the things I could see and do. Most people couldn't deal with having a friend who was a spook magnet. It's a little too close to crazy, I guess. Sighing, I looked her in the eye. It wasn't like I considered Kelly to be my friend. So really, what was there to lose?

"Why?" That was all I said.

Kelly blinked and wrinkled appear on her forehead. She looked like she was going to say something, but I beat her to it. "I can probably explain the how, but it's the why I struggle with."

Kelly nodded. "So let's start with the how part. I'm dying to hear how you pulled off that little stunt."

I pointed to a chair. "Why don't you sit down? You make me nervous when you hover over me." She looked ready to argue with me, but instead took a deep breath and sat. I began to tell my story.

"Ever since I was a little girl, I could see things that others couldn't. These things are spirits, ghosts, dead people, call them what you want." I gazed out the window as I spoke, not ready to make eye contact with Kelly.

"These spirits were always attracted to me for some reason. We have photographs of my early birthdays, with my dead grandmother looming over my shoulder. She's come to me occasionally over the years, but most of the time it's people I've never met before. It's not always clear what they want. There is the occasional one that can communicate pretty well, but most can't. Their communication tools can be described as a blunt instrument at best."

I glanced at Kelly, but her eyes were fixed on something outside. "Several years ago, my mom disappeared while on a medical relief trip—she's a doctor. She'd been traveling through remote areas of Venezuela and vanished without a trace. Last summer, when I was at camp in River Falls, strange things began to happen: A mysterious symbol kept appearing over and over; I was attacked from behind and a bag was put over my head; and another time, I was out running, and for a few minutes the sounds of a jungle became so loud, I wondered if I was still in Wisconsin. One of the creepiest moments came when my roommate and I cut through a field and felt something squishy underfoot. Imagine how freaked out we were when we discovered it was thousands upon thousands of dead frogs. And of course, we were barefoot. All these things were ghostly clues given to let me know my mom had been kidnapped and to point to where she was being held. I figured it out one day as I was looking at a map of the jungles near the

Columbian border. The river matched the symbol that was plaguing me for weeks."

Kelly looked at me now and asked, "So, what did you do?" She leaned forward, waiting for my answer.

"I reached out to a lawyer friend who had military connections. They were able to raid a jungle camp and bring her home." Talking about my mom again brought back powerful emotions, and I wiped away my tears. "She's home with us now."

Kelly's eyes looked moist as well. "That's amazing. But what's going on here at school?"

The moment of truth arrived. "I've been seeing clowns for some reason."

Kelly's eyebrows raised, but she said nothing.

"Lexi and I were driving the other day, and there was one standing in the middle of the road. He was super tall, almost seven feet tall. We both saw it. But it gets worse. They've been all over the school. I'll turn a corner and there would be one. The other day, I was grabbed by the throat and held against the lockers by one. In American History earlier today, it looked like an entire clown parade marched past the classroom. There had to be dozens of them. And..." I paused.

Kelly accurately guessed the reason for my hesitation. "Christina." She stood and leaned against the window ledge, looking at me. "When Sophie and I saw you in the parking lot, you said you had seen someone. It was a clown, wasn't it?"

I nodded.

"Oh my God, this isn't good. I strongly dislike clowns."

"They aren't on the top of my list, either. My father dragged me to the circus the day before school started and there were clowns everywhere. I witnessed a clown confrontation; it was almost a gang fight between clowns. Talk about your surreal moments. Most were the funny clowns you remember from grade school. But there was one that didn't fit in at all with the other clowns; he was over-the-top intense. If you dislike clowns, you would have hated this one."

"I guess," Kelly said. "Do you think your visit to the circus had something to do with what's happening here?"

Nodding, I lean forward in my chair, restless in my seat. "I've never been a big fan of coincidences. My circus visit must have attracted a clown spirit to me for some reason, and now he and a dozen of his closest friends are here, trying to get my attention."

"Sounds like they've succeeded," Kelly said. She folded her arms and continued. "I always pictured ghosts as transparent things that people see from a distance, not some evil force that is capable of kidnapping someone."

"Which is the way things have always been. Most ghosts are sort of here, sort of somewhere else, not capable of physical contact with our world and us. But that's been changing recently. Spirits seem to be gaining more of a foothold in our world, and I'm not sure what it means." I looked out the window at the gray sky. "It could be a sign of something bad to come. I don't know."

Getting to my feet, I joined Kelly on the window ledge. "Some of the clowns I've seen feel exceptionally dangerous and some not so much. Those are more like the clowns you see tossing candy to the first graders at the 4th of July parade. I'm not getting why both extremes are drawn here, though. I'm missing something."

Kelly pulled her hair out of the binder, shook her hair out, and gathered it up again. "Maybe clowns have a herd mentality—which would explain why all the clowns have to crowd into that one small car—so when one shows up, they all want to visit." She made quick work of re-doing the hair binder and checked herself in the window's reflection. Apparently satisfied, she smiled and turned back. "They're ghosts, they don't have to make sense, right?"

"But ghosts, like people, have reasons for what they do. It may not be apparent at first, but it usually makes sense once you figure it out. So I'm left trying to solve the mystery of why a clown wanted Christina. And because I'm the only one who knows they're here, it's up to me to make it right."

Kelly slid over toward me until our shoulders were touching.

"That's not true. You said Lexi knows. And now I do, too. We're all on the same team, and we support each other. It doesn't matter if we're on the field or off, we still have each other's back. So no more of your martyr stuff—I'm in this now, too."

Feeling tremendously relieved on the inside, I wasn't ready to show too much on the outside. "We're not going to hug, so don't get your hopes up," I told her.

Kelly pushed off from the ledge. "You'll be back for that hug," she said as she headed for the door. Pausing, she added, "They always come back."

AT LUNCH, the morning's gray clouds turned black as the rains came. As it often happened during autumn in Minnesota, they never left, and we faced a practice field under water. So Coach Johnson canceled practice. After school, I decided to use the time to work on my Mockingbird paper for English Lit and grabbed a table in the commons. Several dozen classmates were spread around, but I was alone at my table.

My MacBook Air was out, and I made significant progress: I had a title. *The Impact of Class Structure in To Kill a Mockingbird*. Saying it out loud, I liked the way it sounded. How could my paper not be brilliant with such a deep title?

Step one completed, I was ready to roll onto step two. I started typing: The rigid class structure and social stratification of Maycomb County had a profound effect on the events in the novel, *To Kill a Mockingbird* by Harper Lee. The impact of this class structure and the underlying prejudice were especially evident in the trial of Tom Robinson, a Maycomb black man. Because of the strict class system of Maycomb County...

Glancing up, I was surprised to see someone sitting across from me. "Whoa, you startled me."

The boy, looking to be maybe a year older than me, wore a dark green cloth jacket with a checked shirt underneath. He had the bad-boy skater look, which he pulled off rather well. He wore his dirty blond hair long. Pushing it out of his dark eyes, he said quietly, "I get that a lot. Sorry."

"You should be. You could give someone a heart attack sneaking up all ninja-like on them." My comment brought a smile to his face.

"What class are you working on?" he asked after a moment. His voice was soft, in a shy sort of way.

"English Lit. Writing my paper on *To Kill a Mockingbird*."

He nodded. "I had that class last..." he paused. "...Before."

"Before?"

"I meant I had the class before." He seemed a bit awkward, but also sort of sweet.

"I'm Abbey," I said, giving a little wave. "What's your name?"

"Peter." He flashed a little smile.

"Hi, Peter. I don't think I've seen you around here before. But I'm new to Pine Ridge."

"Have you made any friends yet?" he asked, looking around the empty table. "Perhaps not..." Peter's voice trailed off, and he looked lost in thought with a vacant stare.

"I'm getting to know a few, but it's been lonely too." Why I was sharing this with a complete stranger, I had no idea.

Peter looked at me thoughtfully. "I see many people who seem to have plenty of friends yet feel desperately lonely because they feel nobody gets them. It's way more common than you might think."

"Seems I'm not alone in being alone."

Shaking his head, Peter smiled. "Not at all. No matter how lonely you might feel, there is always someone who can relate to you. Maybe you can't talk to them right now, but they are out there. Knowing that should give you comfort."

"Jeez, how old are you, anyway?" I asked. Peter looked confused, and I laughed. "I don't normally get much in the way of life lessons from my fellow high schoolers."

Peter laughed. "Life lessons. That's ironic."

I was about to quiz him when Lexi and Kelly arrived. Lexi dropped her backpack across from me and took a seat next to Peter. "Hey Abbey,"

"What's up, Abbey?" Kelly asked and grabbed a spot on the other side of Peter. She didn't acknowledge Peter.

"Not much. What's on your mind?" I asked her, as I could see something was bugging her.

With a glance in Peter's direction, she said, "I think you need to be open about what's going on. It affects all of us."

Even though I was surprised by Kelly's openness, I shouldn't have been. She was the model of confidence, after all. After the events of the last two days, the time for subtlety had come and gone. I looked around the table. "Something bad has come to Pine Ridge—something that took Christina. And we need to stop it." I turned to Lexi. "What happened yesterday on the road is part of this."

"The clown," Lexi whispered.

"You do remember," I said, holding her gaze.

Lexi nodded, and I continued. "There have been clowns all around the school for some reason."

"I hate clowns," Lexi said.

"Me too," Kelly added. "They scare the living crap out of me."

I nodded. "It's super common. There's even a term for the fear of clowns."

"Coulrophobia," Peter stated.

I nodded. "Like most fears, the fear of clowns isn't usually justified. But what we have here is. One of them took our Christina." I was holding back my tears, not wanting to break down in front of Peter. "I saw a clown in the parking lot that night."

Lexi shook her head. "There's more to it than some psycho killer clown. When we held hands and touched that clown, I felt... something. It was like someone else's thoughts were in my head. I saw things, felt things—experienced things I shouldn't have been able to. It was out of control. Completely out of control," she added with a grimace.

Glancing at Peter, I wondered what he thought of all this. He looked in my direction and asked, "You saw it, too?"

I nodded. "I saw it too, Lexi. But the difference is, I've seen things like this my entire life. I think my grandmother passed on her gift to me."

"Gift?" Lexi asked as she leaned forward.

"Gift. Curse. Whatever. I see dead people. I always have, ever since I was little. And for some reason, these dead people are drawn to me. That's me: Abbey, the spook magnet." Lexi stared at me with her mouth hanging open. "And ghosts aren't friendly anymore. These are definitely not Casper, the friendly ghost."

I glanced at Peter, trying to gauge his reaction, but he wasn't giving me anything.

Lexi pulled her hair back. She paused for a moment before speaking. "So these clown spirits are drawn to you?"

I nodded. "Apparently."

"And they're here at Pine Ridge—because of you?"

I shrugged. "I don't know."

Kelly looked at me. I looked back at her. "Well, maybe," I paused. "Okay, probably."

I turned back to Lexi, and she continued. "The clowns you summoned are putting us in danger."

"That's not fair," Peter interjected. I was shaking my head.

"They took Christina. If that's not putting us in danger, I don't know what danger is." Lexi folded her arms across her chest.

My tears were flowing, but I wasn't going to let anyone bully me. I stood up and jabbed a finger at Lexi. "Look, I didn't summon anyone. Sometimes bad things happen. Sometimes crazy just shows up."

I brushed Lexi's hair back out of her face. "I know you're scared. But, you're not alone. I'm here. This isn't my first rodeo; I've had plenty of experience dealing with this type of thing. Everything's going to be okay. Do you believe me?"

She nodded, her eyes looking watery.

"This isn't my doing, but you can be damn sure I'm going to kick their sorry clown butts all the way back to the spook circus."

Lexi held my gaze for a long moment—and then broke out laughing. "You are one tough chick. And I know you didn't bring the clowns here. Don't worry, I'll be right by your side, kicking butt."

"Me too," Kelly added, "but I'm going to be kicking them from the front side."

We were all laughing as Savannah walked up and proceeded to blow my mind.

She said, "Hey guys," and sat between Kelly and Lexi—right on top of Peter. Except Peter had faded almost entirely away, even though he still held my gaze. His eyes bored into me, a haunted expression coloring his face.

Savannah let out a squeal and fell back off the bench. "Oh, I feel so funky," she moaned as she rolled on the ground, her arms wrapped around herself. "So cold."

The other girls were out of their seats, helping Savannah as I stared open mouthed at Peter—Peter, the ghost. Yeah, that's right. My new friend Peter was a ghost.

Giving me a quick wink, Peter faded out of sight.

GONE LIKE DINOSAURS AND VIDEOTAPE

THE SELFIE WAS UNIVERSAL AT PINE RIDGE. YOU COULDN'T walk anywhere without encountering someone holding their smartphone at arm's length while making a face that was supposed to look both natural and attractive. Judging by most of the selfies I've seen, the duck lips and squinty eyes missed that mark by a country mile.

They were still fun, though. And we all used Snapchat to send them back and forth.

Lexi sent me a Snap. She was at the mall looking at clothes and was asking for opinions. *What do you think of this look?* The top she was modeling in the picture was cute, and I told her that. *That looks awesome on you.* But, something about the scarf she was accessorizing it with didn't look right. *You should re-do the scarf.*

After a moment, she sent another Snap. She'd awkwardly re-tied the scarf, putting most of it on one shoulder. That was just wrong. *It looks like you're hiding a dead squirrel on your shoulder*, I sent back. Lexi sent a brief reply. *LOL.*

Try tying it again and keeping it more centered, I replied. A moment later, she sent another Snap, this time the scarf hung over her shoulders, no knot at all. Lexi held up a finger for my benefit, though. Nice. *Couldn't make it look right.*

Let me show you, I Snapped back.

Pulling out a scarf from my dresser, I stood in front of the mirror tying it the way my mom had taught me. Satisfied with the result, I grabbed my phone. A playful thought came to me and I grabbed a stuffed animal, a chipmunk, and placed it on my shoulder. Perfect. I

Snapped the picture and sent it to Lexi. Couldn't wait to see her response.

Lexi didn't keep me waiting. *WTF*.

Like my friend? I replied.

Seriously? That was creepy.

I wasn't following her, so I texted her back. *It's just a stuffed animal, from the Chipmunk movie.*

Her response was immediate. *NO IT'S NOT*.

Extremely confused, I scrolled back to the picture I'd sent her. I was stunned. It wasn't the chipmunk sitting on my shoulder that bothered her—it was the clown looming over my other shoulder.

I dropped my phone and backed into the corner.

The intrusion left me stunned, but also angry. *Not in my house. And not in my sanctuary.* On a mission, I looked everywhere for the invading clown. But the only clown I found was an old Krusty the clown doll someone once gave me. I took it out to the trash.

Back in my room, I sat on the floor in front of my full-length mirror and picked up my phone. Holding it in my hands, I closed my eyes, focused on my breathing and slowed down my thoughts. I took several calming breaths, wanting to get tuned into that place where I felt more connected with the spirits. It's difficult to explain, but when I focused on the otherworldly plane, a different energy coursed through me. This crackling energy rippled through me, bringing a tingling sensation not unlike a low voltage current. After entering my altered state, I opened my eyes.

There was a haze in the room that made everything monochromatic—no color, just a million shades of gray. I took a deep breath, noting the subtle ozone smell that entered the room. The smell reminded me of the electric bumper car ride at the fair, the way ozone from the sparks hung heavy in the air. My peripheral vision blurred and swirled as I focused on my eyes in the mirror's reflection. What I sought would be in the peripheral, and moving my eyes would almost certainly make it vanish. Concentration was key, as I could only see things obliquely here.

What was this place? If I had to guess, I'd say it was a parallel plane of non-existence where ghosts lurk when they're not trying to impact our world. From what I've seen, most didn't have the ability to enter our world. Those that were able to make an appearance had a calling or purpose that empowered them. Their calling could be almost anything: connecting with loved ones, revenge, confusion surrounding their death, being drawn to a place that impacted their lives, or to communicate an important message. Each spirit had varying degrees of power to affect our world.

I looked for the clown that appeared in my selfie, but he wasn't there. And of course, I had zero idea where they went when they left. Time and distance weren't an obstacle for them. They simply did it.

The buzz of my phone pulled me back into our world. Maybe something to do with the energy leaving my body, shivers hit me as the gray plane was replaced with a full-color version of reality. Looking at my cell, the text was from Lexi, a photo of her with a satisfactorily tied scarf—and my clown directly behind her, a hand draped on her shoulder.

No more texting, I called her, as some things were better communicated by speaking—like the fact there was a dead clown with his hand on her. "Lexi!" I shouted.

"Abbey, we're Snapchatting, not calling. Stay with the program." Lexi had to challenge me on everything.

"Stop. He's there with you now."

"Who?"

"My clown."

"Your clown?"

"Yes. The one from my selfie. He's with you now."

"Really? You're freaking me out." Her voice had lost all of its playfulness.

"Check out your last picture you sent. You'll see." I waited for her.

"Oh my God!" There was a moment of frantic rustling and then she came back. "But there isn't anyone here. I've looked, but there isn't a clown."

A dark thought came to me, creeping into my brain with no warning as most dark thoughts did. What if that clown went viral? Spreading faster than a breakup rumor, fanning out through the school, it could reach most of the school within an hour.

"Lexi, have you been Snapping anyone else? Anyone after me?"

"Just Kelly. And Ryan. I wanted to show off my new scarf that the saleslady tied for me."

"I'll call Kelly, you call Ryan. Tell them not to Snapchat anymore tonight."

"Might as well tell them not to breathe anymore tonight."

"Just do it." After I hung up, I punched in Kelly's contact.

She answered on the first ring. "Go for Kelly."

"There's something happening with the clowns. One showed up in my Snap I sent to Lexi and then it was in the picture she sent back to me." I could hear her breathing, but she wasn't responding. Time to drop the bomb. "Lexi said she sent you a Snap after the clown showed up in her selfie. It might be there with you now."

Kelly let out a loud squeal. "But I didn't open it, I was Snapchatting with Bri."

"Check it to see if there was a clown in Lexi's picture." Things were getting out of hand.

I heard her sharp intake of breath.

That was my confirmation. "Call Bri and see if there's a clown in your selfie. And have her stop Snapchatting."

"Good luck with that."

"Just do it and call me back." I ended our call.

The entire situation had spiraled out of control and I needed a containment plan, some way of reining in the clowns before someone else was taken. But I had zero idea what they wanted and had no idea on how to figure that out. As I discovered in the bathroom, talking to the clowns wasn't helpful, either. They wouldn't answer. And when I grabbed a clown, I'd been overwhelmed with a swirl of impressions that went by way too fast. Nothing to help me figure out why things were happening. If only they were all as easy as Peter to talk with.

Wait, Peter—I had an idea.

In a minute, I was on my bike headed back to school. Never mind that it was dark and cold out, and I lived miles away from school. I needed to get to Pine Ridge tonight. I didn't want to bother my parents, so I ran out with my backpack and said I was headed to Kelly's to study. They didn't need to know I was battling the clown apocalypse and needed to enlist the help of a dead boy from school. Some things were best left unsaid.

And man oh man, that was definitely one of them.

My cell buzzed, and it was Lexi. I answered it as I took a corner hard, my rear tires sliding. With one earbud in, I heard the honking of the angry drivers. I've never been good at following the rules of the road. Yes, I get the fact the cars were a lot bigger than I was, but they needed to watch out for me. I owned the road. And to prove my point, I drove right down the middle.

"What do you know?" I asked. A SUV turned onto the street, but I slid over to one side. I may be a rule breaker, but I wasn't stupid.

"So far, the clowns have shown up in pictures with Kelly, Bri, Mary, Fran, Savannah, Greta, Paige, Julia, Lyndsay, Jaz, Sophie, Haily, and Zecky. But get this: it's not all the same clown, there have been several different ones."

Racing down the hill, the wind made it hard to understand what Lexi was telling me. "Say what?"

"The clowns sounded different from the one that was in our pictures. I had them screenshot them before they disappeared and send them to me. I could make out at least a dozen different clowns. They all sort of look alike, though."

"That's racist."

Lexi laughed. "Good one."

The bad part of riding down a hill was there was always a hill to climb afterwards. Putting the bike into a lower gear, I stood on the pedals as I got to the steepest section. I stayed focused on the steady, rhythmical climb as I muscled my way to the top. At the summit, I worked to get my breath back, enjoying the pumped-up sensation in my legs—it's a soccer girl thing. Lexi must have heard my panting as she waited until I quieted down before speaking again. "What do these clowns want? There has to be a reason why they are coming to us."

Steering onto the school grounds, the parking lot was empty. Pine Ridge wasn't a happening place. "That's exactly what I hope to find out. I'll call you later." I ended the call before Lexi could ask any questions.

Dropping the bike, I tried the front door, but it was locked. I've always found that anything worth achieving would have obstacles in the way. But there was always a way if you had enough determination. And I had plenty to go around.

Back on my bike, I headed for the rear of the building hoping to see a custodian's car. And back near the dumpsters and loading dock, I found two; A beat-up Chevy pickup truck and a decade's old piece of crap car. Custodians meant there was likely a way to get inside. Hopping up on the loading dock, I tried the door adjacent to the overhead door. Success. Not wanting to alert anyone inside, I ever-so-slowly pulled it open.

The dock area was full of shadows, the only light coming from up around the corner. The best part about the darkness was it meant there wasn't anyone in that part of the building. But I soon discovered the bad part when I ran into a pile of crates, knocking them over. The sound echoed through the loading dock area as I froze. Bending down, I rubbed the new souvenir on my shin, listening for the arrival of someone coming to investigate the noise. But after holding my position for a full minute, no one came.

At the corner, I peered around the wall toward the source of the light. The lights were on in this section of the school, while the other direction was dark. I chose the darkness. Slipping off my athletic shoes, I padded down the increasingly murky hallway, trying to be as quiet as I could. Another turn, and the ambient light had gone the way of dinosaurs and videotape.

This was as good a spot as any, so I took a seat cross-legged on the floor. Pulling out my smartphone, I placed it in front of me in case I needed the flashlight app to navigate the pitch-black hallways.

Taking a deep breath, I gradually let it out, my mind focused solely on my breathing. Another breath, letting the calm wash over me. Sitting tall, my hands resting on my knees, I took in another full breath, feeling my heart slow down. Two more deep breaths, and I was ready. Switching my focus, my thoughts moved to Peter, the reason I was there. Picturing his face, I repeated his name in my mind. *Peter. Peter. Peter.*

I could see his face so clearly, it was like he was sitting right in front of me. When I opened my eyes, he was.

"Why didn't you tell me you were dead?" I asked right off.

He answered immediately without a trace of guile. "*Were* dead? I still am dead. But it didn't feel important to tell you at the time. I was happy to finally connect with someone again."

Sitting here in the dark, I shouldn't have been able to see Peter, but I could. There was a soft glow, a muted radiance emanating from him—much like the deep-sea fish that dwell at the ocean's darkest depths. Holding his gaze, we locked eyes for a long moment. I didn't care much for the greenish tinge of his otherworldly glow. Otherwise, I liked his eyes.

"What happened to you?" I asked. It would be good to know how he died.

"Not a clue. At some point, I realized no one could see or hear me."

"That must have been odd."

"Very," Peter replied with a shake of his head. I noticed his hair didn't move.

"Have you tried leaving here and going home? Seeing your family?"

It might be ironic to say he looked haunted, but that was exactly the expression clouding his face.

"You haven't seen them?" It never crossed my mind that he wouldn't visit his loved ones. "I realize it may be difficult to see them now."

Peter's eyes shifted to the ground. I waited as he kept his thoughts to himself. Finally, he spoke, his voice quiet and low. "I don't remember them at all. I don't know where I lived or who my family was." He looked up and I could see the pain in his eyes. "I can feel them, they are part of who I am, but all the memories have been stripped away."

I wanted to reach out to him, but I wasn't sure how that would work.

"So what do you do all day?" I asked, wanting to bring the conversation to a better place. "Wander the halls of Pine Ridge High School?"

Peter's eyes cloud as he hesitated before answering. "I don't seem to have a sense of time. This feels like the same moment I met you," he said. He flickered and shifted a few inches to my right and continued where he left off. "Yet, it obviously is later. I float in and out of moments. That's what I do. There's not much else to do, to tell the truth."

Leaning forward, it was time to give him my best sales pitch.

"Well, Peter, today is your lucky day. I'm here to give you a break from your humdrum routine of haunting this school. This is your big chance to get a life—metaphorically speaking."

"Color me intrigued," he replied, a hint of a gleam in his eye. "Go on."

"I'd imagine the worst part of not having a life, is you don't have a sense of purpose. You hear the stories about the guy who works for his entire life and a month after he retires, he's dead. Without purpose, there was nothing to live for. Maybe that's exactly what you need."

"A purpose." Peters said it matter-of-factly, as if he was trying out the word.

Pressing my advantage, I continued. "I can't begin to know what you need, or if you need anything in your current condition, but I don't believe you're meant to be here. You are between worlds, unsettled, and alone. People were never created to be alone. Have you given much thought to moving on to the next world?"

"At times."

"And..." I prompted him.

"I have no idea how to get there. It's not like there's been a door waiting for me to open. If there was a light, it's not burning brightly enough to see." He looked pained as he spoke. "Or maybe I wasn't supposed to go anywhere. Or worse, it's not the light that I was meant to head for."

"For a dead guy, you're being incredibly melodramatic. So you're deceased, move on." Looking at his blank expression, I wasn't sure he picked up on my intended double meaning.

"I appreciate how you're trying to paint me a primary color picture of what your afterlife is like, but there was an urgent reason I had to talk to you."

Peter raised an eyebrow, which I took as my cue that he wanted me to continue. "As we talked about earlier in the commons, we're under attack here. For some reason, clowns are coming after my teammates and me. They've taken Christina, kidnapped her right from the school parking lot."

"That doesn't feel like a very ghostly thing to do," Peter interjected.

"Well, let me tell you something: they're not all as friendly as you, Casper. I've personally been choked and clawed by angry spirits and witnessed the destructive fury one of these ghostly clowns had boiled up inside him. It wasn't pretty." I shivered at the memory.

"What do you need from me?" Peter asked.

I held his gaze for a moment before speaking. "Your purpose in all this is to intervene. You can go to these clowns and talk to them.

Find out what they're doing here. Find out what they want. They have to want something, after all. Everybody wants something. We need to find out what that something is."

Peter nodded.

"We desperately need to find Christina. I want you to discover what they did with her. Getting Christina back is the most important part of this." I felt a tear running down my cheek. Peter leaned forward, staring at the damp line left by the tear. He subconsciously licked his lips. It felt like Peter was all the way in our world, as I was sure I could smell his scent. Maybe his focus had grounded him. "Say you'll help find her."

"I..." Peter looked to be at a loss for words.

A light went on behind me and I heard the squeak of a wheel. Our time appeared to be over. "Help me," I implored him. "Help Christina."

Someone shuffled nearby now, as the squeaky wheel was right around the corner. I reached out for Peter's hand, and because I was so incredibly focused, I was able to make contact with his hand easily. Gripping Peter's icy flesh in my own warm hand, I squeezed his. "Don't let me down. Don't let Christina down."

He winked out of my world as a startled custodian gasped behind me.

TETHERING THE BLIMP

How many scary movies begin with a deserted motel on a moonlit windy October night?

Far too many for my tastes, but looking out through the dusty window of the team van, that was exactly what I saw. Not going to lie, the sight of the place creeped me out. The door protested with a grating sound as I slid it open and stepped into the cool night. I couldn't help but shiver.

Lexi and Bri were right behind me, the others waking up from their slumber. Honestly, who scheduled these soccer tournaments out in the middle of nowhere? Our team caravanned through the night for more than five hours so we could compete in an all-girls high school soccer tournament at Ripon College.

I grew up loving road trips with my father as we made our way around the country with me being his research assistant and co-conspirator on his writing assignments. For me, the travel was when the magic happened. I grew closer than ever to my father during these trips. We'd play games, he'd quiz me on world events and history, or just talk about life.

Our team trip started as a loud and crazy affair as we sang and laughed at the top of our lungs. A couple of hours into the trip, the volume leveled off as everyone wound down. Lexi and Bri talked quietly about the events plaguing our school, which led to questions about my abilities.

Awkward was the word I would use when I've been asked about it previously. But, since Lexi and I had plenty of shared ghostly history, I decided to open up. After all, they already know I was the ghost girl.

"It's always been with me, this gift. I remember when I was young, lying in bed on a Saturday morning, covers over my head and my hand hanging off the edge of my princess bed. A hand held mine, squeezing it. I assumed it's my mom coming to wake me for breakfast. I turned over, moving the covers, and the weight of the hand vanished. No one was in the room with me. I rubbed my hand, thinking the other hand was warm and comforting, not at all scary. It was just the way things were for me. I suppose I accepted it, much the way someone born with a disability accepts it. It's all you know."

Bri shook her head. "This is so cool," she whispered.

"It's not always cool when you're living it. Spirits of murdered people or the spirits of murderers have come to me at night, asking for help. They don't have a good sense of boundaries. And many are not good at communicating. Some come to act out their violent ends. Picture this, I'm fresh out of the shower, comfortable in my sweats. I'm on my bed, music playing softly and I have my math book out. A scream of terror drowns out everything and gets choked off. Blood splatters my wall and mirror. And not just a few drops, either. I'm talking severed artery, decapitated head streams of blood, spraying all over. All I can do is watch in horror as it runs down the wall. I'm off the bed and out the door as fast as you could imagine, wanting to head off my parents. They never come, as I'm the only one who can hear the screams. This happens every night for an entire week. Same blood-curdling scream, same blood-drenched walls. You can imagine how much I enjoyed those experiences."

"No way..." Lexi said.

"That's not the worst, though. Let me give you another example. I'm out to dinner in St. Paul with my parents. It's this gorgeous mansion made into a restaurant. I stop on the front steps, feeling a weird energy when I put my hand on the railing. My father looks at me, but I wave him on. The energy seeps into me, a dark coldness giving me goosebumps. I want to find somewhere else for us to eat, but what am I going to say? Hey dad, let's have Arby's instead, because the dark energy here is ruining my appetite."

I looked at each of my friends and continued. "So, I go in, super cautious with each step. Dread and anticipation are equal partners as I make my way to our table. It's a Tuesday night on a cold January evening, so the place is half-empty. I remember the vibe of the people's conversations feels strained. There is one couple in particular, sitting next to the stairway, arguing. His face is distorted with anger, and when I catch a glimpse of hers, I see a woman with fear coloring her face. It makes me sad.

"We order dinner and I fill up on the warm rolls the server leaves for us. That's when everything happens. I feel someone holding down my arm on the table. It's like a vise has me pinned and I can't pull away. Of course, I try not to be too obvious with my parents sitting across from me. There's nothing I can see, yet I know heavily corded muscles hold my arm. A slice appears on my sleeve as if someone is cutting away the material. My arm lays there exposed, and I struggle harder to pull free, but to no avail. I see the dimple in my forearm as a sharp point is pressed against my flesh."

Glancing at Lexi and Bri, their faces showed a mix of concern and fear, but I couldn't stop. "My forearm is being scratched so hard I think the knife will cut into me. The thing is, I can't feel a thing—but I want to scream bloody murder because that's exactly what I think might happen. I'm sitting right next to my father as my parents continue their conversation about our healthcare system, oblivious to the fact their daughter is being attacked just across the table."

Bri looked like she was going to throw up. Instead, she swallowed hard and asked, "What did you do?"

Our school bus arrived at our motel and everyone woke up. "I'll tell you later," I said to my two frustrated teammates. After stepping off the bus, we moved toward the flickering sign that designated the motel's office as we waited for the coach to check us in. The rest of the team joined us in a mass huddle for warmth. I glanced around the motel, looking at the office and then up to the overhead sign. "Guys, don't you think it's odd this place doesn't actually have a name?"

Savannah took a step closer. "Could be worse."

"How so?" Ryan asked what we were all thinking.

"It could be the Bates Motel," Savannah laughed. "You can check out any time you like, but you can never leave!"

Sophie looked at Savannah. "I thought that was Hotel California."

"Same difference," Savannah replied with a decidedly evil laugh. "Same difference."

COACH JOHNSON DIVIDED us into groups of four and handed out room keys. I grabbed ours and glanced at the attached tag. In faded letters, it read simply, MOTEL. Figures.

Lexi, Bri, Kelly and I walked down the uneven sidewalk to the last door. Room number 13. Not going to make anything out of that. To do so would be to give into the superstition. It was one thing to know there were ghosts, demons and dark entities, but it's another to give power to the mind's search for significance when there wasn't any. I've always tried not to make too much of coincidences. It would be a long and dark road if I got caught up in all of life's coincidences and superstitions. Still, the door to room 13 opened with a painful horror movie-worthy creak.

After traveling so extensively with my father—and not always to the finest establishments, I've come to realize all motels must cultivate the same smell. You know the one: a smoky mix of tobacco, urine, greasy food and two-week-old diapers. I have no idea why, yet the smell was always the same.

Bri raced to the queen bed furthest away from the door and claimed it with a shout of "mine." She immediately pulled out her iPad, laid down in the center of the bed and started playing.

Lexi walked up to the bed. "Bri, we have to share the bed. There are four of us sleeping in here." Lexi tossed her bag on the bed. "I don't like sleeping by the door, it gives me the creeps. I'll tuck into the back half."

Without looking up from her tablet, Bri dryly replied, "That sounds dirty."

"Not everything is meant to be dirty, Bri," Lexi said as she plopped down next to Bri. "Some things just sound that way."

"You mean like frosting the pastry?" This came from Kelly.

"Exactly," Lexi said with a laugh.

"Shooting hoops," I offered.

"That's weak, Abbey," Bri said. "It's too common of an expression. Try something like jumping the turnstile."

"Or squeezing the produce," Lexi added with a titter.

"Or tethering the blimp," Kelly said and immediately burst out laughing.

Bri laughed now and added, "Sending out for sushi."

I think I was getting the hang of it. "Violating the penal code," I offered. We all giggled as we tried to top each other.

"Quarter-pounder at the Golden Arches."

"Shaking hands with Abraham Lincoln."

"Windsurfing on Mount Baldy."

The conversation went downhill from there.

It was the middle of the night when there was pounding on our front door. I glanced at the alarm clock, worried we'd overslept, but the digital readout said it was 2:22 a.m. The pounding was relentless. Since I was closest to the door, I rolled out of bed first to see what the problem was. I was worried, as no one pounded on your front door in the middle of the night for something good.

I fought with the chain as the pounding continued. "What the hell," Kelly said as she joined me. I got the chain out of its track and turned the deadbolt, feeling the pounding resonate through the door frame. It must be important.

The moment I pulled open the door, the pounding stopped. "What the hell," Kelly echoed her earlier declaration. There wasn't anyone there.

Lexi and Bri had joined us, and we all stepped out into the night. Oddly enough, the same thing happened with the four rooms adjoining ours. Ryan and Fran stared at us from the next room, while Greta and Lyndsay looked around from the room beyond. Past Zecky and Sophie, I saw Coach Johnson, her assistant coaches, and team manager Amy. We all looked at each other with a mixture of confusion, fear and sleepiness. There wasn't anyone else in sight and no place for anyone to hide. Nothing was said, but I know everyone wondered the same thing. How could someone simultaneously pound on each of our doors and then vanish?

THE MORNING GOT EVEN STRANGER. We were scheduled to depart the motel at 8 a.m., as we had our first game at 10:15. Just before 7 a.m., our assistant coach, Paige, stopped by our room. She breathlessly told us plans had changed, and we needed to be on the bus in ten minutes. The girls grumbled, but went to pull on their uniforms and sweats. I followed Paige out and pulled the door shut behind me.

"Hang on a second." I studied Paige for a moment, noting the slight tremble in her hands. She pushed them into her pockets and stared off into the distance. "What's going on?" I asked. "You look like you saw a ghost."

Paige hesitated, and I could see she was weighing her response. She looked me in the eye and shook her head, and started to turn away. "Please," I pleaded with her. "I will understand. I've seen some strange things."

"Okay, but keep this quiet. It began when April—Coach Johnson —got up to take a quick shower. Apparently, she had just gotten into the shower when she heard a piercing scream and felt a burning sensation on her back. She said the scream sounded like it was right in the shower with her. Between her fright and pain, she stumbled out of the shower and rushed into our room to see what was going on, convinced we were in danger. The thing was, we were all still asleep."

"Strange."

"It gets stranger. After she returned to the bathroom, she saw five long fresh wounds that seemed like fingernail scratches on her back. April threw on her clothes and woke us up. She'd said she'd had enough of this motel."

"I could see why. That was creepy."

"It gets worse," Paige said with a shiver. "April said when she came back out of the bathroom, she witnessed a lady with pale skin and long black hair playing with my hair while I was sleeping. Her shouts woke me up from the nightmare I'd been having. I've felt so unbelievably chilled ever since she told me. I can't seem to warm up." As if to punctuate her words, Paige shivered again. A whole-body shiver like she was in the throes of hypothermia.

As I studied Paige, my internal spook-o-meter was seriously redlining. Being the spooky girl, my sense for detecting when the paranormal intruded into our world was highly developed. I could still get fooled, though—Peter being a prime example. But I knew beyond a shadow of a doubt something wasn't right with her. I moved a step closer as I looked into her eyes. Her pupils were unnaturally dilated and there was something about the black of her pupils that seemed to swirl as I stared into them. I shivered.

I'd be willing to bet a million dollars there was more than one person staring back out at me.

GUNS AND HOT CHOCOLATE

As I stared into the pits of darkness that were Paige's eyes, her pupils dilated further and the edges glowed a tarnished silver color. Her face became a blister of red and her nostrils flared with the force of her breathing. If looks could kill...

"Paige," I began, wanting to head off her runaway train of fury before it gathered speed.

"No!" she raged at me, her face contorted with anger. Call me crazy, but I took a step closer. I knew enough to not back down and hand over the advantage.

Looking like there was an internal struggle being waged, Paige's arms trembled. I was confident she wasn't possessed, but almost certain she was being influenced. There's a difference between influence and possession. If you were possessed, you're not conscious and you have no memory of your actions. If you were influenced, you were pushed aside but still aware of everything that happened to you. When you were influenced, you had a strong desire to say and do what the entity tells you to do. It was like the other consciousness took the driver's seat while you were relegated to the backseat, watching, but fighting to get control back.

My suspicions were confirmed as Paige moved away. With a normal person, they would turn and walk away. However, that wasn't what happened. With her freakishly dark eyes burning into me, she moved away, walking backward the length of the sidewalk to her room. I couldn't even begin to describe the creepiness of seeing someone gliding backward. The motion wasn't at all natural. It was wrong.

"Abbey."

I stared in disbelief at Paige and wondered what my next move should be.

"Abbey."

I registered there was a voice behind me, but I was lost in concern for Paige.

A hand gripped my shoulder, and it was Lexi's voice again. "Abbey." I turned to her, seeing the worry on her face. "Something's wrong, isn't it?" she asked.

I nodded. "We need to help Paige."

"She didn't look right," Lexi said, fear coloring her expression. "Normal people don't move that way."

"You saw that?" I looked up at Lexi, trying to gauge her reaction. Sometimes at these kinds of moments, people have had enough and would look for any reason to be somewhere else.

She nodded. "Weird stuff comes your way, doesn't it?" Lexi said. "I'm okay with it, though. Life will never be boring." I guess I shouldn't have been worried about Lexi. Anyone who plays goalie had to be fearless—and a little crazy. Both played well in my neighborhood.

"Well, God bless America. That's what I was talking about." I gave her a high five. "Let's go kick some ghostly butt." Lexi and I marched down to the coach's room, ready for just about anything.

And that's the thing about life, it's such a great teacher. When I forget that a plan—no matter how good it may be—has no real bearing on future events, I'm in for a valuable life lesson. Things don't always go as planned.

The door to the coach's room was ajar, and I pushed it open to survey the room. Coach Johnson and the other assistant, Grace, were packing up their bags. They didn't appear to notice me. Paige was sitting at the small table near the door, with zero expression on her face as she stared at the large metal Maglite flashlight in front of her. I stepped into the room and joined her at the table. Lexi followed but stood behind me.

"Spirits in the Material World" was a best-seller from The Police. My mom liked to play their greatest hits frequently, and I never minded. Looking at Paige, the song came back to me for good reason. As I studied Paige, I had the impression of something struggling just below the surface, something hidden in the recesses of her mind, something from her dark subconscious wanting to be seen.

Paige's breathing had returned to normal, her color had subsided to her usual paleness, and her eyes were vacant. She didn't appear to notice me sitting beside her. I've never been one to let sleeping dogs lie, so I gave her a little kick under the table. Her head slowly, ever-so-slowly, pivoted in my direction. There wasn't anything in her eyes as she looked into mine. Then things changed.

I felt a strange pull in my head. It literally felt like someone threaded a string from my left ear, through my brain, and out my right ear. The feeling left a trail of tingling energy as it passed through my head—not a comfortable feeling at all. That was when I started to feel confused. Lexi was talking, but I didn't hear her. It was as if her voice came from some distant place. At one point, she said, "Abbey, are you getting anything?" Confused and disorientated, I croaked out the words, "I don't know."

Sitting at the table on the receiving end of Paige's unblinking stare, an overwhelming sleepiness came over me, like someone had put a chloroform-soaked cloth over my mouth. I rested my head in my hands and dropped off in seconds. I knew that it was bad, but I was powerless to resist.

I don't know how long I was out, but when I came around and lifted my head, something was very different and very wrong.

My consciousness wasn't alone in my body. There was someone else in my head. For some reason, I knew it was the entity I'd encountered earlier in Paige. I was still totally aware and totally present, but I was no longer alone. I can hardly describe the sensation of being pushed aside in my own body. It was like I was left with five percent of my brain while the entity had the other ninety-five percent.

Coach Johnson walked up to the table and was talking. I glanced up at her and made out the barest outline of her body, but I caught the green of her eyes in the ambient light. For some reason, I felt frustrated and angry with her. The anger built up inside me, and I had a powerful urge to pound my fists on the table and scream, "You're not wanted here. Get out!"

I was surprised at the vehemence of the thought until I realized the anger wasn't mine. It was the entity. She wanted to speak and take action, using my voice and body to do it. I knew I was being influenced, but I was unsure what to do about it. How could I get someone's attention, to let them know there was something wrong with me? I wanted them to help me, but I couldn't speak. I wasn't allowed to.

Lexi could help if I could find a way to signal that I was in trouble. Just then, Lexi moved to the door, leaving me at the table with Coach Johnson and Paige. I was screaming *noooo* inside my head. My only help had walked away!

I struggled to push the energy out of my head, but she was too powerful. I felt like an ant trying to push a school bus down the street. As I tried to fight back, I heard myself making strange breathing noises. Sharp intakes of air, and then my breath got choked off.

Kelly joined Lexi, and I felt her hand on my shoulder. "Abbey, are you alright?" she asked, concern apparent in her voice.

I managed to squeak out, "She's pushing me." I didn't think Kelly or Lexi knew exactly what I meant. Neither said anything, but Kelly gave my shoulder a little squeeze. I was so amazingly frustrated because I needed help, but couldn't say what I wanted to say.

My hands were balled into fists and I got ready to start pounding. I knew it would feel so good to stand and let my rage run free. The *me* in the corner of my head was scared and frustrated because my friends couldn't see how hard I struggled to get their attention.

Then things got worse.

I turned towards Coach Johnson, feeling that the entity inside me was enraged at my coach, wanting me to attack her. Visions of choking my coach flashed through my mind. I was appalled at the thought, but the violent images kept coming. The entity trapping me in my head was furious that Coach Johnson wasn't afraid of her and wasn't showing the proper respect. She wanted me to scream, "How dare you come here and disrespect me! I'm in charge here. You are nothing." She wanted to make Coach Johnson bow before her. Clearly, she hadn't met my coach, an alpha female if there ever was one. Coach Johnson would not be bowing before anyone.

I was in a horrible state, sharing my consciousness with a violent psychopath with control of my body. I was terrified of what she could make me do to my coach. But I was also afraid of what Coach Johnson might do if I attacked her. I'd seen her on the practice field competing with us. She could be ferocious—going in 100 percent on each tackle or challenge—wanting to prepare us for the competitive cauldron that was high school soccer.

From her ferociousness, I saw a glimmer of hope and a plan. I cast mental images of Coach Johnson taking us down, hoping the dark entity inside me would see the futility of attacking her. It seemed to consider this, but then came up with a plan of its own. It wanted me to pick up the Maglite and whack Coach Johnson across the face with it. That was one heavy flashlight, and I knew my coach wouldn't have time to react before she was hit.

It terrified me that the entity was planning a surprise attack that would seriously hurt Coach Johnson. I pushed violently at this entity, trying to eject it from my body. But the violent urges were so overwhelming, I knew I needed help.

Maybe sensing my struggle, Lexi reached out and took hold of my hand. The contact loosened the dark entity's hold on me. I couldn't even begin to express how grateful I was for her touch. When Lexi asked if I was all right, I was able to respond, "No. I'm having trouble."

Kelly cracked a joke, and I started laughing. In that instant, the entity left and I was released from a paralyzing state. Taking a deep breath filled with relief, I stood and looked at the faces of my friends. Things could have gone horribly wrong without them. "Let's get out of here," I said, anxious to get some distance from the dark and entity-filled motel.

THE TOURNAMENT WAS a relief after all the fear and powerlessness I'd felt at the motel. From the first chants before kickoff of, "Whose field? *Our field!* Who's great? *We're great!*" I was all in. Playing without fear and worry was the only way to play. It was so freeing to not worry about making a mistake, but to play for the fun of it.

We won two of our three games and even that one was close as the team from Appleton scored a late winner. Coach Johnson wasn't upset about the loss and told us we had played with all our heart and soul. She said she couldn't have asked for anything more as she made a point of shaking each of our hands. After that, I would have followed her through hell or high water to play for her.

Our trip home was loud for the first hour, and after that, an exhausted team slept the rest of the way back. Me included this time.

I RANG THE DOORBELL. The man who opened the door looked at me with curiosity. He studied me ever so briefly from top to bottom. Not in a judging or pervy way, he simply scrutinized me the way a Target store buyer studied a line of clothing, taking in the details.

"I'm Abbey. Is Kelly home?" I knew she was, as I had just texted her, but I didn't know what else to say. "I'm picking up a textbook."

"She is," he said. "C'mon in." He turned around and there was a handgun sticking out of a holster on his belt. Damn, Kelly didn't tell me her father was a serial killer. "Kelly, you've got a visitor," he called up the stairs. The woodwork on the staircase looked handcrafted. Their home was one of those older homes that still had a current feel to it. There was something about older homes that I liked. They had more character than the new construction ones.

Kelly bounded down the stairs, a history textbook in hand. "Hey," she said to me. "Dad, can you make us some hot chocolate?" she asked.

"Of course, anything for my princess." As he headed for the kitchen, I grabbed Kelly's arm and pointed at the pistol clipped to her father's belt. I gave her my *what's up with that* gesture.

She laughed as we entered the kitchen and said, "My dad is a bit of a gun nut, as you can see." The small round table was literally covered in guns. I counted six as I took in the assortment, thinking he must be planning a bank heist or something worse. I was sure my jaw was hanging open.

Kelly's dad noticed my expression and laughed. "Most cops are gun nuts. When your life depends on your sidearm, you take more than a passive interest in them."

"My father is a cop," Kelly explained unnecessarily. She gestured for me to take a seat and joined me at the table.

"And I'm the firearms safety instructor for the department. The St. Paul police department," he added as he turned the knob on the stove. *Click, click, click,* followed by a *whoomp* as the burner ignited on the gas stove. He poured a liberal amount of milk into a pan and set it on the burner. "A pistol can be ugly and brutish. It can also be elegant—but still deadly."

Totally in awe of the firepower collected on the table in front of me, I said the first thing that popped into my head. "So, where do you eat?" I asked.

Kelly laughed. "Not going to lie, this is a lot of guns even for you, Dad."

Stirring the simmering milk with a wooden spoon, her father chuckled. "These pistols," he said with particular emphasis on the word pistols, "Are for a course I'll be teaching on handguns for women's self-defense. Women are one of the fastest growing demographics in the hunting and shooting market today. Oddly enough, until recently there haven't been many pistols designed for women."

"Us girls have smaller hands, you know," Kelly said.

"Exactly," Kelly's father said. "Women need handguns specifically designed for them, and fortunately, manufacturers are picking up on this and are coming out with more high-quality self-defense handguns than ever."

"Dad, we're not your class."

"I know, but talking through this helps me work out the kinks before I get in front of a bunch of hormonal gun-toting women."

"Dad!" Kelly looked at me and shook her head and turned back to her father. "I take it we're getting paid to beta test your curriculum?"

"Yes, Ma'am. In hot cocoa. Far better than currency in most cultures."

"Not in mine," Kelly said under her breath. I was trying not to laugh as I glanced at her father, trying to determine if he was ignoring Kelly or didn't actually hear her. Either way, it was hilarious.

Pouring the cocoa into three mismatched mugs, Kelly's father set them in front of us and joined us at the table. I took a sip and instantly found new respect for the man. "Oh, this is good," I said.

Looking happy, he said, "Secret ingredient. I add a little mint, but it adds a lot of taste." He took a sip and looked over at me as I reached for one of the pistols and Kelly's father nodded. "Go ahead. They're not loaded."

The handgun fit my hand, and I wrapped my fingers around the grip. It felt comfortable. "So much better than the one I shot before. I've been target shooting with my dad at the Oakdale gun range. He was working on a story and wanted to get a feel for the weapons involved. I remember it being difficult to deal with the recoil."

"Your issue with the recoil is due to the handgun not fitting your hand. It needs to fit comfortably. He held out his hand and Kelly pressed her palm to his, the difference in hand size quite noticeable.

He set his cocoa down and leaned back in the chair. "This is one of the things I'll be covering in the course. If the pistol fits better in your hand, there will be less perceived recoil and you'll have a more enjoyable shooting experience." I could tell it was a subject both near and dear to his heart.

"I like to shoot," Kelly said with a grin. "This one's mine. It's a Ruger," she added as she picked up a slim handgun with pearl grips. She thumbed a switch and dropped the magazine, checking it with a practiced eye before slamming it back in and working the slide. Like a pro.

"Damn, Kelly."

Smiling, Kelly said, "I know. I'm such a badass."

Even though her father shook his head, I detected some fatherly pride going on as well. Kelly's father asked me to hold up my hand. I did, and he slid over another handgun, saying, "Check out this one. I think this might be a better fit."

Picking it up, I wrapped my hand around the grip as he continued. "The handgun has to be reliable and easy to operate. It has to work every time without fail. At the same time, it has to be easy to operate under stress. In a desperate situation, everyone's fine motor skills are dramatically reduced."

"Like in the slasher films, when the girl is trying to get away and drops her keys as she's trying to get the car started," Kelly said between sips.

Kelly's father nodded. "Exactly. That's why the best self-defense handguns are the ones requiring only a few simple movements to operate."

"You don't want to be fumbling with your handgun when some knife-wielding maniac is coming for you," Kelly added.

"Or some homicidal clown," I said as I fist bumped with Kelly.

"Anyway," Kelly's father said after a confused pause, "You're holding a Glock 42, Abbey. It's the latest model and the smallest handgun ever produced by Glock. It has relatively mild recoil due to the smaller cartridges it fires. Not a ton of stopping power, but it will get the job done. With decent aim, you'll stop your knife-wielding serial killer."

"Or homicidal clown."

"Or homicidal clown," Kelly's father confirmed. He hesitated for a moment. "You mentioned that you and your father have been shooting before?"

"Yes, several times."

"It would be helpful to me if you'd be willing to take this to the range and put it through its paces. Make sure it fires reliably before I recommend it to my class."

"Really?" I was excited.

"Really. But I'm not handing over a handgun and a box of cartridges to a high schooler. I would need your father's okay first, and then I would want to give it directly to him to carry. No offense, but..."

I shook my head. "No worries at all. He's actually waiting out in the car."

Kelly's father laughed. "Why didn't you invite him in?" he asked with surprise.

"I thought I'd be just a minute. And Dad was totally into some public radio program he was listening to in the car."

"Have your father come in," he suggested. "It would be a relief to talk to an adult and have an actual intelligent conversation for once." He had a twinkle in his eye as he spoke.

"Hey," Kelly said with mock indignation and a grin, "I'm sorry you can't keep up with our discussions of current events."

Her father gave me a playful look. "She doesn't realize there's a difference between pop culture and current events. A huge difference."

"Not in my world," Kelly said as she stuck out her tongue. We were all laughing as I stepped out to get my father. I thought about our handgun discussion as I tapped on the glass to get my father's attention. Possibilities...

A girl could never be too prepared.

SNERT WAGON

"I ALWAYS LIKE WATCHING THOSE GHOST HUNTING SHOWS," LEXI said as she steered her Ford Escape onto the freeway. A horn honked behind us, and Kelly laughed.

"You are the worst driver. Ever. Just get us there alive," Kelly said. She turned and waved at the driver behind us.

Sitting in the backseat, I was happy to go on an adventure with my friends, even if it was a stupid adventure.

"You know those shows are fake, right?" I asked. "You never actually see anything happen. It's always the camera filming someone in a dark hallway when someone yells, 'Holy crap, something touched me!' Then the camera jumps and focuses on the man's face and his look of shock. Or you hear a door slam off camera," I said. "Both are so easy to fake. And there's no way to prove he wasn't touched, or that someone off camera didn't slam the door."

Lexi steered us onto 35E as we made our way south. "But they have those voice recordings of the spirits. What about that?"

Shaking my head, I said, "You mean those static-filled electronic voice phenomena (EVP) recordings?"

"Yeah, I heard them say 'he's here' and 'get out' in the last episode," Lexi said. "It was spooky."

"Did you really, though?" I asked, as we drove toward downtown Saint Paul. "It's all in your interpretation. Meaning, it's only after they say the words they want you to hear, that you think that's what was said. It's all suggestion."

Kelly turned back towards me. "I gotta agree. I'm like, that didn't sound like 'stay away' or whatever they said. If you go back and listen again, it sounded just as much like, 'snert wagon.'"

Lexi lost it in the front seat as she snorted. "Snert wagon?" And then she was belly laughing. Both Kelly and I joined in for the next few miles.

When our laughter subsided, Lexi turned on the radio, and right away an eighties favorite came on. "Turn that up," I shouted. The sound of Whitney Houston's "I Wanna Dance with Somebody" flooded the car. The song was infectious, and soon we were all singing along with the chorus. It was one of those times when all of us were shouting as we sung along with the queen of eighties music.

Ahh, good times.

"You sure like your eighties music, don't you, Abbey?" Kelly asked.

I nodded as "We're Not Gonna Take It," by Twisted Sister came on next. "I got my love of eighties music from my mom," I said. "We'd always play it and dance around the kitchen. When she was kidnapped in South America, it was the music that gave me strength to keep going. Both my dad and I really struggled without her." I wiped away a tear. "But it's been great having her home with us. And she's promised to stay close to home from now on."

"That must have been tough. I see why you love the music," Kelly said.

Leaning forward almost into the front seats, I said, "It's not only that. The music feels like a soundtrack to my life. Don't we all need a soundtrack?" There were affirmations from my two teammates. "Imagine we're on the field and the other team is being overly physical."

Kelly blurted, "Like South Saint Paul."

"So South Saint Paul," Lexi agreed.

I laughed. "Yeah, like that. We're getting fed up, and the ref isn't calling anything. After getting knocked down for the umpteenth time, I hear you call out, 'Abbey, we're not going to take it.'" I turn to Kelly. "And then I call out, 'Hey Kelly, we're not going to take it.' Pretty soon, the whole team is saying the same thing and then next thing you know, we're pushing back. Hard. Because we're not going to take it."

"Yes!" Kelly said pumping her fist in the air. "That's what I'm talking about. We're tough, and we're not going to take it anymore."

"And you know we'd win that game, wouldn't we?" I asked. "Nothing's Gonna Stop Us Now," I said throwing out another eighties song just because I could.

"Damn right," Kelly said.

"Language," Lexi said with a laugh.

Kelly looked over. "Lexi, you're such a snert wagon."

And then we were all laughing until we got to our destination on Saint Paul's most prestigious avenue.

HOME to the longest stretch of Victorian-era homes in the United States, the four-and-a-half-mile stretch of Summit Avenue was a visual delight of old homes. Sometimes my father and I would drive down and take a walk on a sunny Saturday afternoon and drool over the amazing architecture. I was no stranger to the area, but I had no idea why Lexi had brought us here. She had only said we needed some adventure in our humdrum lives.

"Lexi, why are we here?" Kelly said, glancing around.

"See that big house?" Lexi said as she pointed to the massive structure we were parked in front of. Of course, pretty much all the structures were massive around here.

"Can't miss it," Kelly said. "It looks creepy."

Lexi laughed. "It's supposed to be creepy," she said as she pulled up her phone. "Listen to this. The Griggs mansion on 476 Summit is rumored to be one of the most haunted houses in Minnesota. The four-story, 24 room, Victorian mansion was built by Civil War veteran and grocery king Chauncey Griggs in 1883. The most notable ghost is said to be that of a young maid who hung herself from the fourth-floor landing in 1915, and some claim the mansion is haunted by at least six entities."

"Six?" Kelly asked. "How could they possibly know that?"

"Because they are trained paranormal investigators, silly. They know these things. Now, let's go meet some of these entities," she said as she climbed out of her car. Not wanting to miss out, we were both out of the car right away.

The imposing mansion sat back with a long stone sidewalk path leading to the street. We stopped and stared at the massive sandstone structure. I couldn't help but shiver as I looked at the windows, wondering who—or what—might be looking back.

"Lexi, how are we going to get inside?" Kelly asked. "Don't people live here?"

"I've got it covered. The place has been split into three units and all the residents are staying somewhere else. My uncle is remodeling the place and said because they are resurfacing the hardwood floors starting tomorrow, the residents have moved out for a couple of days —at least the living ones," she said with a twinkle in her eyes.

"Lexi," I said, as I shook my head. "You've outdone yourself. This is a cool idea."

We moved up the sidewalk and took the steps up to the landing. A realtor combination box attached to the iron door handle had the keys stashed inside. Lexi lifted it up while Kelly shone a flashlight at the buttons. I wasn't surprised little miss preparedness would have a flashlight. I was surprised though, when she handed me one too.

"You do know the code, don't you?" Kelly asked.

"Of course I do. Uncle Mike always puts a six in front of the house number. So, the box code would be 6476." She punched in the numbers and there was a soft click. Lexi pulled open the front plate and there was a set of four keys inside.

There was something about what Lexi said that raised a flag, but as soon as she unlocked the front door and we stepped inside, I forgot about it. The smell of sawdust and mothballs tickled my nose. Kelly pushed the door shut behind us with a loud click that echoed around us. My goosebumps were alive and well.

The open foyer was lit by a single lamp that sat just inside the entrance. Lexi flipped a switch that turned on the wall sconces, lighting up the wallpaper and framed landscapes. Woodwork unlike anything I'd seen was used for great effect, making the place look magnificent and opulent. We took a few steps into the room, the wood floors creaking under foot. I stopped and bounced my weight a little, feeling the floor give as I made creaking sounds that carried and echoed throughout the ground level.

"Abbey, you're our paranormal expert. Do you see anything? Feel anyone here?" Lexi asked as she moved closer and looked into my eyes.

"The only thing I'm feeling is you stepping on my foot," I said as I nudged her back. "Give me a little space, if you don't mind. You silly snert wagon."

Lexi backed up, a loopy grin on her face.

Stepping away from my friends, I moved out into the expansive open space and tried to clear my mind. My mind wasn't having it as every time I glanced toward Lexi I started cracking up. Shrugging, I pointed toward the staircase.

"Let's move up a floor." I tried to project confidence, like this was part of my plan.

The others followed as I took the steps slowly, running my hand over the smooth wooden handrail. I wanted to get a feel for the place. In my experience, homes often have an energy to them that gave each structure a unique feel. Have you ever entered a home and felt calm or a welcoming energy? I don't think that was Feng Shui—the Chinese pseudoscience which claims to use energy forces to harmonize individuals with their surrounding environment—as much as it was the residual energy from the people that lived and died in the home.

These energies can linger a long time.

Unfinished business can keep a spirit in this world, dooming a spirit to wander endlessly where they died. Some repeat the same motions they were doing before they died, like an echo of the past. Some can have actual interaction with the living. Those are the most fun—and the most dangerous.

We were halfway up when the front door slammed and heavy footfalls sounded below us. We looked at each other wide-eyed.

Still a little clueless, I said, "Maybe it's your uncle."

Lexi shook her head. "He doesn't know we're here."

I should have known.

"Move," Kelly hissed, gesturing for us to get our tails moving up the stairs.

On the second-floor landing, we paused and looked for a place to hide. The footfalls moved toward the staircase, the same staircase that would lead to us. Kelly pointed toward the stairs, gesturing for us to go up again. We didn't hesitate. We climbed.

When we got to the third-floor landing, we moved to the only door. It had the number three on it. It was locked.

"The keys," I whispered to Lexi. "Use the keys."

She fumbled with the keys, pulling them from her pocket. Lexi found the one marked 3 and opened the door. When we were safely inside, Kelly put her palm against the door and eased it shut. After hearing the satisfying click of the lock, I started breathing again.

The room was empty besides the stunning Steinway grand piano pushed over near the windows. I assumed the furniture had been shoved into the bedrooms for the floor resurfacing.

I turned on Lexi. "Your uncle doesn't know we're here. Lexi, that means we're breaking and entering. Last time I checked, that's against the law." I was fuming, that was, until Lexi did a Lexi.

"How often do you check? Was it recently? Maybe they changed it." Her earnest expression melted me. How could anyone stay mad at someone so adorable?

"C'mere, you," I said and wrapped her up in a hug.

"Who is out there?" Kelly said with an eye up to the peephole. "I don't see anyone."

"Let's open the door so we can see who's out there," I suggested, reaching for the knob.

"Wait, are you nuts?" Kelly said stepping between me and the door. "You don't know who's out there."

"Exactly why I want to open the door. How else are we going to find out?" My logic game was strong.

"Abbey," Lexi said, "I'm not sure that's such a good idea. What if it's my Uncle Mike? He's not going to be happy with my life choices."

"Lexi, you're a goalie. No one is happy with your life choices," Kelly said with a grin.

"Guys," I said, "What if it's NOT Lexi's uncle?"

Both looked at me with wide eyes.

"Let me put it out there that it would probably be the best-case scenario if it was Uncle Mike. Sure, he'd be mad, but that's it." I looked at my two friends. "It could be a lot worse if it was anyone else. I think we need to know exactly who's out there."

Kelly looked as if she was going to argue with me, but then something else happened.

The piano began to play.

Surprisingly, the music was fast, energetic, playful, and rhythmic —not at all the music one would expect from a haunted piano.

Worst of all, the music was loud.

Yanking open the door, I gestured for Kelly and Lexi to get their butts moving. We ran for the stairs anxious to get away from whoever was playing the piano. With the music cascading loudly out the open door, all attempts of sneakiness were abandoned. We took the stairs two at a time until we reached the fourth-floor landing.

The fourth-floor landing.

The infamous place where the young maid suffering from depression over an ended romance hung herself.

I couldn't help but shiver as a feeling of foreboding enveloped me. Looking to Kelly and Lexi, they felt something too.

"I don't like this," Kelly said, her eyes darting around. "Something bad is going to happen. I can feel it."

Lexi wrapped her arms around herself as she shivered. "I'm scared."

"It's this place. The maid died right here a long time ago, but she's still here. I can feel her. Sometimes really powerful energies will remain long after the person has died and will affect the living." I turned in place, my arms outstretched, my eyes closed. "The energy is so dark, it's like being trapped in a deep well of despair. There's no way out and no end to the suffering. Hope has died."

"Abbey."

"I can't get out. I can't stop it." My eyes wouldn't open.

"Abbey, we're here."

Hands latched onto both of mine, fingers intertwining and squeezing. Friends coming to my rescue. Friends to support me and make me stronger. My spirit rose, leaving the dark, the deep, and the despair behind.

I soared.

"Guys, I think we can help her. Close your eyes and picture what I'm telling you."

My eyes fluttered open. A willowy blonde girl wearing a maid outfit that was not of our era stood there looking self-conscious. She wasn't much older than me. Her hair was severely pulled up, and her eyes revealed much pain and sadness in her short life.

Describing her as best I could, I told my friends everything that stood in front of me. When I was done, I told them to keep the picture in their mind while they opened their eyes.

"Well, hello there," Lexi said with the breathless voice of a young girl seeing the Disney castle for the first time.

Kelly didn't say anything, she simply stared.

The young maid looked back at us, which surprised me. She was in our world—or maybe we were in hers—but the possibility of interaction was real. We could talk to her. And she could talk to us.

"Hello," I said to her as I gave a little squeeze to both my friend's hands. "It's nice to see you."

The maid blinked and opened her mouth, but that was as far as it got. If I had to guess, I'd think she hadn't spoken in a long, long time.

"It may be difficult to find your voice at first, but can you tell us your name?" I nodded reassuringly.

She looked at me with wistful eyes and spoke. "My name is Marina."

Well, there you go.

"It is our pleasure to meet you, Marina. I'm Abbey."

"And I'm Lexi."

Kelly was still silent to my left.

"And this is Kelly," I said with a nod. "She's a shy person." Which is probably the biggest lie I've told since I looked at my reflection in the mirror and told myself I looked like a strong confident woman. I know, my self-talk game needs some work.

Studying her, I took a step forward. "Marina, can you tell us about yourself? Where are you from?"

"I'm...I'm from...Northfield. I grew up on a farm with my two sisters." She looked a little wistful, so I asked her questions. Keeping her engaged would keep her here with us.

"What was that like living on a farm?" I'd always been a suburban girl.

"We were always doing something. Picking blackberries for mom to bake pies. Roaming the hills helping dad search for a lost cow and her new calf. We made hay, carried pail after pail of milk, planting the gardens and butchering chickens. We walked to our one-room schoolhouse, and Sundays were for visiting." Marina looked off into the distance as she remembered her childhood.

"What was it like coming to the city here?" I asked.

Her eyes regained their focus. "It was amazing. All the big homes and buildings. So many people. I'd never seen so many people, except maybe at the county fair."

"How did you come to work here at this house?" I glanced at my friends and they were as riveted as I was, listening to this dead girl tell her story. The intense feeling of foreboding had subsided and was replaced by a warm vibe that made me think of sunshine, a summer breeze and fields of wildflowers.

"I was living in a rooming house near the stockyards and the mum came. She was looking for maids for the well-to-dos. Living on a farm, you do everything, so I knew how to clean. And I'd rather do it in a fancy place than another barn that smelled of cow manure."

"Makes sense to me," Lexi said.

"Did you like being a maid here?" I asked.

Marina nodded.

My father, the journalist, had taught me to avoid asking the yes or no questions just for this reason. You don't learn anything from a nod. Ask open-ended questions, he'd say, and they'll open up for you.

"Marina, what was your favorite part of being a maid here?"

Her face brightened, and I saw her beauty. She had striking pale blue eyes. "At first, it was the exploring as we cleaned and helped the house staff. I'd never seen such a place. So many rooms, so many things to see and touch. I made a good friend, Sarah, and we shared a staff room in the basement. We'd do everything together. We made a game of hide and seek as we moved through the floors cleaning. Mum didn't mind as long as we had our chores done and didn't make too much commotion."

I held her gaze. "Marina, what didn't you like about working here?"

She hesitated, with a stare of pain.

"Marina?"

Her eyes dropped down. "It was the master. He was mean to us girls. I never liked how he looked at us. It was contempt that a lowly farm girl would be allowed in his house."

I nodded, wanting to steer the conversation to what drove her to hang herself. "Did having a romantic relationship help you over those tough times?"

Her eyes clouded while her eyebrows furrowed. "Romantic relationship?" she asked.

"Yes, there was a story that said you were despondent after a romantic breakup." Lexi squeezed my hand. She'd told me about her own breakup the year before. I knew how painful it could be.

Marina scoffed. "Well, stories can be lies, too. I've never been romantic. Never wanted to."

Kelly glanced my way, confusion on her face. This didn't make sense. I could understand how the facts were distorted over the years, but the dark energy that surrounded this girl told a story of pain and death just the same. Something bad happened to her, right where we were standing.

I tried a different tactic. Sometimes, being direct is best. "Marina, can you tell us how you died?"

Her eyes narrowed and her beautiful face distorted into a grimace. The sunshine and flowers were gone and the icy fingers of impending doom were back with a vengeance. Lexi gasped, and I immediately saw why.

A rope noose hung from the wooden post at the top of the stairs.

Maybe being direct wasn't the best idea after all.

"Marina," I said as my voice quavered. "Why did you hang yourself?"

The blue fled from her eyes. Only an inky blackness remained. She no longer looked the part of a sweet country girl. She looked like pain personified. Lexi and Kelly squeezed my hands to the point of hurting.

"I didn't!" she raged. "He did," she roared.

A thin man wearing a black suit stood behind her.

"Holy crap," Lexi said in a quiet voice.

A strong wind picked up—unusual for being inside a house—and swirled Marina's hair. The wall sconces burned brighter than any light I've seen, and the black suited man floated eerily toward us. He looked like one of those creepy undertakers from an old horror movie. I thought I was going to pee myself.

I shouted to be heard over the roar of the wind. "But why, Marina? Why would he do that to you?"

But instead of Marina's voice, it was the unusually gravelly voice of the black suited man. "Because the farm girl was going to tell. She should have known her place." He spat out the words.

The three of us exchanged glances, horrified, as we realized the reason for the maid's pain.

Something not everyone knows about me, but they learn if they are around me long enough, is that I have a strong sense of outrage. When a person is used and abused by someone of authority, my blood runs hot. No one—alive or dead—should be treated the way Marina had been treated. The way he was treating her in front of us. Consequences be damned, I had to do something.

"You," I barked. "You, in your undertaker suit that smells of sweat and desperation, are a vile piece of garbage. You've haunted this poor girl—this sweet girl—in life and death. It stops now."

"Get him, Abbey," Kelly said next to me. Lexi gave me a reassuring hand squeeze. I love my friends.

"This girl is under our protection and she will no longer be fouled by your presence." I made a show of sniffing while making my best Mr. Yuck face. "Quite frankly, you smell like a shit wagon and you should be hauled away. Far, far away from here."

"Yes," Kelly said. "You stink."

"Like cow crap," Lexi said with more enthusiasm than people often have when they're talking about animal feces.

As one, we stepped to the old man. "I'm commanding you to vacate these premises. Take your sorry ass and leave immediately. Go," I shouted, and with Lexi's hand in my left and Kelly's in my right, we made contact with the ghost of the unpleasant man and shoved him backwards. His eyes were locked on mine as he hung in balance at the top of the stairs. But our shove had been enough. With a look of fear, he toppled backwards and fell. We watched him careen down the centuries-old staircase, and just as he should have hit the bottom...he didn't.

He was gone.

The light bulbs on the wall sconces flashed brightly and

shattered, sending glass everywhere, leaving us breathing heavily in the darkness.

Flipping on my flashlight, I was startled to see Marina standing so close to us. Her dark eyes stared into mine. Her face was devoid of expression. I had no idea what she was thinking, or really, if she was capable of thought in her current condition. All I knew was there was more to do.

"Marina," I began. "You are free. There's nothing binding you to this place. You're free to move about the cabin."

"Abbey," Kelly called from my right. "She doesn't know about airplanes."

"Sorry, that's a reference you wouldn't understand. What I'm trying to tell you, is there's a better place for you. A place that's warm and inviting. A place with a warm summer breeze and fields of wildflowers. A place with your sisters and your parents. A place where your friend, Sarah, waits for you."

Tears rolled down Marina's smooth cheeks.

"Marina, there's a light. This light is your beacon, your path to home and family. Love awaits you in this light."

I turned off my flashlight as there was more than enough light to see now. Marina's face lit up with golden light as she smiled, her crinkled eyes squeezing out the last of her tears.

"Marina," I said fighting my own tears, but losing the battle. "Go now."

With a shimmer of sparkling light, Marina faded from view.

"Oh, Abbey," Lexi said as she wrapped up Kelly and me in a massive hug. "That was the most beautiful thing I've ever witnessed."

Kelly tried to say something, but her voice caught in her throat.

"I know," I said with the wonder of what just happened. "I know."

At least there weren't any clowns.

YOU CAN'T STOP ME

I WAS DREAMING AGAIN.

Moving along a hallway in measured steps, a hand slid along the pebbly surface of the brick wall. The hand I saw wasn't mine, yet I was seeing through the eyes of the hand's owner. We caught a glimpse of someone going around the corner ahead of us. I felt the urgency as we sped up to get to that corner. The edges of my vision blurred, but the center of my vision was sharp and locked in on the girl as she moved down the secluded hallway. She neared another corner, but was too distant for me to recognize. There was something predatory about the way I watched her. My heart beat faster, and I heard the heavy breathing of the stalker I shared the experience with —an experience he seemed to enjoy. Things would not end well.

We turned the corner and saw the girl step into a dimly lit classroom. We were right outside the room as the lights flickered on. I recognized the classroom as one of the biology labs. A sense of dread rose—there was something about the way she moved that made me feel I knew her. There was only one person I knew at my new school who would be at home in the biology lab. It may not be her, but my growing trepidation told me otherwise.

The hand reached for the door and eased it ever-so-slowly open. I felt us step into the entrance and peer at the girl. She wore a lab coat and had her back to us. Her blonde hair obscured her face as she turned to the side as if listening for something. My host held his breath. After a moment, the girl shook her head and turned back to the table. The stalker let go of the breath he'd been holding.

Her head shake was enough. I knew who she was, and I tried with every fiber of my being to scream out, "Bri!"

Skinny, sweet, hilarious, socially awkward Bri. I had to warn her that her life was in danger from that creeper. But I wasn't in control. He was—and he took a step into the room. Bri was alone, her attention solely on her lab project and had no clue what was approaching her.

My mind raced. I needed to protect Bri. But how? I tried everything I could to impact the horrible situation, but it was like watching a scary movie and yelling at the screen. No matter how loud you yell, "Don't go in there," you know she was never going to hear you. And she would go in.

My host took another step forward.

I wanted to scream—no, I needed to scream. I was frustrated, angry and scared. Bri was one of the sweetest people I knew. I remembered the game when she had received a yellow caution card. It was our third or fourth game of the season and we were playing North under the lights. Bri played forward and was matched up with a beast of a defender who played her hard. Every ball that went Bri's way, the girl was all over her. Grabbing, bumping, not giving an inch. Late in the second half, Bri pushed back once and was shown a yellow card. I was astounded that Bri, of all people, would get a card. It would be twice as likely that your grandmother would be arrested for pushing around a gang of punks on a street corner. Never Bri. This should not be happening to her.

Another agonizingly slow step towards Bri.

His eyes were the eyes of a predator, and they did not waiver. Bri was his prey.

Feeling the burning hot intensity of his gaze on my friend, there could be only one outcome—and I needed to stop it. Maybe diverting his attention would offer Bri a chance. I focused on the large glass and chrome beaker on the table next to us. Every ounce of my brain— every neuron—focused on that beaker. I wanted him to touch it, take his focus off Bri. Maybe he'd make some noise and offer her some warning.

He took another step, just feet away from her now.

And then...his focus moved away from Bri to the beaker. I was stunned. Please, let it work. God, I'll even start going to church again. *C'mon, make some noise.*

His hand, ever-so-slowly, reached for the beaker, wrapping his impossibly long fingers around it. As he lifted and judged the heft of it, I caught a glimpse of his reflection on the beaker's chrome lip. A glimpse was all I needed. And my mind was blown.

It was the scary clown from the circus.

Images of that night at the circus ran through my head, remembering the terrifying visage of the dark clown. Many people are scared of clowns for no reason, but one look at that one and you'd have your reason. His dark eyes promised evil, and you knew there was something seriously wrong with him. There was madness there.

The other circus clowns were terrified of him. That should have been a tip off for me. When a clown was scared of another clown, you know something wasn't right.

As with most dreams, reality wasn't real as the face of the clown shifted and melted into a different clown. Sharp, pointy teeth and a scarred visage on this one.

The sound of the beaker shattering on the floor to Bri's left pulled me back to the present. Her head whipped around as Bri let out a shout of shock. The clown took advantage of the diversion, immediately closing the gap to grab her from behind. He was all over her: one hand covering her mouth, while the other arm wrapped around her throat. Her cry was cut off instantly. The sound of her whimper broke my heart.

The only saving grace was that Bri couldn't see the face of her attacker. Seeing his face—one not even his mother could love—would put her over the edge.

He pulled her off the stool, tipping it over with a loud clatter. The sound echoed around the deserted lab. She flailed her arms trying to get loose. But if you ever saw Bri, a little wisp of a girl, you'd know she had no chance. With virtually no effort, the clown dragged her to the door and paused. By the way he cocked his head, I believe he listened for something. Voices approached.

Yes! It was the break Bri needed. I couldn't picture the clown fighting off multiple people while holding onto Bri. The voices approached the door, shadows on the other side of the frosted glass. Please, let it be a teacher.

I felt the clown tighten his grip on Bri and pull her to the side of the door. "Make a sound and I'll twist your head off," he hissed in Bri's ear. "Understand?"

Bri nodded.

The door opened and two boys stepped in, heading for the far-right side of the room. Animatedly discussing which superhero could take the other in a cage match, they took no notice of the evil lurking just inside the room's entrance.

"Spiderman is quicker. No way Wolverine could even catch him."

"He doesn't have to catch him. Just slice him with his claws." Idiots.

The clown pulled Bri around the corner and out the door, her heels dragging on the tile floor.

As if the entire experience hadn't been odd enough, the clown said something under his breath. Barely a whisper, but it chilled me to my core. "You can't stop me."

As my brain disengaged from the clown with two faces, I felt any hope of helping Bri slip away. I was powerless to help my friend. Exasperated and afraid for her, I shouted out my frustration. "No!"

The problem, as I discovered, was that I was in class. Sitting near the back, watching a video during English Lit, I must have dozed off. I was still exhausted from the tournament. For the briefest of moments, I hoped my shouts were in the dream. Mr. Karp clarified that in a hurry and dashed my hopes when he paused the video, asking, "Are you alright, Miss Hill?" There was genuine concern in his voice. I felt everyone's eyes on me as they waited for my reply. Everyone was so quiet.

The problem was, I had no idea what to say. So I said nothing.

Mr. Karp held my gaze for a long moment. "Maybe you should visit the nurse," he suggested.

"Maybe I should." I gathered my things and rushed from the room.

"I'll go with her," Kelly said behind me. "Make sure she gets there okay." She joined me in the hallway, a look of apprehension on her face. "What is it?"

"It's Bri, she's in trouble." Grabbing Kelly's hand, I pulled her down the hall. Breaking into a sprint, we took each corner hard, navigating the sparse traffic we encountered as we raced for the lab. I feared for Bri.

Reaching the lab, I pulled open the door and raced in, Kelly right behind me. The two geeks were still in their discussion as they hovered over a burner. "The Flash would run circles around him. And create a vortex in the process that'll suck away all the oxygen."

The other boy poured some liquid into the tube on the burner. "Batman is smart, though. He's crafty. He'll pull something out of his utility belt to trip up the Flash."

The first one snorted. "That's all you got? Tripping him?"

"Hey, Einstein," I called out. "Did you see anything here?" The boys looked at us with that deer in the headlight look. "Wait, what?"

"Over here." I walked them over to where Bri's stool laid on its side with shattered glass on the floor nearby.

"Whoa. When did that happen?" The boys crowded around us. "I didn't see anything."

"I bet Batman would have noticed."

Time slowed as my mind raced. There are people who bring light and life to our world. They bring a spirit of kindness and hope that energizes the people around them. And then, there were these two. School book brilliant, they lacked any real-world smarts. Put them in a dollar store and they would have no idea how they got there or how to get out. These two were a complete waste of space.

Knowing it was a dead end, I sprinted for the door, desperately hoping they were still on the school grounds. "Go check the lot. I'll go to the woods behind the loading dock."

An hour later, I was exhausted and frustrated and afraid. Sinking to the ground, I broke down and cried. I was still sobbing when Kelly found me.

"I couldn't find her. Our friend is gone. That maniac took her, and he's going to kill her."

"We'll find her first," she promised. "And Christina too. And then we're going to kill that clown."

I shook my head. "That might be hard to do if he's dead already." Kelly's open mouth told me she hadn't even considered the possibility.

"We better call the police," I said getting to my feet. "We're going to need all the help we can get."

FRIENDS AND RELATIONS

Several deputy sheriffs showed up, but nothing happened. No miracle.

When they first arrived, I'd told them that Bri said to meet her in the lab, but all we found was her backpack and cell. The broken glass seemed to concern them, but they said all they could do was be on the lookout for her. If someone had seen something, the woman deputy said, then they could act with more urgency. For all we know she said, Bri had cut her finger on the glass and went for a band-aid. She gave me a little smile and patted my shoulder.

The woman deputy had talked slow and over-pronounced each word as she introduced herself as Deputy Francis. She must have thought I was in first grade. If there was one thing I hate, it's when an adult talks down to me. With all my travels accompanying my father around the world, let alone having a doctor for a mother, I was not your average teenager. I knew I was bright and could almost certainly guarantee I was considerably further up the intellectual food chain than that bleached blonde.

My father taught me when you become frustrated with someone, you couldn't let it show or color your responses. A journalist needed to keep the information flowing even when the interviewee wasn't as bright or cooperative as you would prefer.

His tried-and-true technique was to smile and nod with each infuriatingly idiotic statement and think happy thoughts about the person's demonstrated shortcomings. I needed to put his coping technique to the test.

"I'm sure she got sidetracked and forgot her things here." I nodded. *This woman was clear proof that evolution CAN go in reverse.*

"We'll give her parents a call. She's probably already home watching TV." I gave her a reassuring smile. *The wheel's spinning, but the hamster's dead.*

I knew things from my dream vision I couldn't reveal like that the clown dragged her out of the classroom. They had to search the area, at least. "But you have to..."

The woman held up her finger and said, "Shhh." Putting her arm around me, I caught her wink at her partner. "This is a matter for law enforcement. We deal with this kind of thing all the time." *Poor woman. She had obviously fallen out of the stupid tree and hit every branch on the way down.*

"Why don't you girls go home and get started on your homework? I'd hate to have your grades suffer for nothing." I was running out of coping thoughts as the deputy pushed the limits of my endurance. One last thought popped into my brain: *She's a few clowns short of a circus.*

I cracked up at the absurdity of the moment. I covered my smile and started to cough, barely able to stop a laugh from coming out. I turned away and coughed even louder. Kelly came to my rescue as I was about to lose it.

"Let's get you some water." She latched onto my arm and pulled me toward the door.

"Thank you, Officer Friendly," Kelly told the deputy as we stepped into the hall.

"It's Deputy Francis," an exasperated sounding voice call out behind us as our coughing overtook both of us.

It was difficult to think about playing soccer after what happened, but I got the team concept and didn't want to let my teammates down. Entering the locker room, I took a hopeful glance towards Bri's locker, but it remained closed, and she was nowhere to be seen. The atmosphere should have tipped me off. Word had spread, as the room had a somber feel.

As we prepared for the game, there was almost no conversation. Heads were hung and smiles were upside down. I didn't like our chances of winning the game.

But the night had two things going for it: We were playing Woodbury, and we got to play under the lights. Each of those factors by itself would usually generate tons of excitement. You'd hear girls talking smack and speculating about who may be in the crowd. If you were thinking cute boys, you'd be right on the mark. Girls noticed these things. It was also unseasonably hot for a night game.

Coach Johnson strode into the locker room, paused, and looked around. "Whoa, we are one sorry lot. This is possibly the biggest game of our season and we're going to walk out on the field with our heads hanging. We may as well hand over the conference bragging rights to Woodbury right now. Let's skip the embarrassment and head home early. At least I can catch 'Dancing with the Stars,' so the day won't be a total loss." She glanced at each of us, waiting for some reaction. She got none.

"This is also the last game of our season. With two girls missing, Christina and now Bri." Coach Johnson's voice broke. She paused for a moment before continuing. "We can't in good conscience continue. Soccer is important, but it's not worth risking your lives over. Don't worry about your safety tonight, we have the stadium covered. You'll see plenty of law enforcement at the game tonight."

"It makes me feel better that they like soccer too," I said. It looked like Coach Johnson was going to say something, but then she got the joke.

I got a nod before she continued. "So tonight, we go out there and we play our last game in front of your families, friends and classmates. And you know the place will be full of Woodbury supporters. They're going to be loud, they're going to be mean, and they're going to make the game harder than it should be. But does that mean we should give up because the game is difficult?"

Coach Johnson searched our faces.

"Does that mean we should give up because there's no playoffs for us?"

She looked around the room and shook her head.

"Let me answer the question for you. No, we should not give up. Ever. Because there's someone else watching tonight. Remember when you were a little girl who fell in love with the game? Over the years, you've had hours upon hours of practice, dozens of coaches who've pushed you and inspired you, and probably a million touches of the ball. You've sweated, cried and celebrated over the games won, lost or tied. That little girl is still inside you, the same one that dreamed of playing with her friends, playing for her school, and playing in big games. She's inside of you, watching...play for her."

Tears ran down my cheeks, as well as several of the girls. But the room was silent. At last Lexi raised her head. "Coach?"

Coach Johnson took a step toward her. "Yes?"

"But Bri." Lexi's voice cracked as her words came out.

Taking a deep breath, Coach Johnson took a knee in front of Lexi. Her voice barely above a whisper, "Bri may not be our best player, but she has a heart like no other. Her gift is caring about others and putting them first. I've watched Bri help her teammates after a tough game when she could barely walk herself. Yet she offered comfort and a shoulder to lean on as both players limped off the field."

"I remember that," Fran said quietly.

"How about when we played White Bear Lake, and the rain was coming down in sheets, and no one wanted to play? Bri was the first one on the field."

"And she took that spectacular dive into the massive puddle in front of the bench."

"She looked like a seaplane coming in for a landing."

Laughter now.

"But she got all of you to do it too," Coach Johnson said with a smile. "And then you guys were all fierce on the field after that. No monsoon of a rainstorm was going to stop you from kicking White Bear Lake's tail."

"We beat them 5–0." Sophie smiled. "That felt so good."

Coach Johnson moved into the middle of the group. "Put your hand in and let's do this for Bri."

I felt myself getting caught up in the power of the moment. There was electricity spreading as we joined hands. "One, two, three. Bri!" we yelled together and moved out into the hot evening air, ready to take Woodbury down.

THE STANDS WERE jam packed full, as was much of the sidelines with standing room only. The visitor stands had more fans than I've ever seen, but our home section was a sea of blue and gold. Maybe word spread that this was our final game, and everyone wanted to be there to see it. The sheriff's department sure was there in numbers. Deputies lined the edge of the field roughly thirty feet all the way around, though none faced the game. Their loss. It was quite the game.

I spent much of it dealing with Woodbury's twin forwards. Actually twins, the two girls were both tall and fast. They played off each other well, kind of like they've been playing together all their life. Wearing numbers 9 and 11, they figured in just about all of Woodbury's attack.

With 30 minutes to play, the ball got passed to 11, who I was covering. Right away, there was Lexi behind me with a familiar command, "Don't let her score."

I didn't need Lexi's reminder, as I hadn't planned on letting her score. I kept touch distance from her, as I didn't want to let her turn with the ball. Instead, she passed the ball to her trailing sister, 9, and spun off me looking for the return pass.

They say the eyes are the window to the soul, but in soccer, they are the key to reading intent. 9's eyes gave away her intention, and I was there to intercept the pass.

With the ball at my feet, I surged forward, taking the open space. My head was up as I evaluated my options. Julia was wide, making a run down the right side of the field. I hit a curved pass that put the ball into her path. She picked up her pace and got her foot on it. She passed it to Haily, who pushed it past her closing opponent and sent it back to Julia.

Kelly was on the left side of the field, calling for the ball as she streaked in at an angle for the back post. With her next touch, Julia hit a hard crossing pass that eluded the feet of all four Woodbury defenders. The pass ended up on Kelly's foot, and with a simple redirect, the ball sped past a diving Woodbury goalie and into the back of the net. The goalie slammed her fist on the turf with frustration.

"Nice work, Abbey," Lexi said with an accompanying fist bump. I nodded, as nothing compared to the feeling of helping your team score a goal. The team dynamic was a strong bond, and I liked it. A lot.

It was a Hollywood ending. It was still over ninety degrees, and we were up by the one goal late in the game. It'd been tough as Woodbury was playing a physical game trying to even up the score. Every ball was met with a physical challenge that sent me to the turf on more than one occasion. Woodbury was relentless as the game clock wore down with less than ten minutes to play. They were literally throwing their bodies into each challenge, and the center referee wasn't calling anything, obviously preferring to let the game play out.

And then everything changed.

Without warning, the sprinkler system came on, spraying the field like a rainstorm. The ref looked over to the coaches, who held up their hands and shrugged, conveying that there was nothing they could do. The second the ref blew his whistle three times, announcing the premature end to the game, both teams screamed and ran for the sprinklers. I slid across the wet grass, loving the feel of the water. It was a moment of complete joy, a moment of being a little girl again.

WALKING BACK to my locker basking in the glow of the win, every step reminded me of the knocks I'd received. It was the toughest game—and most satisfying game—I'd been a part of so far. I was moving a little slower than normal, though. Okay, more like a sloth after a particularly difficult day of slothing.

The halls were dark as I turned the corner and used my phone's flashlight to see my locker combination. An involuntary groan escaped when I reached down for my backpack. No doubt about it, I was going to be extremely sore tomorrow, I realized, as I straightened up and closed my locker.

I wasn't alone.

"Oh," I called out involuntarily, startled to find Peter leaning against the adjoining locker. He wore jeans, a flannel shirt with a white tee underneath, and a smug smile. "It's not nice to scare someone," I scolded him with an accompanying waving finger.

"I was operating under the assumption you didn't scare easily." His dark eyes held mine. He still had that smug smile going.

"Well, a lot of things have changed recently," I said as I turned and walked away leaving him standing there. "This clown apocalypse is getting to me," I called over my shoulder.

Turning the corner, Peter was there waiting, of course. It was difficult to express my attitude by walking away from him when he was always going to reappear in front of me. I stubbornly turned around. He was there again.

"What?" I held up my hands in mock surrender. "What can I do for you?"

Peter sort of flickered, reminding me that he wasn't actually part of our world. "You're the one who asked me to do something for you. Find out what the clowns are doing, talk to them."

I nodded, instantly interested. "And..."

His downward gaze told me a lot about his results. "Nothing. I can't find one—not a single clown—anywhere here."

"Seriously?" I asked. "They're not hard to miss. Just look for the crazy hair, red nose and questionable fashion choices."

"They must not be on the plane where I exist. Maybe spirits are not meant to interact. Interaction is for the living." His face had turned somber.

"But we interact."

"You're special, though," he replied.

"Short bus special? Eat the paste special?" I said trying to lighten the mood.

"You are the only one who has ever seen or talked to me. That kind of special."

"I've been thinking about that same thing." I took a step closer. "All my life, I've seen dead people and been able to communicate with them in a primitive way. I've never been able to sit and have a normal conversation like we've had—like we're having now."

Peter nodded, but didn't reply.

"So why is that? This is uncharted territory for me."

Looking directly at me, he said, "For the life of me, I have no idea."

I fought back a smile. "I see what you did there."

He showed a hint of a smile before he continued. "Maybe we're better connected somehow." He shrugged as he tossed out his speculation.

"What would make us better connected?" Though I wasn't expecting an answer.

Peter ran a hand through his hair. "It could be that my energy better resonates with you. Maybe I'm closer to your dimension than the others." He paused. "Or maybe you had something to do with my death."

I held up a hand. "I can assure you I had nothing to do with your death. Besides, you have no memories of how you died, right?"

"No..."

"Well then, let's get to the bottom of that mystery." I sat right down on the school floor and pulled out my iPad. "My father has been an investigative journalist my entire life and I've often helped with his research. He's told me he wouldn't be where he is today without my awesome research skills."

I pulled up Google. "What's your last name, Peter?"

His expression remained blank.

"You don't remember that either?" He shook his head. Okay, no last name then. That should make things more challenging.

"Let's start with what we know. Peter. Pine Ridge. Student. Death," I said as I typed my search query and hit the button.

Nothing relevant came up. "Hmmm."

"What is it?" he asked.

"Got nothing that looks right. But I'm just getting started." I pulled up the school website. "These dot edu websites hold a treasure trove of data if you know how to look for it."

Peter crouched by my side, looking on, wrinkles creasing his forehead.

"Hmmm. Nothing here either."

"Maybe you don't know how to look for it," he said with a hint of a smirk.

"Shush," I said. "Professional at work here."

I got on the Pioneer Press website. The Pioneer Press was St. Paul's largest newspaper and the closest major paper to Pine Ridge. Checking their archives, there were several possibilities, but nothing that seemed to fit. Where else could I find news about our school? The nearby town of White Bear Lake had a small paper that had published area news for a hundred years, even reporting on the gangsters who'd come to Minnesota to summer on the lake back in the day. But nothing of consequence showed up, other than a mention of their new digital archive. It said their newly restored archive would be available on the first of next month.

I could really use that archive now.

Checking the time, I saw it was going on 8:30 p.m. No one should be at a small paper like the White Bear Lake Press unless...

"Hold on, I have an idea." I checked the newspaper's directory looking for the prep sports writer. This time of evening would be his prime time for writing up the day's games. I searched for his byline and found his cell number. These small-town papers were all about access, unlike the larger papers that employed gatekeepers to keep people using the proper channels.

"I'm calling someone that could help," I said as I called Bradley Prose, Prep Sports Reporter.

"Brad Prose, Prep Sports," I heard when he answered on the second ring.

"Evening. This is Amanda Bynes, I'm a researcher on the Pioneer Press crime beat. I'm following up on a cold case from several years ago and in the spirit of inter-departmental cooperation..."

Peter raised an eyebrow.

"Could you enter a brief search into your new digital archive? It would be a huge help." I guessed that the paper's staff would have advance beta access to the archive.

Prose hesitated for a long moment. I purposely remained silent to keep the impetus on him. He cleared his throat. "I don't see what it could hurt." My hunch was correct, he did have access.

"I'll make sure our managing editor is aware of your cooperation. You never know when that awareness may come in handy." It was a fine line to walk. I wanted to entice him, but also be subtle enough so he was the one to connect the dots. Let him realize the potential benefits of establishing a relationship with a much larger newspaper.

Except of course, it wasn't a real connection, and I didn't know the managing editor, and I had nothing to do with the Pioneer Press. I should have felt guilty about misleading Bradley Prose, but I didn't. That put me firmly in the "ends justifies the means" camp.

"I've got the database pulled up. What are your search terms?"

"Peter. No last name. Pine Ridge High School. Student. Death." I tried to cross my toes to go along with my already crossed fingers. Please, please let the search work.

"I do have a result with a strong correlation. It's from 1965 though, so more than a few years ago."

I glanced at Peter, who was now sitting beside me. He did that flicker thing where he winked out and reappeared an inch over. Holding my hand over the phone, I asked, "Could you have been from 1965?"

I got a shrug.

"I can email a PDF of the story over to the paper, if you'd like," Prose said.

No, you shouldn't, I was thinking. "Could you just read it to me? See if we're on the right track."

"Sure." Prose cleared his throat as I put the call on speaker. "Student Dies at Local High School. The story is dated Thursday, November 11, 1965. A 15-year-old student at Pine Ridge High School died Wednesday after a fall down a flight of stairs.

"Peter John Vickrey of Juniper Street in Pine Ridge died of head trauma received during the fall. He was found at approximately 2 p.m. and had last been seen at his 12:15 p.m. class. Although his death was ruled accidental, questions were raised why Vickrey was in the area of the building where he was found.

"Sheriff Bill Hudson spoke to reporters. 'Vickrey's classes should have kept him in the South wing, yet his body was found in the North wing on a back staircase that was rarely used.' The sheriff went on to say that unless a witness came forward, the circumstances around Hill's death would remain a mystery.

"Vickrey is survived by his parents, John and Meredith Vickrey, as well as siblings Elise and Jennifer. Funeral arrangements are pending."

My eyes bored a hole into Peter. For his part, Peter looked back at me with a blank expression. It was like looking into the eyes of a goldfish. There was nothing going on in there.

Prose cleared his throat. "That's it, Ms. Bynes. Is this what you were expecting to find?"

I was trying to wrap my little mind around the big news. "Uh, no. Not at all what I was expecting. But I thank you, Mr. Prose. Appreciate your time."

Peter was giving me a look of expectant confusion as I ended the call. "What?" he asked.

"I'm sure that story was about you. Utterly convinced, in fact." I wanted to reach out and hold his hand as I broke things down for him. "Your name is Peter John Vickrey."

He nodded. "Feels right."

"And Peter, you died in 1965."

"So?"

"Do you know what year this is?" He shook his head. "Peter, you died nearly 50 years ago."

"Really?"

"Really. You've been wandering the halls of Pine Ridge for 50 years. You'd be 65 if you were still living."

His face had a surprised expression. "Oh."

"And the head trauma may explain why you don't remember anything from your past."

"Makes sense."

I paused. "But there's more going on here." I held his gaze. "Maybe I can help you with your recall. It looks like your middle name came from your father, John Vickrey. Try to picture him and your mother, Meredith."

I studied Peter. His eyes were closed, his forehead wrinkled with the effort of concentration. "Can you do it?" I asked in a soothing voice.

"I...see them." He smiled, and I gave him a moment to enjoy the memories.

"You also had two sisters."

Eyes still closed, his smile broadens. "Yeah, Elise and little Jen. Jen's stubborn and sweet, like a little sister is supposed to be. Elise is my older sister. She is...was...haunted. She could see things that we couldn't. It made life difficult for her."

"Peter." His smile had faded.

"Peter."

He opened his eyes. "Hi. You and I were never formally introduced." I hold out my hand, which Peter ignored. "My name is Abbey Nicole...Hill."

Peter's forehead was wrinkling again. He hadn't made the connection yet.

I continued. "My grandmother was named Elise Hill, though her maiden name was Vickrey." Peter's eyes narrowed. "Elise had a son, Constantine. He's my father. My grandmother Elise had a sister, Jennifer. And I remember hearing stories about a brother who died when they were young. His name was..."

"Peter," he finished my sentence. Now he had it.

"Exactly. Which means you and I are related."

PETER WINKED out of existence after my announcement. Being related explained why I was able to communicate so well with Peter. No oblique symbols or subtle messages, I could simply talk to him. I wish he could help with the clowns, but for some reason he was separated from the other spirits. As I stepped out into the warm evening air, I thought I knew why.

ANOTHER STEP TOWARDS THE ABYSS

THE PARKING LOT WAS DARK AS I WAITED FOR MY FATHER TO pick me up. Still a little shy about my new soccer career, I hadn't asked my parents to come to my games. Sure, they asked how it was going almost daily, but I was going to wait a little longer into the season before I invited them. I wanted to make sure I knew what I was doing first. It would have to wait until next season now.

When I texted my father to pick me up, I mentioned I had some news to tell him. Couldn't wait to tell him I'd met his uncle Peter.

A sound.

I listened. Maybe not a sound, but something had pulled my attention away from my phone. I tucked it away and surveyed the lot, making sure I was alone. There was no sign of the earlier massive law enforcement presence. Considerably after hours, the parking lot lights were off, and I relied on the ambient light as well as the little light from the moon that was trying to peek out from behind the clouds. There was only one car left in the lot, which belonged to a lacrosse player. His piece of crap car hadn't moved for over a week. The warm air blew in fog from the surrounding forest.

With my father coming soon, I didn't want to go back inside to wait. Thinking of the door's latch sound when I left the school, going back in wasn't an option, anyway. I took a few steps along the sidewalk wanting to get closer to the lot's main entrance and nearer to traffic. Quiet as a graveyard in the lot, the fog didn't do anything to discourage the graveyard impression at all. Stopping to look back across the lot, I felt an electric tension. Without a doubt, something was going to happen.

The Talking Heads had a hit in the Eighties called "And She

Was." At first, I thought it was about a girl who floated over her neighborhood, but the song was actually about a girl the band leader David Byrne knew in high school who dropped acid in a field by a Yoo-hoo chocolate drink factory. I thought that was so surreal when I'd first read about it. Apparently, I had no idea how surreal life could get as every hair I had stood on end.

With a loud *whoomp*, the overhead parking lot light in the far back corner turned on. Mounted on a two-story pole, the fog kept the parking light's radius tight beneath it. *Shouldn't all the lights be wired to the same circuit?* I'd never seen just one light turned on. The entire lot should be lit up when the switch was thrown. Yet, there was just one burning. Ahh, the joys of paranormal activity.

Whoomp. Another pole lit up, this one a little closer. Was there something dancing at the light's edge down on the lot?

Whoomp. Another. Where was my father? I looked around with rising anxiety.

Whoomp. Again. The pattern obvious as there was a diagonal line of lights beginning with the back corner of the lot moving in my direction. I caught a hint of movement towards the light that most recently turned on. Moving towards me.

Oddly, I was reminded of the spotlight dance from Rosa's Quinceañera. Rosa was my neighbor, and there was a great party for her 15th birthday. When she entered the darkened room, a string of lights winked on as Rosa danced. It was both beautiful and cool. But this was the complete opposite. And for the record, not once did I feel like wetting myself at her party.

Whoomp. Still another light was added to the line. As I searched the edges of the light for any movement, there was a loud sound of metal against metal. Steel striking steel.

A figure stood at the base of the pole. He raised an arm and slashed violently toward the pole. Whatever was in his hand hit the metal causing a cascade of sparks as the light winked back out. One thing I'd learned from my history class, there came a time in battle when retreat was the best strategic move. Especially when faced with a superior opponent—or a rampaging killer clown. Historical precedent aside, there was no pride lost by moving to a better position. I turned and ran as I heard another loud *whoomp* behind me.

I ran hellbent for the parking lot entrance. Pushing my sore muscles to work harder than during the game, I gave it everything I had. I knew my life depended on my speed.

With no cars in sight, and miles of emptiness to my left, and a large horse farm across the road, I had one option. I turned right, heading towards the fire station and gas station several blocks down. Daring a glance behind, I was surprised that there wasn't anyone giving chase. But I knew I wasn't safe. Not even for a minute.

Tired and winded, I pushed myself to keep moving towards the gas station. The dark and forbidding woods on my right ended as I reached the edge of the church property bordering the school. Thankfully, it was all open terrain after that with no place for someone to hide. Ahead, a car turned in my direction from the stoplight. Hoping for rescue, I was off the sidewalk and running into the road directly at the car. Waving, I yelled, "Stop, please, stop."

The frightened face of an elderly woman came right at me as she honked and screeched to a stop just missing me. Her window was down, and she yelled something about teenagers today. She threatened to call the police right before she hit the gas and raced off.

"Go ahead, call the police," I yelled after her. "Call them right now." But she was gone, and so was my chance for escape.

Survival instincts kicked back in, knowing I was too exposed. I took a few jogging steps towards the gas station just past the church, and stopped.

At the edge of the woods, a dark shape silhouetted by the church parking lot lights waited. Even though it wasn't moving, I was almost sure it was the same dark figure I caught glimpses of beneath the lights in the school lot.

My chest heaved as my heart thumped like it was trying to beat its way out of my body. I froze in place as my eyes locked on the shadow-figure some fifteen yards away. All I saw was a black mass, but it felt alive and threatening.

Options ran through my head. I wanted to run, but if I moved towards the gas station, he'd catch me. If I headed in any of the other directions, I'd be moving away from people, safety and rescue. I didn't like any of my options.

I felt the weight of his eyes as they sized up his prey. Me.

I turned slightly away as if glancing back to evaluate my options. I wanted to hide what I was doing as I reached for the phone in my back pocket. I pulled up the iPhone's phone app, keeping the phone out of his view.

My last call was to my father, and I touched the screen to redial him. I knew I couldn't put the phone to my ear or use the speaker, because that would force my stalker to act. When you're in the jungle, you don't want to do anything that makes the lion pounce. Acting as if I was adjusting the shoulder strap on my backpack, I tucked the phone underneath to hide it. I should be able to hear and be heard if my father ever picked up. And why wasn't he there yet?

The voice I heard wasn't the voice I expected—or wanted—to hear. It was my mother. "Hello, Abbey."

"Mom..." Not sure what to say. She knew some of my past occurrences, but had no real idea the dangers my abilities regularly brought to my life. My father and I had agreed it was better that she didn't know. The world she lived in was logical, methodical and scientific.

"Sorry, we're running so late. We stopped off to pick up a pizza at Wildwood Pizza. We knew you'd be hungry after the game. You played great, by the way." I had no idea my parents were at the game.

"We'll be back to pick you up soon. Your father is inside paying for the pizza." Wildwood Pizza was one block further down the street from the gas station. That meant they were close. So close.

As I listened to my mother, I'd swear the shape had moved slightly away from the forest's edge. "Mom..."

"We ordered Canadian bacon and pineapple. Your favorite."

"Mom..." I stared intently at the black mass, convinced it was staring just as intently back at me.

"It's okay, no need to thank me. I try to look out for you. I do owe my life to you, after all," she said, referencing the rescue from the South American cartel. I wished she'd hurry up as I saw something move by the figure's midsection. If I had to guess, I'd say it looked like a glint of reflected light on a steel blade. A long steel blade.

Things may not end well.

"Hang on a second, your father's back," she said. "How much did you tip? That's not enough, don't you think? Here, go back and give them this." I heard rustling from the speaker. "Your father. He only tipped $2 for a $16 pizza. I sent him back in with $2 more."

I was absolutely beside myself. She sent him back in? Unbelievable. Watching the figure, I knew our standoff would be ending shortly. Taking a step back, there was movement from the steel blade. I knew I'd trigger something bad with any further movement away. That left me with only one real option to postpone the clown. I took a step toward him.

"Okay, Abbey. We're on our way. Hang tight."

I was hanging on—by the proverbial thread.

I took a second step towards my fate, knowing it was a fine line I was walking. My fate could be death, or something worse. Or it could be escape. But the only way to find out was by taking another step forward. And I did.

"Are you still there?" she asked. "We need gas." OMG.

It was all I could do to not scream into the phone as I took another step closer to the clown.

"Should we stop now or pick you up first?"

I was going to lose it. I know I was, but I reigned it back in. My voice was tight and controlled as the words came out in a staccato cadence. "Pick. Me. Up. First."

"She wants to be picked up first," I heard her say to my father. "We'll be there in a moment."

I took a fifth step towards the abyss. The shadows took shape as I got closer. It was a human figure. Another step closer and he also took a step away from the tree line. The streetlight illuminated him even more. Not that there ever was a doubt, but it was the clown. The same grotesque one that took Bri. And there was a very long knife clenched in his fist.

A horn broke the staring contest between the clown and me.

My parent's jeep idled beside me. My father had his window down. "Hey, let's go. I'm starving."

Without hesitation, I jumped into the jeep. My father raced off into the night, leaving the killer clown in our rearview mirror.

CHEERIOS OR CAPTAIN CRUNCH?

TURNER PICKED UP ON THE FIRST RING. "WE NEVER TALK anymore."

He let me hang for a long moment, before adding, "What's up?" In other words, he was asking why I called. I wanted to hear his voice, but I wasn't ready to tell him that. Everything had been strained between us, the tension palpable.

"I...I just wanted to say hi." I sounded stupid and added, "I don't think our texting is working."

An understatement if there ever was one. "Don't You Want Me" by The Human League, another song in my near-endless Eighties playlist came to mind. I wanted him so bad, wanted what we found over the summer, but did he want me?

A pause. A super long, awkward as a church fart, kind of pause. Turner spoke quietly. "Agreed. And I know you've been busy. New school, new friends, new boys..." Wait, what?

"I've been busy, but not with boys."

"You mentioned earlier that the boys were clowning around with you..." He drew out the sentence, leaving a noticeable pause. Whoa, really? Turner was jealous?

I couldn't help but laugh at the absurdity of our miscommunication. Looking out my bedroom window at the gray clouds chasing across the sky, I needed to set him straight.

"No, not boys clowning around," I reassured him. "I was referring to actual real clowns. Or possibly ghost clowns. But never boys clowning around." I was still laughing. "Turner, is that what you've been thinking all this time?"

"Well..." I pictured him with his furrowed brow as his dark eyes gazed into my soul.

"Let me set you straight. My first day at school, after my first soccer practice, I saw a clown at the end of the hall. I thought, this can't be normal." I turned over in bed, thinking it was time to get up.

"Does Pine Ridge have a school clown club? Sort of like a chess club." He didn't sound like he believed it either.

"Hardly." I was smiling as I rolled out of bed and got dressed, pulling on a pair of shorts. My Boston Strong t-shirt went on over my head and I missed Turner's comment. "What was that?"

"I asked if your school mascot was a clown. Ours is a jaguar."

I padded through the kitchen, stopping to grab a cereal bar. "Not that I'm aware of," I replied with a giggle. Talking with Turner always made me happy.

"I take it you've seen the clown more than that one time." Not a question.

"I've seen them a lot. Sometimes daily, sometimes just a few times a week." I scribbled a note to my parents that I was running up to school for an errand. I could hear Turner crunching in my ear.

"Cheerios or Captain Crunch?" I asked as I opened the garage door.

He laughed. "Nope, Cinnamon Toast Crunch." A pause, and then Turner asked, "You said 'them,' so it's not the same clown each time?"

"No, not always the same clown. There's been a lot of different ones showing up." I put in an earbud and climbed on my bike, coasting down our driveway. "It gets a whole lot worse. Two of the girls from my team have gone missing in the last several weeks. And neither has been found."

"Whoa, seriously? Is there a clown connection to their disappearances?" he asked.

"There has to be. I caught a glimpse of a clown when Christina was taken and I had a clown experience with Bri's disappearance." I shivered at the memory.

"Clown experience? What do you mean?"

"I was dreaming—this incredibly vivid dream—of being inside the clown as he grabbed my friend from the school lab. And that's exactly how it happened, so it had to be more than a dream." I slowed to let a car turn and then followed it down the block.

"Wait, you were inside the clown?"

"I can't explain it, but I was actually in his head as he kidnapped my friend."

"I don't know what to say other than I am so sorry." Turner sounded sad.

I took a left and then a quick right. "Last night was the worst, though."

"How so?"

"The nastiest of the clowns came after me." I jumped the curb up onto the sidewalk, approaching the same gas station I was so desperate to get to last night. "He chased me and had a knife. A very large knife."

I could still see him standing near the edge of the woods, tense with the expectation of a kill. Even though I was never able to see his eyes, my imagination filled in the details. Blood-red eyes, hate burning with a fire that only my death could extinguish.

"Holy crap." Turner took another bite of cereal and I heard his crunching. "Did Pine Ridge have a history of clowns before you got there?"

"Not that I'm aware of. But who talks about clowns?" A dozen of the school's cross-country team passed in a group run. I nodded. Not a one acknowledged my presence, such was their focus.

"You are the spook magnet. Ghosts really like you." Turner knew my history with ghosts.

"'Like' isn't the best word. They are frickin' drawn to me like paparazzi to a Kardashian. And it's not nearly as glamorous as it sounds." Passing the church, I asked the question that had bothered me for a while. "Clowns. Why does it have to be clowns?"

"I get it. A lot of people are terrified of clowns. I think it was from that Stephen King novel," Turner said before pausing. "Maybe ghosts are taking the form of clowns to scare you. Or to send you a message."

I stopped at the school parking lot entrance, not yet ready to revisit the scene of the knife-wielding clown. "No, I believe they actually were the spirits of clowns. Not spirits posing as clowns."

"There's something that I don't get," Turner said. "How is it possible these ghost clowns were physically able to kidnap someone? Those two girls were athletes, so they would have put up a fight."

"Knowing Christina and Bri, yes, they would have put up a massive fight." They were soccer players after all.

"From what you've told me before, I didn't think the ghosts were here enough in our world to grab anyone, let alone two fit athletes," Turner said.

The gray clouds had stopped their chasing and were now gathering as the sky darkened. "It doesn't sound like business as usual for the ghosts," I admitted.

"It doesn't sound normal at all," Turner agreed.

Thinking back to the past year, I had to shake my head. "There is no normal. Not anymore. These ghosts are getting more potent or maybe I'm the one that's grown stronger. Maybe I'm the one that is more in their world."

I continued pedaling into the parking lot, which was a lot less eerie in the light of day. The same piece of crap car from last night was the only vehicle left in the lot. It wasn't going to move without a tow truck—or an act of God.

"Hmmm," Turner said slowly. "So, before school started, you'd never seen a clown before? A dead clown, I mean."

The *woosh, woosh* sound of the school's wind turbine bothered me for some reason. Maybe it was the fact that above the calm, there was a lot of turmoil. On the ground in the parking lot, the air was still, no breeze to speak of. Overhead, it was obviously different. The blades were a blur from the winds above ground level.

"No, I've never come across a ghost of a clown previously."

"Okay, what about live ones?"

"Well, I was dragged to the circus the day before school started. My father was working on a story about clowns and wanted my mother and me along. After sitting through several too many shows, I went exploring. Okay, maybe I bent the rules a bit and went behind the scenes. I wanted to see what goes on backstage."

"No. You?" Turner shared my disdain for stupid rules.

"I know. Hard to believe. But going backstage and wandering through the maze of circus tents was the best part of my circus visit. That was, until I saw a group of clowns that were arguing."

"Can't say I've ever seen clowns argue," Turned said.

"Nobody has. That's not the public face they ever want us to see."

"What were they arguing about?"

"They were arguing about one of the clowns," I told him. "They mentioned the name Rellik. It was getting pretty heated, and I thought it was going to get physical—at least until Rellik made his appearance. The clown argument stopped dead when he stormed through. The other clowns feared him. And when he stopped and stared at me, I could see why. He was the kind of clown people are afraid of. Dark and scary, in other words."

"Hmm. Don't you think it's odd that a family circus would have such a clown entertaining children?"

"Good point, I never considered that. I was relieved to get away from him." I shuddered.

"What was the name of the circus? I might do a little research." Turner's voice brightened as he said this.

I knew his little research would be extraordinarily thorough. From what he'd shared with me, Turner's planning and research skills allowed him to pull off some mighty elaborate pranks. He told me about a prank where every day he went out onto the football field wearing a striped shirt, blew a whistle, and threw birdseed on the ground. Of course, with the birds trained to expect birdseed, when a penalty was called at the school's first football game, there were birds everywhere. He said the bird chaos delayed the game for quite a while. Although his pranks were harmless, they've also gotten him into trouble. Hopefully, Turner had learned, and in the future he'd use his considerable powers for good and not evil.

"It was called the Surini Brothers Circus & Traveling Roadshow."

With a, "Get back to you," Turner ended the call.

I needed to see for myself that the events of last night truly happened, and I headed across the school parking lot to the one light post that would tell me what I needed to know. I slowly circled the towering post as I studied it.

Deep, ugly gashes were cut into the metal pole. One of the cuts was so deep, I could see the interior of the pole. The gash was framed by scorched metal, the metallic coating blackened. Last night's eerie spotlight dance ended with the shooting sparks as a result of the clown's fury. One thing was obvious as I looked at the wanton destruction of school property. The blade would have done considerably more damage to me than the pole. A warning I'd take to heart.

THE RETURN OF TURNER

"Hey," the familiar voice said on the phone. It was Turner, and his voice had that breathless quality he got when he was excited about something. "So, I did some research."

That was quick. "And...?"

"What are you up to?" he asked.

"Nothing. But don't leave me hanging here. Find anything interesting?"

"I sure did. I found the circus. It's down in Iowa." He sounded proud of himself.

"Go on."

"I got to thinking," Turner said. "Everything began with your circus visit. So let's go back. Let's go to the circus."

His idea was elegant in its simplicity. Go back to the circus.

"I'm in," I replied.

Most people knew what a circus should be like. Animals, peanuts, trapeze artists, sideshow barkers, cotton candy, jaunty music, thrills and applause. But the Surini Brothers Circus would have clowns, too. Big ones, little ones, happy ones, and sad ones. All sorts of clowns. And unfortunately, one very scary clown.

That was the part I wasn't looking forward to.

Turner was at my door within the hour. I opened it and he was standing there. *Turner was at my door!* I had no idea what to do. Should I hug him? Give him a kiss? Shake his hand? When self-doubt clouded my decision-making ability, I turned to my mouth. Just keep talking and everything should work out.

"Well, you got here fast. There were speed limits posted along the way, weren't there?" I asked somewhat facetiously.

"I was careful," he replied with a shrug. I liked the twinkle in his eye.

"You know, that doesn't answer my question—or I suppose it does." I missed him more than I wanted to let on.

It was the first time I'd seen him since our camp experience. My eyes took a stroll over the tall figure standing in front of me. His dark hair was worn long. A white t-shirt—snug in all the right places—showed off his broad shoulders, and his ripped jeans held my attention longer than they should. All my feelings for him came to life. I couldn't be the cool one any longer and I jumped into his arms, my arms around his neck, and my legs wrapped around his.

"Ahem."

I buried my face in his neck, enjoying Turner's scent, savoring the feeling of being in his arms again. The last several weeks had been difficult for a lot of reasons. Emotions coursed through me as I relived the pain of us growing apart. Sometimes texting wasn't the best way to communicate. Relief was near the top of my emotional list as Turner held me like he'd never let me go again.

"Ahem."

"I missed you too," he murmured in my ear as goosebumps—the good kind this time—rose on my arms. The pent-up emotions of the last few weeks threatened to boil over. I wasn't going to cry, I told myself as I felt a tear leak out of my squeezed-shut eyes. One tear didn't mean I was crying. But another found its way out and I was thinking this wasn't how tough girls were supposed to act. Anyway, a tear or two—or several more—was still not crying.

"Ahem."

I took a deep breath and pulled myself together. A voice started to register in my brain. Recognition was sinking in, along with the awareness that I'd heard it a few times now. Up to now, it was quite distant like when I was younger playing with a friend in a culvert on a country road and her voice was far removed and echoing. Like that.

"Ahem."

There it was again, much clearer now. With considerable effort, I pulled my head from Turner's neck and glanced around to find my father standing there. He had a bemused grin on his face.

My legs picked that moment to lose their grip, and I slid down. Oh, how I wish they had retained their ability to hold my weight. Quite awkwardly, I melted into a heap at Turner's feet.

I could tell my future grandchildren that was the exact moment that I first identified with the ostrich's desire to put his head in the sand and disappear. Yeah, I know they didn't actually do that, but I liked the visual.

"Oh hi, Dad." I was on my back looking up at him.

Giving me a reassuring smile, he said, "Hi."

I gestured to the boy standing over me. "You remember Turner. From camp."

I swear to you, he stepped over my prone body and shook Turner's hand. "How are you? School going well?"

My turn. "Ahem."

They ignored me and Turner replied, "It is. My teachers are fun, and I'm especially enjoying my art class. I've been learning to paint with oils. Very liberating to throw gobs of paint on a canvas, and see it come together."

"Ahem," I said again.

My father was doing his best not to look down. "A man needs to have a creative outlet. Without one, we'd all end up going into politics, or worse, become lawyers."

"Dad!" I knew it's every father's God-given right to embarrass his daughter in front of a boy, but I didn't have to give in quietly. "Hey, can I get a hand here?" Both of the men in my life offered a hand and pulled me to my feet in a flash. Giving each of them the look, I knew they wouldn't dare speak of this moment again.

"What are you kids up to this afternoon?" my father asked, gracefully changing the subject. He looked pleased with himself. "Mall, movie or both?"

Turner shot me a subtle nod. "We haven't checked the movie listings yet, but—" I held up a hand cutting Turner off in mid-sentence.

"This is too important. We need to be straight up here." I glanced around. "Let's go talk out in the driveway."

I led as the boys followed me out the door. Outside, my father faced me, arms folded across his chest. I was mirroring him several feet away and Turner leaned on his still pinging Chevy S10 pickup, hands in his pockets.

Not waiting, I began, "Ever since we visited the circus, I've been seeing clowns. Mostly at school, but not always. Some of my friends have seen them as well. They've come to me in remarkably lucid dreams, inside a mirror, walking the school hall. And they figure in both Christina's and Bri's disappearances." I took a step closer to my father, his eyes showing his concern. "Because everything started after our visit to the circus, we're going back to that same circus hoping we'll find our answers there."

My father stroked his chin with his thumb, a gesture that signaled his deep consideration. "I hadn't realized the circus was back in town."

"It's not. It's in Mason City."

"Iowa?" Unease colored my father's face.

"It's only three hours away."

My father nodded. "But, it's not just the distance. You'd be heading into the mouth of the monster."

"Dad, I got this. I'll be safe—especially with Turner along. And really, the danger is here, not in Iowa. We want to get answers."

"So, what are the questions you need answers for?" I had to remember that my father was a reporter, and he was always going to ask tough questions.

"Fair enough," I nodded. "Okay, in no particular order, why clowns? Why me? Why the sudden interest in my school? What do they want? Why start now? And how do they get so many clowns in that little car?"

A hint of a smile warmed my father's face. "I may be able to help with that last one. However, the others..." His smile faded, and he became serious. "Would you like me to come along? Your mom wants to go antiquing today in downtown Stillwater, but I could miss that."

I shook my head. "As I said, I've got this, and besides, I have someone to watch my back," I said, nodding at Turner. "And the ride down will give us a chance to get caught up. Unless you want to listen to us catch up for the six hours we'll be in the car."

Laughing and shaking his head, my father said, "I never thought I'd be saying this, but I'd rather spend the day antiquing."

I gave my father a big hug. "I'm glad you're my father," I said.

"And I'm glad you're my daughter," he replied. This was an exchange we've had many times before. He always wanted me to know how much he valued me. Having such a solid foundation was a great way to grow up. From scary clowns to mean girls, I could take on everything life—and death—threw at me knowing I had his unconditional love.

"Let me know when you get there. And be careful," he said as we left the safety of my home behind. George Michaels' "Father Figure" from my eighties song playlist fittingly danced across my mind.

TURNER ACCELERATED onto the ramp for 35E. A dozen miles and we'd meet up with 35W and then it was a straight shot down the interstate to Mason City. The radio played a classic rock song I'd heard a million times before, yet I didn't know its name or even who sang it. We all have things in our lives that exist in the background without us ever examining them. It might be a song, it might be a person, or even a habit of ours. Always back there, never to see the light of day.

"Where do you think we're going to get our answers from?" Turner asked, pulling me back to the moment.

"Who. You mean *who* are we going to get our answers from."

Turner looked as if he was going to say something. He paused and said it anyway, "Grammar police got me again. Okay, who? Who are we getting our answers from? Clowns?"

"Nope. Harmony."

"Who's that?"

"Harmony French. She's a woman I met backstage. She's a mystic. She knew things about me."

Turner gave a skeptical laugh. "That fortune teller stuff is all fake. They pick up on your reactions and your body language. Give them a little information and they're off to the races and into your bank account. Complete frauds."

"She's different, though," I protested. "Harmony knew stuff. She knew about me. About you."

He gave a quick glimpse in my direction. "Me?"

"Yeah."

"Well, that's different then," he said with a grin. "Seriously, can you trust her?"

"Yes. Enough to find out if she has the answers we're looking for. I want to hear what she'll say about the clown apocalypse I'd been facing." I paused, reflecting on my visit with Harmony. There had been some sort of connection between the two of us. I'd felt it, and she'd said as much.

Turner stepped in on my moment of reflection. "You said this mystic knows about you. Let me ask then, how well do you know yourself?"

"Huh?" I managed to say in reply. Leave it to my philosophical boyfriend to ask these sorts of questions.

"An unexamined life is not worth living. Socrates said this," Turner said. "I know there are various interpretations, but here's mine: You can't coast through life. There needs to be intentionality.

And to be intentional, you need to ask questions of yourself. Know why you're doing something."

"Elaborate, please." I turned in the seat to look at Turner.

"Why do you suppose you interact with ghosts?" He glanced in my direction.

That was easy. "It's a family trait that's been passed down."

Turner shook his head. "That's the *how*. Answer the *why*."

I didn't get where he was going with his question. "What do you mean?"

"I'm asking *why* do you interact with dead people? You could choose to ignore them."

My turn to shake my head. "I couldn't. It's not possible."

"It's not possible because the ghost comes to you like a baby whose needs are expressed so loudly you can't possibly ignore them? Or do you mean that you're not wired to ignore someone—living or dead—when they need help?" Turner changed lanes, moving past a car full of girls in a Kia Soul. They were all watching us.

I hesitated as I pondered my reply. "It's both. Probably in equal amounts. They won't let me ignore them, but I feel compelled to help them. I mean, who else could?"

"True."

"But there are times I hate dead people—okay, most of the time—because they completely disrupt my life. Sort of like that friend you see only once in a great while. They sweep into your life with their baggage, cause a lot of commotion and turn your life upside down. Then they vanish, leaving you to clean up and deal with the consequences."

The partly cloudy sky was getting less partly cloudy and more fully cloudy as we traveled south. "Except, instead of ending up with the tattoo you'll forever regret, you end up with nightmares and emotional trauma."

Turner glanced over and stared at me. "How old *are* you? You sound like you're thirty."

I couldn't help but laugh. "That comes from my parents. When one is a doctor and the other makes his living from using the English language, mature language is a household requirement."

"I get that," Turner replied. "Are the ghosts ever dangerous?"

"They can be, if they're angry about something. But sometimes there's more than ghosts I deal with. Let me tell you a story."

"Okay," he said. "We have nothing but time."

"I'm at home in bed, when in the middle of the night I hear a creak. Sitting up in bed, I listen for it again. The moon brings enough light for my sleepy eyes to make out the shapes of my room. Thankfully, nothing moves, and I think it's just the house. But then I hear a closer creak. Something's coming for me.

"I slide from the covers and move to the doorway. I don't want it in my room. Another creak, ominously mere feet away, and my goosebumps rise. My heart rate shoots up as my fight-or-flight response kicks in. But my body knows I wouldn't be going anywhere. I'm a fighter."

Turned nodded. "You don't have to tell me."

The story brought back feelings, and I couldn't help but shudder. "When I stepped into the hallway, it was right there. The towering figure of a man enveloped me, and right away I had trouble breathing. A howling roar like a tornado surrounded me. I've learned from experience that that noise is for me alone. My parents wouldn't be pulled from their slumber by any sound the ghostly thing made. So powerful and disorienting, I had to fight back or be consumed by the noise. Of course, resistance wasn't exactly easy as the large figure had little in the way of actual mass—I was able to see right through him.

"Focusing everything on my right hand, I needed to make enough contact with the thing to keep it away. The focused concentration gave me the strength to push it back. The howling subsided to a seventy-miles-per-hour-motorcycle-ride-without-a-helmet experience. Not perfect, but it was a step in the right direction. But then, things changed for the worse when the figure melted into something else, something dark and indistinct."

"Whoa," Turner said.

"The attack was sudden and vicious, as it sliced my t-shirt open across my stomach. The pain mixed with concern about waking my parents—having them there would not be a good thing. My belly looked to have a four-inch-long gash running across it. My concentration slipped, the roar returned, and a foul odor had joined it. Even though it was inches away from my face, I could no longer recognize it as once being human.

His expression spoke volumes. "Damn."

"The pain focused me, and I was determined to fight back. With renewed strength, my right hand made physical contact and I pushed it back. Summoning everything I had, I added my left and took a step forward, feeling it retreat."

Semi-trucks dotted the right lane as we sped past in the left.

"I wanted to know what I was dealing with, so I looked into the depths of this new dark thing, searching for something recognizable, a face perhaps. Its features were shrouded, like it was partially there, partially somewhere else. But, as far as I'm concerned, it needed to be completely somewhere else."

There was nothing but fields and telephone lines outside, but I kept looking out as I told the story.

"The swirling mass took shape. Its eyes formed first, dark pools of hate. The thing had a mouth, rows of sharp teeth, a tongue slithering over them as it grimaced. I could almost taste the hatred emanating from the thing. I needed to send a message and get this thing back to where it came from. 'Get out!' I shouted and shoved the thing down the hall. With a scream born of hate, pain and death, the sound cut into my soul before it echoed and faded. The walls on either side were sliced deep as unseen talons fought for purchase as it was forced out of our world. It was not a moment too soon, as I was wiped out and slid to the floor, exhausted."

I glanced at Turner and grinned. "But I kicked its ass."

"Yeah, you did." My cheeks felt warm at his words.

"Now I have this souvenir." Turner glanced over as I lifted my shirt, exposing the faded scratches.

"Eyes on the road."

Turner put his eyes back on the road.

"Dangerous girl," he said with a shake of his head.

"You have no idea," I replied with a giggle. "I can go from princess to warrior when I need to."

Let's hope I didn't need to.

COMMON SENSE BE DAMNED

CAR RIDES MADE ME SLEEPY.

Somewhere amid all the endless cornfields, I'd dozed off and woke up with a hazy memory of a bad dream. With no specific recollection of events, I was left with a feeling of dread. Something bad pursued me relentlessly in my dream, and there was nothing I could do to stop it. I yawned and stretched as Turner smiled at me. "Hey, sleepy."

"I have to pee," I replied. It was late afternoon, and the sun had peaked hours ago. Gray clouds slid in to hasten the already shorter days that we experienced in late fall. "Can we stop soon?"

"There's a truck stop ahead that I've visited before. We should be there in a few minutes. You have to love a good truck stop. The restrooms may be a toxic waste dump, but the food is usually good." Turner wore a silly grin. "Hope you've mastered the fine art of peeing while standing up."

I could barely reply as I cracked up. "All those squats will finally pay off."

I've always enjoyed our banter. That was one of those intangibles about being with someone you were truly comfortable with. You could be yourself, make stupid jokes, laugh—snort even—and your friends would embrace you for who you are. Simple acceptance. No drama, no judging. There almost certainly would be teasing, but that was good attention—my favorite kind of attention. I couldn't help but smile at the moment Turner and I were having.

"I had no idea you were training for the truck stop Olympics."

"Oh, I compete every year."

"Really?" Turner glanced over at me, a twinkle in his eye. "What's your favorite event?"

"It's a toss-up. Between the week-old hot dog throw for distance and the truck stop waitress bubblegum bubble blowing contest."

Turner's grin grew. "I would have thought it would have been the bathroom stall graffiti art contest. You've always been one to express yourself in unusual ways."

"I thought it best to wait another year. They don't start teaching anatomy at Pine Ridge until next year."

Turner laughed as he took the exit, the large sign of the Flying J Travel Plaza standing out in the flat terrain of endless farm fields, an endless sea of soybeans and cornfields all the way down Interstate 35 into Iowa. At least until harvest time, which should be soon.

Turner steered the aging pickup past the rows of semis. Dave's Trucking, Walmart, Heartland Express, another Walmart, Old Dominion, Target, Stevens Transport and FedEx. Life on the road must be lonely being away from loved ones. Before I had the chance to start making up country music lyrics, Turner pulled into the end slot and shut off the truck.

"There's a nicer bathroom inside by the restaurant or a closer one around the corner out here."

I was already headed for the corner. "I can't wait any longer. I'll meet you inside."

Turner chuckled behind me. "Use a wide stance," he called out. "It helps with balance."

Pushing the stained door open, I found an empty three-stall bathroom. I headed for the far one, hoping it would be the least used. I wiped off the seat and soon found relief. However, the odor permeating the place was an especially repulsive one. The combined smell of waste from a hundred or more people had left behind a distinctive odor. I wouldn't be lingering.

When I stepped out of the stall, I stopped in surprise. There was a doorway that hadn't been there earlier.

The new door was on the wall adjacent to the toilet stalls and directly across from the two yellowed sinks. The steady *drip, drip, drip* of the ancient faucet would normally trigger the hand washing response after using the bathroom, but not this time. My brain was otherwise occupied.

The new doorway should lead to the outside—the parking lot was on the other side of the wall—but that wasn't what I saw. Instead, the interior of a colossal industrial building was visible through the doorway. Several stories high, the place was a wreck. The cracked concrete floor was dotted with puddles the size of small lakes. A light fixture hung askew from a single frayed cord, and much like the faucet behind me, there was a steady drip adding to the puddles.

Drawn to the doorway, I entered. Common sense be damned.

The air was damp and cool, the obnoxious odor of the toilets replaced by a moldy smell. I had clearly gone somewhere else. But what was this place? And why was I there?

It's been my experience that when spirits want to communicate, it didn't involve something straightforward like speaking. Spirits had drawn me into other places before, wanting me to experience something.

I know what you're thinking, and I was thinking it too. Was I actually there? Or was the experience all taking place in my mind? Was there something in the brownies?

If it was all in my head, it was unusually vivid and amazingly real. The temperature changed, and the smells were different. As I kicked at a puddle, my shoe got wet. It wasn't my imagination. I was actually there.

Needing to find out why, I stepped inside.

Making my way into the building, I moved carefully around the puddles and debris. Beyond the sound of the dripping water, there was something else. Pausing, I strained to make out what I was hearing. I took a step or two further and whatever it was got louder. Curiosity kept me going further into the building.

I moved across the open expanse and approached an intersection of hallways. The light diminished, and I wasn't feeling so safe in my current location. A sudden worry hit, what if the doorway was no longer there? I didn't want to be trapped in that forsaken place. I spun around, but the doorway was still there. As relief coursed through me, I caught a flicker of movement to my left. There was something in the shadows and I knew I wasn't alone. My goosebumps rose.

Taking several more steps, I held my breath and listened for the sound. Ever so faintly, there it was—the sound of someone crying. Not the wailing sound of someone hurt or scared, but the sound of someone who had cried for a long time. It was the sound of despair. And it was most definitely female.

"Christina? Bri?" I called out. "It's Abbey." My voice echoed in the large space. Hearing the furtive sounds of movement behind me, I spun around expecting the worst, but found nothing. Circling warily, I caught a glimpse of movement across the room from me. I had the alarming feeling there may be more than one creeper in here with me.

Keeping my gaze fixed on where I last saw the movement, I called out again. "Bri? Christina? Can you hear me?" The crying continued. With a glance over my shoulder, I headed toward the crying.

There comes a time in life when you are forced to either give in to your fears or face them. When I was in third grade and living in our old house in St. Paul, I heard something. It was a creak, the sound of weight being put onto an old floorboard. My parents were outside on the front porch, as I could hear them talking about one of my mom's cases. Instead, the creaking sound was coming from upstairs.

I remembered hesitating at the bottom of the staircase, terrified of what might be up there. I considered telling my parents about the sound, but I didn't. It felt pretty mature, as I thought of it now, but I hadn't wanted to give in to my fears. I didn't want to be afraid of every sound I might hear in the future. And the only way not to live in fear of what might be up there, was to go see what was up there.

It was definitely one of those facing your fear times.

The crying brought me back from my memories. The sound

came from the hallway down to my left. There was just enough light to see the outlines of the debris strewn around the hall's entrance. Whoever used this place was clearly not a neat freak.

I made my way carefully around the debris, staying close to the sides of the hallway. The feeling of dread was with me much as it was when I took those first few steps up the staircase in St. Paul. I had to know the source of those creaks. Moving down the corridor, I was less terrified now than I was then—I remember my heart was threatening to pound its way out of my chest—but I approached a perfect ten on the wariness scale. I knew I was putting myself at risk, but that was what friends do for each other. If Christina and Bri were here, maybe I could help them.

A creak just ahead put me in full stop mode. Frozen in place, holding my breath, I willed myself to blend into the shadows. The crying that brought me down the dark corridor was no longer audible. What I heard instead, was the sound of someone approaching.

I took a step closer to the wall.

Creeeeeeak.

Imagine hearing the drawn-out sound of a door ever-so-slowly opening. I trembled. Swear to God, it would chill you to your bones. It was like how Michael Jackson's "Thriller" started out with a creaking door, thunder, footsteps moving closer, and a mysterious howling in the distance—all things that will raise the most reluctant goosebump.

The door continued its long and slow swing, hitting the wall. The impact resonated down the hallway and was followed by the unmistakable sound of someone stepping into the corridor. While there wasn't enough light for me to see who'd stepped out, I prayed there wasn't enough light for me to be seen either.

Nothing happened for a moment while I held my breath. I knew someone was in the corridor with me, maybe twenty feet away. *Twenty feet.* There were circumstances where a distance of twenty feet felt like an eternity away.

This wasn't one of those times.

This twenty feet meant I was only a step away from death. I was so close that the smallest sound I made could be the end of me. Unable to hold my breath forever, I was forced to breathe. But I tried to make it slow, even, and most importantly, quiet.

I thought back to that moment in St. Paul as I'd slowly climbed the stairs. Feeling the weight of each step, I moved closer to the source of those creaks. Outside the bathroom, I'd hesitated, knowing something was just around the corner. I held my breath for as long as I could and waited. But knowing I couldn't avoid the confrontation any longer, I'd stepped around the corner.

A creak pulled me back to the present. Each little movement of the thing here in the corridor sounded amplified. I heard it moving away from me, bringing me a tiny bit of hope. Seizing the opportunity, I backed away. Each step was slow and measured as if my life depended on it—which I strongly suspected was true.

My mission was clear. Do not trip over the debris, stay silent and get as far away as possible from the hallway creeper.

It felt like each step backward took minutes to make. Maddeningly slow, I looked behind to position each foot away from all obstacles, with the dim light giving me outlines of the debris. I swiveled my head after each step to look forward to see if the thing in the corridor was moving. The troubling part was that I couldn't see anything at all, there was nothing but pitch black in front of me. After an eternity, I reached the entrance of the corridor. I absolutely needed to get out of the corridor and get around the corner to safety.

The experience in St. Paul flooded through me like I was back there again outside the bathroom. The second I stepped around that corner, I was presented with a gray figure standing just feet away from me. I hesitate to describe it as a ghost, but that was exactly how I remembered her. Towering over me, she was washed out like a photograph left in the sun. I wasn't afraid once I saw her, and gave her a smile. Her eyes were kind as they met my gaze. Although my smile wasn't returned, I had the feeling she approved of me.

"I like taking baths," my seven-year-old self told the dead woman. "Do you like baths?" I asked ever so curiously.

The woman held my gaze, her twinkling eyes showing she still had some life even though she was no longer alive. That was a learning moment for me that I carried with me every day of my life. It wasn't just catching a glimpse of a ghost. No, there was more to the spirits being here in our world. The dead can affect the living.

At that moment, back in that bathroom in St. Paul, the dead woman had affected me. With a swirl of gray shades, she passed right through me.

"Whoa."

I couldn't say with absolute certainty that was my exact expression, but it was in the ballpark. The moment she entered me, I felt something that was palpable, something that was both cold and warm, something that infused me with energy. My every nerve and fiber tingled. I could feel her energy, saw her memories, and knew without a doubt that the afterlife was very much real. Pretty heady stuff for a child to realize.

I was convinced that was the day my life took a left turn.

Now, in the damp of the industrial building, I swung myself around the corner, out of sight. Slumping against the wall, relief sapped my nervous energy. The doorway leading to my escape was a quick sprint away. Hope at last.

Of course, hope could be fleeting.

A white shadow, formless and slightly translucent, stood at the doorway across the room. It was a humanlike silhouette, but with no definition whatsoever. Its body melded into one long mass as it reached from the floor to the top of the doorway. It had no legs or feet, yet it moved in my direction, gliding slowly across the floor. Periodically, something bubbled at the end of where the head should be. It looked like melting flesh as it happens, creating a face in great torment.

The face pleadingly stared straight into my eyes as it continued to melt. My tummy felt like I'd dropped while riding a roller coaster.

As it moved ever closer, my skin felt as if an army of ants with needles for feet were marching across my entire body. The shadow thing continued toward me and paused. It stood idle, the only movement was the continual emerging and melting of its tormented face. Its eyes never left me—unsettling to the extreme—but terror rooted me in place.

To make matters worse, more of the white shadow things appeared from the doorway. One after the other, they passed through the door and glided across the room, each with a unique expression of agony, pain and anguish. All of them were different, and yet they all inspired the same feeling of dread deep inside me. Each moved to take a place standing next to the previous one until they encircled me.

They stared, never moving for what felt like hours. And I was held in place. Whether by fear or by common sense, the result was the same.

And then things went from worse to worser.

Someone approached from the corridor behind me. Since I was frozen in place, I didn't look around. A shadow moved into my peripheral for a moment, then became much, much more. Dressed in the darkest shades of crimson and black, eyes sunken pools of fury, a grimace of hate underneath his painted smile, was a clown.

LIKE A SLOTH ON VALIUM

A CLOWN. WHY DID IT HAVE TO BE A CLOWN? I HATE CLOWNS. And seeing one there blew me away—and quite honestly, scared the crap out of me.

Standing a mere foot away, the clown stared toward the doorway. It was like he was waiting for something. There was something familiar about this clown, but I couldn't say I've ever seen one with such terrifying makeup. The area around his eyes was painted with the darkest red. It looked more like blood than any makeup you could find at the clown store. There was madness, bloodlust and fury painted on his face. The scary clown wasn't moving, and I had no idea if he knew I was there. I was inches away from his fury.

I wanted to move, but the white sentinels, silent and horrifying, surrounded me.

The clown held his vigil for a long moment and then turned my direction. I was locked onto his horrifying visage as his face came back into view. His jawbone clenched and unclenched as his nostrils flared. His eyes narrowed into slits and he sniffed. He turned further toward me as he continued sniffing the air. Taking another step closer, he seemed to smell something. I suspected it was me he'd locked onto, but he didn't see me for some reason.

My sigh of relief was tempered by a new sound. Something moved in my direction.

My eyes darted around as I tried to place where the sound came from. I didn't see anything moving, and it took a few seconds to triangulate the sound. It came from the shadows across the room. Just as I thought I couldn't handle anything more, something emerged from the black shadows.

Something wicked this way comes.

As it moved at a snail's pace out of the veiled shadows into the light, I saw limb-like appendages that were wiry and freakishly long. The muscles pulled at the visible bone from under the skin as it dragged itself across the floor, revealing more and more of its horrifying appearance. It was completely black, devoid of any color.

That featureless face moved closer and closer. Everything about it was elongated. Moving like a sloth on valium, it slowly reached out a hand and dug its gnarled claws into the ground to pull itself along. It pushed through the circle of shadow things and headed in my direction. The tears flowed freely as I tested my muscles in an attempt to flee. A vain attempt, it was as if every muscle had locked up. My mind was frantic, and my breath was ragged and raw as each breath set my throat aflame. The dark thing continued its insanely slow trek towards me.

My eyes jumped to the clown, looking for his response to the demonic creature. With his back to the advancing horror, he didn't appear to notice me or the surrounding white sentinels. He certainly wasn't aware of what was coming for me.

The creature rose behind the clown, towering over him. Bones crackled with every move it made. Its neck extended further, as its vacant face was only inches away. The face cracked and tore, opening up to reveal a mouth. It lifted its head and cocked it to the side before letting out a terrifying screech as a bloody drool of slime made its way to the floor. As the drool slowly elongated and oozed down, I couldn't take my eyes off it. I could seriously puke.

On this day of horrifying surprises, I was shocked.

Instead of coming for me, the dark thing reached out for the clown instead. Enfolding its arms around the clown, it melted into him, all traces of the creature's existence disappearing. Watching the creature merge into the clown, one would think that was what happened, but I didn't think so. The creature's energy merged into the clown and made it into something worse. Not a winning combination for those of us fighting for good.

For some reason, "Freaks Come out at Night" from the eighties band Whodini came to mind. If I thought clowns were terrifying, this mashup of clown and freaky creature were far worse. I could honestly say I'd never been so scared. And then the unexpected happened again.

THE CLOWN DIDN'T MOVE for several beats, as his dark eyes narrowed. And then, as if listening to music only he could hear, the clown swayed to a soundless rhythm, head tilted back. Arms swinging, body loose and spinning, he floated in the center of our odd little circle.

When he made it to the first of the white shadow things, the clown swung an arm through it with a violent swipe. At the point where his arm impacted the shadow thing, the white turned pitch black and sucked out the rest of the white. He continued his dance, spinning and striking each of the white shadows as they let out a gut-wrenching wail. My ears burned as the sound grew so loud that I felt sorry for the entities.

As they faded into wisps in the dark and disappeared, their screams lingered and echoed in the cavernous room. And then silence, save for the sound of the clown's breathing.

Completely still, his macabre dance of death was complete. Rooted in place, the clown's heavy recovery breaths resembled a post-gallop sprint of an aging racehorse. Now that all the shadow figures were gone, there was only one person in the cavernous room of horror with the clown: Me. And for the life of me, I had no idea why I was untouched.

"Abbey." It was Turner, who had come up behind me.

I turned and looked at Turner as he stood in the doorway of the ladies room. Glancing around, the odd and horrifying building had...

well, for lack of a better expression...had left the building. I was back standing in the restroom and there was only one doorway. And that was the one where Turner stood.

"We've miles to go. We need to leave."

Shaking my head at the absurdity of life and death, I followed Turner out into the fresh air.

I could never do drugs. I am a drug.

A TICKET TO THE FREAK SHOW

IT WAS TWILIGHT AS WE MADE THE STATE LINE, LEAVING Minnesota and crossing into Iowa. Far off in the distance, lightning flickered behind a colossal bank of clouds, a massive storm mounting. Far removed, I could enjoy the beautiful lightning for its raw power. Growing up afraid of storms, I'd watch all the weather reports so I'd know if and when a storm was coming. Rationally, I knew the odds of being injured in a weather-related event were similar to winning the lottery, but my irrational side usually exerted its dominance, and fear took control. Being much older and wiser now, storms didn't hold their power over me, but the old fears lingered.

"That storm could be fifty miles away. You can see forever in the prairie," Turner said. I shared my fear of storms with him when we were at camp. He was smart enough to know I still worried. "And I bet the storm is headed away from us."

"Most likely," I repeated as I kept a wary eye on the thunderheads. A cumulonimbus cloud. Solely as a survival mechanism, I researched and learned as much as possible about the weather. It had seemed a good idea at the time. Not that we're exactly tornado alley in Minnesota, but we average around forty every year. A few years back, we had close to fifty tornadoes in one day. That was the day I decided knowledge was power.

Mason City was the first decent-sized city on Interstate 35 after crossing into Iowa. Turner said the circus was located on the edge of town on the Cerro Gordo County fairgrounds. I knew we were getting close to Mason City as the frequency of road signs increased. Gas stations, fast food, hotels, diners, Woodsey's Pest Control.

Growing up with a father that traveled a lot, we would play the

178 | ALLAN EVANS

sign alphabet game. The rules were simple: be the first to shout out the letter as we move up the alphabet. "A, Avenue" or, "B, Best Western." Even though we'd be competing for each letter, there wasn't an overall winner or loser, we simply played to unleash the competitive beast inside of us. The game could move pretty fast—at least until we got to Q and prayed for a Dairy Queen to show up soon.

As we exited the freeway and saw the circus tents off in the distance, my stomach quivered. I felt the growing energy as tangibly as I would the chill on my skin on a brisk December morning.

The grass parking area was a sea of pickups and cars, but clearly truck dealerships had the most business there in Iowa. Turner parked his truck at the first spot inside the entrance and we were out and moving right away. A distant rumble had me scanning the skies. The thunderheads had moved closer despite Turner's assurances to the contrary. I was sure of it.

The circus must be in progress as we were the only ones moving in the lot. Cutting between the vehicles, we stepped onto the main path leading to the circus entrance. I grabbed Turner's arm and pulled him to a stop.

"What is it?" Turner asked warily as he looked around—looking right past the clown that waited just ahead. He didn't see it. Turner had been through the spooky stuff with me before and could read my body language. He didn't need to see it to know there was danger ahead.

A tall clown stood to the left of the path. With a painted smile that didn't match his serious expression, red hair and a polka dotted outfit, the clown stood motionless like a sentry. His eyes were intensely aware, however, and stared directly at me.

The wind picked up as the distant lightning flashes became less distant, but still far enough away that there was no accompanying thunder.

Taking Turner's hand, I pulled him close to my side. "There's a clown. Right there." I said nodding in the direction of the circus sentry. It was at that moment that I became aware of another clown, positioned directly across the path from the first. This new clown was even taller than the first. Grim and deadly serious, his expression countered his jubilant costume. That macabre counterpoint may be exactly what had scared people most about clowns—unless said clown was carrying a foot-long butcher knife like the clown had last night. That would be scarier.

Turner became aware of my stiffening body language. "What's going on?" he asked evenly as he looked around.

"I know you can't see them, but there are two now. Two clowns." I nodded to my right. I wasn't sure why I was only nodding, but it felt like I'd be inviting danger if I was overt enough to point.

Following my gaze, Turner looked in the direction of the second clown, but not right at it. "I don't see anything," he said with obvious concern in his voice. "What are they doing?"

Getting into a staring contest with the second clown, I replied. "Nothing. They're standing there across from each other. Oh crap..."

"What?" Turner asked, squeezing my hand even harder than I was squeezing his.

My voice was slow and measured as I replied—not wanting to spook the gathering herd. "We have a third clown now. Next to the first one."

Turner's head swiveled in that direction. The new clown was shorter than the others. Wider, too. Bluish hair, striped costume, red nose. Penetrating eyes, he stood motionless and watched. Watching me.

Holding Turner's hand, I thought of my recent clown encounter on the road with Lexi. Maybe I could help Turner see what I was seeing. Why should I be the only one having fun?

"There's a way I can help you to see the clowns too. Are you game?"

"I am," he said without hesitation. My brave boy.

"I need you to clear your mind."

"Easier said than done," he said with a trace of worry.

"I know. But you need to, so focus on this clown," I said as I touched his cheek and turned his head to the right. Of course, now there was a new clown there, joining the second on the right of the path. Two and two now. "Four clowns now," I said, my hand in his.

Leaning into Turner, I looked up at his eyes. "Picture this in your mind. The clown is tall, maybe six and a half feet tall. Thinner than a supermodel. He's got an orange clown wig. Bright red smile painted on his thin face. Exaggerated eyebrows that suggest a look of surprise and a single tear below one eye. Keep your eyes shut while focusing your mind on his image."

His eyes squeezed shut, his eyes moving back and forth behind his lids. I was on my toes and whispered into his ear. "Open your eyes. Slowly." His eyes fluttered open as his body tensed. "See him?" I asked.

He nodded.

Squeezing his hand, I felt our shared energy. I had no idea how it worked, but I was able to share some of my ability. "See any of the others?"

Turner's head swiveled as I continued to study his face. He nodded again. "There are more. A lot more," he said with a quavering voice.

Glancing away from Turner, there was way more than I expected. Try tripling that number and you won't even be halfway there. Clowns lined both sides of the path all the way down to the main gate. One hundred yards of clowns standing across from each other, each staring at me with an unwavering gaze. Okay, it was more than a little creepy.

The air practically crackled with the clowns' combined energy. Their presence was especially strong here—we were on their turf.

"Now what?" Turner asked, his grip tightening.

"We keep moving." I took a deep breath and took a step forward. "We have a circus to visit."

Turner didn't move. When I glanced back, worry clouded his face. "Are we safe?" he asked.

"If they wanted to harm us, we'd already be dead."

"Actually, that's not very comforting."

"It is what it is. But, they're here for another reason. So, let's find out what that is."

Turner stepped forward. "Okay, I'm in. Let's roll."

The sky picked that exact moment to let loose with an ominous roll of thunder as the winds grew considerably more powerful. Leaves swirled around us. The gathering storm was no longer far away as we entered the gauntlet of dead clowns.

Every shape, size, color, and even every sex of clown lined the path. Rigid as statues, twice as dead as a MySpace page, and eyes as alert as a department store security guard, the clowns watched our every step. Except it wasn't "we" that was under scrutiny—it was me. Not afraid of eye contact, each of the clowns stared deep into me.

"Turner," I whispered. We were walking slowly along the clowns, still a long way from the entrance.

"Yeah?" he replied just as quietly.

"Are they staring at you too? They keep watching me." I glanced at the closest one to my left and of course, he stared at me.

A long moment passed before he answered. "No. They're only looking at you."

"Lucky me." The large one on the right held my gaze as I passed. I nodded at him, but he didn't return the gesture.

"Maybe it's not a bad thing," Turner said after a pause.

"I don't see how it could be a good thing. It's creeping me out." As much as I didn't want to look into their eyes, I couldn't help it.

"I keep thinking of the time I was at the airport for my trip to Boston," Turner said. "There were cops from all different cities everywhere. There had to be a hundred or more. It didn't make sense until they assembled into an honor guard to send off the family of a slain policeman to the National Law Enforcement Officers Memorial in Washington, D.C."

The clown on my left had to be the largest clown I'd ever seen.

"Turner, now may not be the best time to share your vacation memories."

Turner stopped, which was the last thing I wanted to do in the midst of the clowns. "Don't you see?" he asked. "These clowns are lined up—and I mean exactly—like the cops at the airport. Abbey, this is an honor guard."

We reached the front gate and approached the ticket booth. The woman behind the window looked to be in another place as her eyes stared into the distance. Stocky, dark haired pulled back into a bun, she sat alone with her thoughts. I had to say hello several times before her eyes focused and looked in my direction. She wasn't looking at my eyes, though. She was staring at my mouth. For some reason, I immediately disliked her.

"Two, please," I said as I pushed a twenty into the opening of her window. Her pale hand shook as she reached for the bill. I glanced over at Turner, and based on his expression, he shared my concern. "Are you alright?" I asked the woman. Her hands trembled so much, it bordered on a seizure. I had zero idea what to do if she said no, but it never came to that. The woman tore two tickets off a large roll and held them out.

I hesitated as her head lifted up and her voice, low and wet, spat out, "Our last guests. Enjoy the show." She made a choking laugh as she tossed the tickets towards me. Her laugh changed into an obscene parody of laughter as she slammed down the clear plastic door over the window slot. Turner literally dragged me away from the ticket window freak show as I was rooted in place.

No one waited to take our tickets at the gate.

"What was that?" Turner asked as we entered, his voice ragged and with more than a hint of panic. "What the hell was that?"

"Absolutely no idea," I managed to reply. "There's a lot more going on here than I thought."

Looking at me with wide eyes, Turner asked, "What do you mean?"

"I mean," I started as I looked warily around, "clowns might not be the worst thing we face tonight."

Ominously, R.E.M.'s eighties classic, "It's the End of the World as We Know It (And I Feel Fine)" played in my head.

Several circus roustabouts lingered near the yellow rope that marked the restricted areas. Like laborers in any field, these roustabouts were here for their strength and not any skill you'd want to talk about in mixed company. Heavily muscled and wearing several days' worth of dirt and grime, they laughed loudly as they hung out, in no hurry to move.

"They are standing exactly where we need to go and we don't have a lot of time." I said, as I checked out the swirling clouds overhead. The nearby audience roared their approval under the big tent.

"Then we need to find them something else to do," Turner said with his trademark *I'm-up-to-something* grin. "Get moving as soon as they leave. I'll catch up." Not waiting for my reply, he fast walked over to the roustabout group.

Turner walked awkwardly forward. When he addressed the men, he tilted his head even more awkwardly. "My friend, Tommy," Turner began in an overly loud voice that suggested someone of limited intelligence. "He's mad because there was no toilet paper. Tommy's down there peeing on your tents," he said with a dramatic gesture away from the men. "Tommy said he's going to poop right in front of the big tent, too."

Without hesitation, the men broke into a run in the direction Turner had indicated. The only problem, one of them grabbed Turner's arm and pulled him along.

Turner...

But I couldn't waste the opportunity he'd created and ducked under the rope. With each turn through the maze of tents, it got quieter as the familiar music and crowd noise was left behind. Not sure where I was going, I trusted my gut instinct. A left here, another left, now a right. After my last right turn, I found myself in a large meadow of trailers similar to where I'd met Harmony French.

Walking into the center of the meadow, I found Harmony's trailer, but I didn't find her. Her dog barked when I knocked, but no one answered. For lack of something to do, I took a seat by her firepit, glowing embers all that were left of a recent fire. I grabbed a stick and poked at them. There's something about a fire that's always captivated me. Grabbing several pieces of wood from the stack, I tossed them on top of the embers, hoping I could resuscitate her fire. Moving the wood around until a corner was buried in the embers, I blew on it to speed things up. Smoke was my reward as the wood caught fire.

"Glad to see you're making yourself at home," a familiar voice said behind me. I played it cool and didn't turn around.

"Well, someone let this fire go out. And since I happened to be in the neighborhood..."

"And you were feeling neighborly," Harmony said with a laugh. She walked around and sat across from me. Her red hair was piled high with a scarf tied into it. She wore a silk blouse with vibrant colors that magically popped with her eyes and hair. The pattern reminded me of a Van Gogh painting when you zoomed way in. The effect was engaging and would totally be on point in any fashion magazine.

"I'm a giving person," I said, as I poked at the fire, moving the logs around. They didn't need moving, I just liked to play with the fire. I mean, who doesn't?

Gazing across the fire, Harmony studied me. Her fingers steepled as she looked into me. After a long pause, she said, "I see there has been both good and bad in your life since we met. I told you that you would be tested."

I couldn't help but grin. "This is when I would usually say that you have no idea how much I've been tested, but I suspect you have a pretty good idea."

Harmony nodded. "But we both know there's more to come. The

outcome will be determined by how the events unfold and not all will be under your control." The fire had caught, and the flame's reflection danced in her eyes.

I shook my head. "It feels like very little is under my control."

"In life, control is overrated. And mostly an illusion." Harmony held my gaze with a warm look. Not an ounce of confrontation or condescension. Simple acceptance. "Tell me what brings you back here."

Where to begin? "After we met in August, I began to see clowns. Not real, human clowns, I saw these ghost clowns appear and disappear wherever I was. Dead clowns in my school, dead clowns inside mirrors and dead clowns in Snapchat photos."

"Oh dear."

"It gets worse. The dead clowns kidnapped my friends."

"That would be most unusual." Her brow furrowed.

"Everything about them is most unusual." I was getting frustrated and angry. "Why come to me? And why don't they go away?"

Harmony didn't answer. Instead, she studied me. I didn't say anything as I feared losing control and didn't want to yell at her. Though, I suspected I didn't need to say anything as I was transparent to her.

"There's certainly something about you. A light that shines intensely across many spectrums. This light is your soul," she said, leaning forward. "You're a beacon to those that have crossed, you're a conduit from their new existence back into ours. They come to you because you know. You know they still exist, and that means you could help them."

"Help them? Help them how?" The flames danced in front of me.

"Help them to affect outcomes here. Things they cannot do."

"So, you're saying the clowns want to affect change here," I said matter-of-factly.

She nodded. "Not how I would have put it, but yes, they do. Death has changed them. Alive, their mission was to entertain. In

186 | ALLAN EVANS

death, they may have found a higher purpose. But, alive or dead, their fundamental nature would remain the same. They don't become evil because they died. Once a clown, always a clown."

I let the stick slip from my hand. "But how do I know what they want?"

Harmony stood and moved in my direction. She sat on the arm of the Adirondack chair, putting a comforting hand on my shoulder. "Let me ask a question. All this began after visiting our circus?"

I nodded in response.

"The answer is obvious," she said as a crackle of thunder echoed overhead. "You need to talk to our clowns."

KILLER

I COULDN'T HELP BUT STARE AT THE TOWERING CLOWN.

Easily four feet taller than me, wearing stilts made him one tall clown. After all I'd been through, I should have been intimidated by him, but I wasn't. His sparkling eyes were kind, and his genuine smile was larger than the painted one underneath. "Hello, little lady," he said with a chuckle. "How's the weather down there?"

"Looking like rain," I replied with a glance at the green-tinged clouds.

"I'll let you know. The rain will get to me long before the drops get down to your level. You're a short little thing, aren't you?"

"I'm not that short," I protested, but enjoying his teasing all the same.

"Maybe if you tried standing up."

"I am standing," I said with hands on my hips.

"Oh, dear." He shook his head with mock sadness. The tall clown had a friendly and engaging way about him, even as he mercilessly teased me. I could see why Harmony left me with Stilts, as she introduced him. She had said it was all-hands-on-deck and headed off to get ready for the show's finale. Harmony surprised me when she ran back and kissed me on the forehead.

"God blesses those that stand up for others," she had said before leaving again.

The tall clown leaned down. "Try standing on your tippy toes. See what that does." When I hesitated, he cajoles me. "C'mon, c'mon."

I played along and got up on my toes.

With a dramatic shake of his head, he pronounced, "Nope. No

good." Leaning even closer, he peered at my feet. "Maybe you're standing in a hole. Try moving back there," he suggested, pointing behind me.

I stepped back and there was something there and I was falling backward—until I was caught by another clown. A third clown, down on his hands and knees, caused my fall.

"My friend, Clooney, sure has a way with the girls," said the clown who caught me, and helped me back up.

"They're always falling for me," the crouching clown said with a belly laugh. "And not my friend, Crackers," nodding to the one who caught me. Clooney gracefully got to his feet and took an exaggerated bow.

"They might fall for you, but I was a much better catch," Crackers said with a wink. His costume was all polka dots, a bright red bowtie and shoes so large, he couldn't fit in a phone booth. Not scary in the least.

"You're both show-offs," Stilts, the tall clown said, shaking his head in an exaggerated disapproving way.

"But you have to admit, that being a show-off is exactly what we're supposed to be as clowns." The remark from Clooney was accompanied with a high five between him and Crackers.

"You got me." Stilts stepped over, putting a hand on my shoulder. "Ms. French said this one is a friend. Though she has to be my shortest friend by a country mile."

"Hey, I'm not that short," I protested.

Patting my head, Stilts said, "Yes, you are." There was a sweetness about him that I liked. I was reminded of my favorite uncle who teased me mercilessly, yet I always enjoyed the attention.

Stilts straightened as he adjusted his outfit and proclaimed in a loud voice, "We need to be big about this."

"Someone needs to be," Crackers interjected.

"Short people need love too," Stilts continued. "We need to take the high road."

"Guys, I'm five-foot-four-inches tall."

"We'll need to protect her from the dwarf tossers. It's our civic duty." Clooney fist bumped with Crackers.

"That's the least we can do for a friend of Ms. French's," Crackers nodded with authority. "She asks so little of us."

"I'm really not that short," I offered.

Stilts patted my head again. "If only wishes were reality."

"Then I'd be living on the beach with Mrs. Crackers, a full-size chocolate fountain by our zero-entry pool." Crackers looked up with a smile on his face.

A roar came from the crowd as the show's intensity picked up, the finale not far off. Time was running out. "Guys, I need your help."

"Anything for our vertically challenged friend. But we need to be out in the plaza when the crowd is released. Have to say our goodbyes." He wiped away a fake tear, and then for effect, blew his nose loudly into a large handkerchief.

"Can I ask you an unusual question?" I prefaced. This subject was always difficult to approach with someone. Not everyone accepted my world without judgment. Most believe I was either, A, kidding or B, trying to get attention or C, simply had lost my mind. For the record, the correct answer was D, none of the above.

"You can try, little lady," Stilts said. His eyes offered enough acceptance that I continued.

"Do you believe in ghosts?" I looked at each of them expectantly, as they looked at each other in turn. Here it comes.

Clooney shrugged, "I guess I don't *not* believe in them. My Aunt Petunia used to see her dead uncle strolling through her garden when the moon was full. Me, I've never seen one."

"Well, I have." I held Clooney's gaze. The other two moved a little closer. I seemed to have their attention, though it may be a train wreck *can't-take-your-eyes-away* kind of thing. "Really. For my entire life, ghosts have been coming to me. They seem to be attracted to me for some reason. I'm sort of a spook magnet. I can see them when others can't."

Crackers looked around. "Wait, are there any here with us now?"

"No. All clear on the ghost horizon," I responded without a glance. "Ever since I visited your circus, though, I've been seeing clowns. Ghost clowns."

I waited for their skeptical reaction.

Stilts looked down at me, an unreadable expression on his painted face. Crackers cleared his throat. "You kids eat way too much processed foods. It's a scientific fact that it can make you delusional."

I took a step toward him. "It's the truth. I've seen them all over. At school, at home. Hundreds of different ones, but I've also seen the same few clowns over and over." I wish I had a picture to show, but the clowns that were in our pictures disappeared as all Snapchat pictures do.

"Describe one." Stilts' kind eyes gave me the comfort to elaborate. I began with the tall one I'd seen the most.

"There is one clown in particular I've seen a lot. He's tall, going on seven feet. Thin as a goalpost and hunched over, he's dressed as a tramp with a well-worn hat, black coat and tails. He's got the red nose and drawn in beard, but no white face."

I caught Crackers and Clooney sharing a look and moved in on Crackers, pointing a finger. "You know him, don't you?"

"Lenny." Crackers nodded and looked up at Stilts.

"Lenny?" I asked Stilts the question.

"Lenny," Stilts began. "He died during a performance last winter. We were in Myrtle Beach."

"Lenny," Clooney repeated the name with obvious reverence. "Lenny was a clown's clown. He cared about the art of clowning more than anyone I've ever met. There will never be another one like him now that he's gone."

I shook my head. "He's not that gone. I've seen him several times." Clooney gave a visible shiver. "There's another one I see frequently. This clown is short and incredibly wide, he's almost square, he's so wide." Now Clooney was giving a look to Crackers, who nodded in return.

"Brick," Clooney said. "His name was Brick."

"Was?" I asked, though I already knew the answer. From the direction of the big tent, I heard a loud collective gasp. Must be the high-wire act.

"Brick had a heart attack two years ago. When he collapsed, the paramedics could hardly lift him onto the gurney." Clooney nodded.

"Brick was the most physical comic I've ever seen," Stilts said.

Clooney took a step forward. "I'm convinced," he said with another shiver.

I faced the group, my arms folded across my chest. "Okay, here's the big question. Any idea why your dead clowns would be coming to me ever since I visited the circus in St. Paul?"

"St. Paul, you say?" Crackers asked. A look was shared between all three of the circus performers.

"You know something, don't you?" I took a step closer and held Cracker's gaze. They didn't realize it, but I could be quite the force of nature when I put my mind to it.

"Well..." Crackers looked up at Stilts, asking a non-verbal question.

Stilts was obviously processing things in his head. After a moment, he sighed. "One of our clowns left the circus when we were in St. Paul. He disappeared without a word."

"Maybe a good thing," Clooney said.

"No doubt about it," Crackers added and Stilts nodded in agreement. "Better off without him."

"He was new to our circus. This particular clown didn't fit in very well." Stilts adjusted his shirt. "You see, sometimes clowning brings in the wrong kind of person. There was definitely something off about him."

"Off is not even close to describing how wrong he was," Clooney said as he kicked the dirt at his feet.

"Agreed," I said with immediate reaction from all three. They look confused.

"I saw him," I confirmed. "Don't shoot me, but..."

"We don't make a habit of shooting people here," Crackers said as he pulled out a pretend pistol from his pretend holster.

I held up a hand to shush him, then continued, "I was at the last show of the evening in St. Paul. I'd snuck beyond the roped off area to explore and heard an argument the clowns were having about someone. Someone everyone seemed to be afraid of."

"That was us. And his name was Rellik," Stilts offered.

"Yes, Rellik. Odd name for a clown," Clooney said. A crackle of thunder wasn't too far off and the wind picked up again.

Stilts watched the sky as he replied. "He said it was a family name, going back generations in Hungary. You see, many of us are clowns because clowning runs in our families. Clowns may have a bad reputation in the entertainment industry, but it wasn't always that way. Clowns entertained on prime time in television's early days. Emperors and royalty were fascinated by the clown's humor and often kept them as part of their trusted court."

Folding his arms, Stilts continued with apparent enthusiasm for the subject. "Clowns, being in trusted positions, could get privileged information out in times of war. They've been used as espionage agents in a number of instances."

"I had no idea," I told him, though I actually knew it because of my father's clown article—the very article that started my clown apocalypse. Sometimes I found it better to let adults believe they were more knowledgeable than me. Whether true or not, it kept them sharing information. It didn't hurt to have them underestimate me as well.

A rumble of thunder interrupted, louder this time. I needed to get back on track. "As I said, I was there on your last night in St. Paul, a Sunday night. I remember it vividly. The argument was heating up until Rellik made his appearance. Everyone froze when he came out of the tent. It was like all of you were afraid of him."

"Well..." Clooney looked away.

"I'm not saying we were, or we weren't, but there was something in his eyes. It spoke of bad things to come." Crackers shuddered.

"It had gotten worse since he came to the circus the month before," added Stilts.

"He'd become fixated on Tang."

"Tang?" I asked.

"Tang," Stilts confirmed. "She's one of our acrobats. Petite, about your height, and looked younger than she is. It started with Rellik never missing her performances, always watching from the shadows. He constantly lurked around her trailer. We were worried about Tang's safety."

"That's why I told some of her troupe to watch out for him," Crackers said. "I heard they confronted Rellik earlier that night. I don't know what happened, but those acrobats can be physical when they're provoked."

"That may explain his rage when we saw him," Clooney remarked. "If looks could kill..."

"That's when he saw me," I said.

"What?"

"I was backstage in the shadows, afraid I'd be discovered. And then the scary clown stopped right where I was hiding." I shivered. "He knew I was there. He stared at me like I was..."

"Lunch?" Crackers said with a trace of humor in his voice.

"Just about," I confirmed. "Like the fat kid staring at pizza, ready to devour the entire thing in one bite. It was like I wasn't a person to him, but something to consume."

"What did you do?" Stilts asked. There was obvious concern in his voice.

"Don't judge me, but I ran. As fast as I could."

Crackers shook his head emphatically. "Absolutely no judging here."

"That was a good call. You don't want to be in Rellik's crosshairs," Clooney added. "Tell me though, could he have followed you home? He has a demonstrated history of fixating on someone."

It hadn't occurred to me that a real clown might have followed me home. "He could have. I ran fast, and when the show ended, I was swept up in the crowd with my parents. I doubt he could have followed us all the way back to Pine Ridge."

Stilts held up a hand. "Maybe he didn't have to." He pointed to my Pine Ridge soccer sweatshirt. "What were you wearing that night?"

Oh crap, I thought as I remembered that night. "I was wearing my pink Pine Ridge High School hoodie." I ran my fingers through my hair. "The one with my last name stenciled on the back."

There was a long moment of silence as we considered the implications. I shook my head. "I've seen a lot of clowns, but I haven't seen him. I would recognize that horrible painted face of his."

Stilts put a hand on my shoulder. "Don't be so sure. Clowns don't always paint themselves the same every time. Many change their look as their moods change. Some evolve over time. Many stay the same, locked into one character that they've learned to play to perfection. But Rellik had many faces. You may not have recognized him with a change of makeup and costume."

I was having trouble breathing as I considered the possibility that it was Rellik that took Christine and Bri. That was worse than a demonic ghost clown taking them for some reason. Humans could be far scarier than ghosts.

Stilts gave my shoulder a tug and said, "Let's go find Tang. She may have more insight on Rellik."

We found her just outside the big tent, lined up with the other acrobats, waiting for the show to conclude. I remembered when we left the circus in St. Paul, the performers were applauding us as we left the big tent. It was a cool and memorable way to leave the grounds. I haven't often been applauded in my life.

Stilts pulled Tang aside as I studied her. She was of Asian descent, shorter, with long black hair. Lean and muscular, she was beautiful by anyone's standards. She listened intently to what Stilts said as he leaned precariously over. She nodded and then looked in my direction. Stilts waved me over.

I held out my hand. "I'm Abbey. Nice to meet you." I got a firm handshake in return.

"Tell Abbey about Rellik," Stilts prompted her.

"He was a creeper," Tang said with a hint of an accent. Her English was good, but clearly not her original language. "Can't say I was sad to have him gone."

"I get that," I said. "I heard he was stalking you."

Tang nodded. "I hadn't noticed him at first, but Antonio pointed him out one day. He said that clown is always there. After that, I'd see him standing in the back at every show, watching us. Watching me. I started to see him everywhere around the circus. It happened too often to be a coincidence."

"Did he ever say anything to you?" I asked.

She shook her head. "Never. He stared at me like I was some prize he had to have. It was his eyes that scared me the most. I kept getting the feeling that something was going to happen sooner rather than later. His intensity was building as time went on." She tucked her hair behind an ear. "If Crackers hadn't said something to the guys, I truly believe he would have done something."

Looking at me with obvious concern, she asked, "Is he after you now?"

"It's starting to look that way," I said as a feeling of dread washed over me, and I shivered.

Taking a step forward, her brown eyes locked on mine. "Be careful. There's something seriously wrong with him, like there's something evil festering below the surface. I don't think it's possible to underestimate what he's capable of." She shuddered.

I reached out for her hand and gave it a squeeze. "At least he's my problem now. You're safe." It felt like I should give her a hug, and I did. Her arms were solid as I thought that I needed to get to the gym more often.

As I awkwardly disengaged, she hesitated. "There was one more thing you should know about Rellik. I figured it out after he left."

"What's that?"

"His name," she said. "It's spelled backward."

"Backward? Oh crap," I blurted as it hit me.

Killer.

*

"I KNOW why the dead clowns are coming to you," Stilts shouted to be heard over the rising noise levels. It was the crowd cheering their appreciation of the show's finale, but there was more than that happening. It sounded like an approaching freight train, not that I remember seeing railroad tracks.

I moved closer to Stilts to hear what he was trying to tell me, when a familiar hand touched my shoulder. "Hey, found you," Turner exclaimed. "What did you find out?"

I nodded towards Stilts, who leaned down best he could, given the height of his stilts and the strong wind. "I know," he began again.

A flash of lightning, with an immediate crack of thunder lifted our gaze as the crowds poured out of the big tent. The green-tinged clouds moving in a peculiar circular pattern, the approaching roar, and the breeze that become a strong gale all came together in my mind.

"Tornado," I shouted. "Get to shelter."

The eerie and frightening whine of the tornado siren cut through the noise and pandemonium reigned. People screamed and ran with no clear direction of where to go. Where do you go in the middle of a field of tents? The approaching roar gathered in intensity. Beyond a freight train now, an almost animal-like snarl joined the sound, bringing back the all-too-familiar feeling of panic that bad weather could ignite in me.

But I wasn't that same little girl who cowered in fear. I'd learned action was the best response, as it gave me a sense of control. Control may well be an illusion, but it could also save our lives.

Grabbing Turner's hand, I shouted to be heard, "We have to move."

"Where?" he questioned.

Remembering the ditch as we turned into the fairgrounds, I pulled him in the direction of the parking lot. "There's a culvert at the parking lot entrance," I shouted. Lightning flashed and illuminated the massive twister bearing down on us. Dust and debris swirled around the base of the tornado. In my efforts to cope with my weather phobia, I read up on tornadoes, as they were the worst of the worst as far as I was concerned. However, what I learned didn't allay my fears.

The dark funnel of a tornado could destroy solid buildings, make a deadly missile of a piece of straw, uproot large trees, and hurl people and animals for hundreds of yards. Heavy objects like machinery and railroad cars were often lifted and carried by the wind for considerable distances. In 1931, a tornado in Minnesota carried an 83-ton railroad coach and its 117 passengers over eighty feet through the air, before dropping them in a ditch.

It felt wrong to be running toward the tornado, but the culvert was the only shelter I could think of. The tents were not an option. We might as well find a mobile home park.

Running hand in hand with Turner, I watched the twister's erratic motion as it skipped and danced. Even with my heart pounding, our survival depended on our cool heads. Get to shelter, my mind repeating the mantra as we sprinted. Get to shelter.

We were out of the main gate, running down the drive. Not a clown in sight this time. No longer quiet, the evening air was filled with the roar and siren. A family ran in front of us, obviously headed for their car. A small girl wearing a purple flowered top, maybe ten years old, fell directly in front of us. I let go of Turner's hand, scooping her up as her father turned back to look for her. Pushing her into her father's waiting arms, I shouted, "There's a culvert at the entrance. It's the only shelter."

Shaking his head, he shouted back, "No. I've got my half ton," as he pointed at a seriously badass pick up. More at home at a monster truck show than a county fair parking lot, it was black with neon green graphics, six-foot-tall tires, chrome vertical exhaust stacks, a steel cage in the bed, and enough attitude to keep a TMZ reporter interested for months. It could be the perfect escape vehicle. Could be...

And suddenly, the twister was there. Listening to a survivor describe a tornado's roar on the news, I didn't think they did it justice. The sound was so deafening it consumed you, making it a surreal experience. My survival instincts took over to keep us moving. We dove into the ditch and monkey-crawled toward the large culvert's opening.

Turner got there first and turned to wait for me. I yelled for him to get inside, even though I knew he couldn't possibly hear me. He picked up on my spastic gesturing and crawled in, with me right behind him. I needed to know what was happening and looked out the culvert's opening. Flying debris was everywhere as the howl echoed through our makeshift shelter. My ears popped as I felt the metal of the culvert pipe shaking. I wasn't at all ashamed to admit that I was shaking too. Think of a Chihuahua in Frostbite Falls, Minnesota kind of shaking.

Without warning, the perfect escape vehicle crashed upside down directly in front of the culvert entrance. The windows blew out, and the same small girl was thrown clear, landing on her back. Consequences be damned, I made for the entrance, but my leg caught on something. I twisted back to look for the cause and saw it was Turner holding onto my foot, a horrified look on his face. Accurately reading my desperation, he released me and I was out of the culvert in a flash. The maelstrom buffeted my entire being, and the wind threatened to lift me off the ground as I fought to reach the girl. When I grabbed her arm, she locked both arms around me in a bear hug. Unlike the drowning swimmer latching onto their savior, her vise-like hold was a good thing as it allowed me to crawl back to the culvert.

Turner was out of the entrance, one hand on the pipe, the other reaching for us. He grabbed my outstretched hand and pulled so hard I felt something pop in my shoulder. We swung into the culvert as the tornado was upon us. The ground heaved, and the seam separated on the pipe, giving us something to hang onto. My hands were next to Turner's as we held on for our lives.

Eyes squeezed shut as the debris whipped against us, though we had no way to protect ourselves. It felt like forever, but it was likely only seconds as we endured the twister's pounding. The girl's face was buried in my neck as she clung onto me. If she was crying or screaming, I never knew.

In a tornado, no one can hear you scream.

And just like that, the buffeting debris was gone, the wind diminished and the howling freight train had moved on down the track. In the deathly quiet, my fingers unclenched and we slid down the side of the large pipe, exhausted beyond anything I'd ever felt.

We held each other, the Thompson Twins' "Hold me Now" running through my head as eighties songs like to do. Both Turner and the girl trembled as we clung to each other. No one wanted to let go.

Sirens of the approaching emergency vehicles grew louder as I pushed the hair from the girl's face. Looking into her eyes, I whispered, "We're safe. We are safe."

The girl looked anxiously toward the culvert's entrance. "Daddy," she croaked, the words coming out in pained sobs. The overturned truck was gone. "Daddy..."

WILE E. COYOTE

My father stared at me with his mouth literally hanging open.

I was sure I was quite the sight with all my ripped clothing and one arm in a sling, let alone all the scrapes and bruises that covered my knees and face. Not at all the pristine condition he saw me in earlier that morning. But, hey. You try surviving a tornado and see how you look.

Driving back, we debated whether to come directly home, but Harmony's advice regarding my father kept running through my head, "He's stronger than you think. Trust him." My father studied me with concern. He could tell when I was about to cry and hurriedly closed the gap between us. I received a hug that bordered on painful because of my sore body, but I didn't care. At all. As someone who tries to take on the problems of the world—and the netherworld—it felt nice to be loved and supported once in a while, so I relaxed and lived in the moment.

"Tough day at the circus, I see," he said, obviously trying to lighten the mood. Pushing back the hair from my face, he looked me in the eye. "Clearly, I was justified to be worried about your circus visit."

"Maybe," I agreed. "But it wasn't because of the clowns. They were nice, actually. It was the tornado that wasn't so nice."

"Really?" My father's concern evident as his eyes threatened to water. "What happened to your arm?" he asked.

"It's my shoulder," I corrected as I tried raising my arm with a wince. It was still painful, and the ER doctor said it would be for several days. He also said that given the circumstances, things could have gone way worse. I had to agree with him. "The tornado was veering right at us and we found shelter in a culvert at the main entrance."

"Smart."

"But then Abbey left the shelter just as the twister was on us." Turner threw me under the bus.

"Maybe not so smart," my father said.

"But you haven't heard the whole story. A little girl needed saving. She was thrown from her parent's pickup, and I was close enough to grab her." Thinking back to that moment, I shuddered.

My father smiled. "You did the right thing. Always help those..." He paused so I could finish his thought.

"...Who can't help themselves. I know Dad." This was a guiding principle in our house. It's the reason my mom joined the Doctors Without Borders organization in the first place.

"So, what happened next?" my father prompted me to continued.

"I grabbed her, and we tried to get back to the culvert. The wind was so strong it lifted me up. But Turner grabbed my arm and pulled us to safety inside the culvert."

"I guess I pulled a little too hard. Sorry," he offered.

I smiled and touched his arm. "We might not have made it without your help. Don't worry about it."

My father ran a hand through his hair and sat on the stairs. He looked at us and asked, "Was the trip worthwhile? Did you get the answers you hoped for?"

I looked at Turner and he shrugged.

"We met Stilts, who you can guess by his name is quite tall."

"I met him when we went to the circus earlier," my father added. "He's the senior clown with the Surini Brothers Circus. Nice guy."

"He was," I agreed. "After we talked for a while, he said he thought he knew why the clowns were coming to me. But that's when the tornado hit. It's crazy how random tornadoes could be. This one touched down in the parking lot and then skipped over the main part of the circus. We looked for Stilts afterward, but we could never find him again. Didn't see him at the hospital either."

"Hmm," my father said as he stroked his chin. "So, Stilts said he had an idea why the clowns were coming to you? Maybe we can recreate his thought process. What had you told him?"

I took a seat next to my father, letting out a groan as I sat. *Getting old*, I thought, *getting old*. "We talked about the scary clown I saw when we were at the circus in St. Paul. His name was Rellik."

"Which is Killer spelled backward," Turner chimed in.

"Not a good sign," my father said with his usual keen grasp of the obvious.

"Not at all," I answered. "Most importantly, Rellik saw me that night we were there in St. Paul. And I was wearing my Pine Ridge hoodie with my name on the back."

My father groaned. "Not good, either."

"It gets worse. Rellik disappeared from the circus that same night."

"But he's alive, right? He's not a ghost clown like the others you've been seeing?" My father looked at me with confusion.

I pondered his question for a long moment before answering. "No, he was alive—the other clowns saw him too."

Turner paced as we talked and held up a finger. "Maybe something happened to him after he left the circus. Got hit by a bus or trampled by a rogue elephant," Turner suggested with a chuckle.

I shook my head. "No, Rellik's still alive, and that could explain some things, too. Ghost clowns can haunt mirrors and disappear in front of me, but a live clown—a psychotic clown—could be responsible for Bri and Christina's disappearance."

My father nodded his head. "This disturbed clown sees you, finding something about you that lights his fuse and sets him off. He knows your name and your school. Maybe he watches you as the fire builds in him. He's ramping up to the right moment, sees your soccer friends and takes several of them, waiting for the right moment to take you as well. Frankly, I was surprised he hasn't come after you yet."

"I..." My hesitation was all he needed to know.

"Wait, Rellik has tried to take you?" By the expression on his face, my father already knew the answer. "When?"

"It was last night after our game. When you and mom went to go pick up pizza. I had come out to the lot to wait for you and I saw someone with a knife. He was mostly in the shadows, but he'd sort of dance into the light underneath the lampposts. I heard the sound of his blade striking the metal of the posts. He was moving in my direction, stalking me, as I headed out into the street."

"That's why you were out there when we came to pick you up," my father said. "I was wondering."

"You came at just the right moment. I don't think I had much time left."

"You should have said something. I would have called the sheriff." He shook his head, worry coloring his face.

"At the time, I thought it was another ghost clown. What would law enforcement do with that? If I tried explaining that to a cop, I might be the one who gets locked up."

"True." My father put a hand on my shoulder. "You've had a rough couple of days. Hopefully, it's over. Now that we know Rellik is alive and out there, we can do something. The sheriff can get a manhunt started to find Rellik and the girls."

Turner cleared his throat. "But it's not just Rellik. All sorts of clowns have been coming to you. And all of them are ghost clowns. We saw almost a hundred of them down in Iowa."

I nodded in agreement.

"They were lined up at attention on either side of the main drive into the circus," I told my father. "They just stood there. Turner's right, there had to be a hundred of them."

"It was like the honor guard I saw at the airport," Turner added. "They were lined up to honor a soldier.

"For me, the most interesting part was when I was talking to the

Surini Brothers clowns and describing some of the clowns that I've been seeing. They recognized them as clowns who had died." I leaned forward, trying to get a kink out of my sore back.

"Were they scary clowns as well?" my father asked. "Did they embrace the dark side of clowning?"

Studying my father, I was unsure if he was kidding with his melodramatic question, but decided he was serious. "That's the thing, no. These clowns were well-respected and described as being genuinely nice."

"Hmm," my father said, as he pondered the facts we've laid out. I've come to understand my father enough to let him think things through when he goes into his deep thought mode. I kept silent to let him process things. Harmony said to trust him as my mind drifted back to my last meeting with her. She said the clown's fundamental nature wouldn't change with their death. Once a clown, always a clown. We also talked about the reason many ghosts come to me: because I can help. And...

"Oh crap," I said.

I knew, and it felt so obvious that I should have realized it long ago. My father and Turner looked at me with concern.

"The clowns," I began as I stood up. "They're coming to me because I can help them, but they've been trying to warn me about Rellik, too. There was something seriously wrong with him and they know it. He's perverted clowning and the ghost clowns have been trying to warn me. Trying to help me. These clowns have spent their lives entertaining others. They don't want people hurt—or kidnapped —especially by a fellow clown." I started moving toward the door.

"So, these clowns want your help?" my father asked.

"Sure looks that way. But maybe they can help me, too. We need to get to the school to find out."

"Why the school?"

"That's where the attacks happened and where the clowns are most often. There has to be a reason."

"Good enough for me," my father announced. "I'll drive. I have an idea of a plan. We'll talk about it on the way."

I wasn't going to refuse his help. All hands on deck.

I STOOD out in the open under the light of the harvest moon in a star-filled night sky. A rare shade of blood red, the moon was unusually large and bright in the night sky. I prayed the moon was the only blood I would see tonight as I noted the crimson cast my outstretched arms had in the light. The crisp autumn air felt cool on my bare arms. A glance over my shoulder reassured me that my backup, Turner and my father, were across the parking lot, waiting and watching. My father's plan was simple. I was here to communicate with the clowns to find out where Christina and Bri were. Nothing else. My father and Turner would follow discreetly. They would be there to help if I needed it. The beauty of the plan was, it put me front and center to lead the way. And of course, the problem with the plan was it put me front and center when anything happened.

"Brick," I murmured, saying the stout clown's name that I'd seen multiple times. There was no particular reason that I'd chosen Brick from all the clowns I've seen. He was easy to picture, and I had to start with someone.

"Brick. Brick," I said evenly as I turned in a circle, my arms outstretched as I pictured Brick, the short and stocky clown. "Brick, I need your help," I said in an almost sing-song voice. "Brick, Brick, come quick."

And when I turned toward the woods, he was there. Thick as a brick, square as a lakeshore rental cabin, he stood in front of me. His piercing eyes were locked on mine. I took a step closer and said, "Stilts sends his regards." Brick nodded.

"Do you know why I need you?" I asked.

Again, Brick gave me a nod.

I took another step toward him. "Then show me," I requested.

His massive hand pointed a finger at me, then swung it toward the heavy woods behind me. I looked into his eyes and nodded in understanding. He gave a little wink, and I instantly knew I was doing the right thing as I headed for the trees.

The tall clown, Lenny, waited for me on the hill. Unusually tall and thin, he was as distinctive as distinctive could be. Right behind him was the stand of pines used in the school's logo. Pine Ridge High School was built in a basin with a thick forest overlooking the school directly to the north, and the stand of pines sat at the edge of the forest.

After I climbed the ridge, Lenny tipped his hat to me. Wiping the sweat from my eyes, I study the freakishly built clown. If Brick was a square, then Lenny was a pencil. Tall, thin, and angular, he ushered me forward with a dramatic wave worthy of a game show spokesmodel.

I moved forward, but the problem was, there was nowhere to go. There was no opening in the trees. Beyond the outlying Pine Ridge signature trees, the forest looked absolutely impenetrable. I turned back to my guide and shrugged. Lenny rolled his eyes at me in mock annoyance and pointed a finger at me.

"Who me?" I asked.

I got a vigorous nod as he took a few surprisingly graceful strides toward the treeline and crooked a finger at me in the classic "come here" gesture. When I got to his side, he pointed to a trampled patch of grass and gestured for me to move forward. Taking a step onto the grass, I was forced to push a massive low-hanging branch aside. Completely hidden until I stepped in and moved the branch, I discovered a path running off at an acute angle. Unless an especially enterprising—and frankly, lucky—sheriff discovered the path, the authorities hadn't searched there. The path would have been impossible to see even in the daytime. I was left wondering whether my backup would find the path, either. But with my cell reassuringly tucked in my pocket, I could reach my father when I needed to.

208 | ALLAN EVANS

I turned to give Lenny a thumb's up, but he was gone. His job must be done. No point in me waiting; I stepped into the forest. The trampled path quickly gave way to a rocky path that followed a ridge winding its way deeper into the forest. Where I was headed, I had no idea.

The smell of the pines and the haunting refrain of a nearby owl almost made it an enjoyable hike. Almost. If it wasn't the middle of the night and I wasn't being led by dead clowns into who knows what, I might enjoy it.

The rocky terrain brought me along a ledge overlooking a plummeting drop to the forest below. As the bare stone walkway marked the path through the near-impenetrable undergrowth, I had only two options for directions. Since I could say with certainty that I wasn't going back, going forward it was. I was on a mission to rescue my friends, and I could be relentless. A not-so-far-away coyote picked that moment to utter his distinctive and eerie howl.

As the path declined, the trees opened up, and relief blossomed as I emerged from the forest. Stepping into the meadow, I paused to examine my new surroundings under the light of the moon. The meadow was large and rolling with a stand of trees in the middle. Looking across to the sides, there was more of the thick forest. When I turned back around, I found I was no longer alone. I had a large clown standing in front of me.

Pointing across the meadow to the stand of trees, the clown gestured for me to go in that direction. Wearing a yellow hat at a jaunty angle, this wasn't a clown I remembered seeing before. With tufts of red hair sticking out, a large red nose and face makeup, he wore a plaid jacket with an unusually large flower adorning the lapel. I decided to give him the respect he deserved and stepped closer.

"Thank you for helping me," I said as I held his gaze. He hadn't moved—his arm still was pointing in the direction he wanted me to go. His expressive eyes blinked and looked as if they might tear up. He gave a little wink, and I headed for the stand of trees. Glancing back, he was gone.

Another coyote howled, even closer this time.

When I arrived at the stand of trees, I saw my destination. Down the hill and across the meadow stood a dilapidated corrugated steel building. When I say dilapidated, picture a rusty, pieced together, falling apart, roof panels blowing in the breeze, piles of material stacked haphazardly, kind of dilapidated. There was even an ancient doghouse half buried under a bunch of rebar. The large building was a series of connected structures all in the same state of disrepair.

It had to be the place.

There was movement to my right, and I froze. A dog had stepped into the meadow and watched me warily. He looked to be about fifty pounds with light gray fur. As his tail lifted into the moonlight, a black tip came into view. The dog's ears were wide, pointed and erect. As it bared its teeth and let out a menacing growl, I realized it wasn't a dog. It was a coyote.

Getting to the building seemed my best course of action. But, when I took a step toward the structure, the coyote took a matching step towards me. And at that moment, another coyote stepped out into the meadow to join the first. This one was slightly larger and stared at me for a long moment before it lifted its head and howled. The sound was eerie and piercing—and worse, it was answered by still another coyote.

The answering coyote wasn't far away. I couldn't distinguish which direction, but the mystery was rendered moot when a dozen or more coyotes raced across the meadow and joined up with the first pair.

Could my night get any worse?

Buoyed by the pack's arrival, the first coyote took several steps toward me. These were not the tentative steps of an animal checking out the situation, but the confident steps of a predator ready to take down its prey. Tail down, teeth bared, and clearly only one objective was on the beast's mind, and I was the prey in question.

Quick aside: my mind was capable of processing multiple options in a nanosecond. As possible scenarios raced through my synapses, I also thought that since these coyotes were nocturnal, that would make me their breakfast, rather than dinner.

Sizing up my options, my best protection was my father's Maglite flashlight. A foot in length and constructed from solid aluminum, it felt good in my hand. But was a flashlight enough to deter a dozen coyotes? There may be another option, but I had to save it.

Squaring up my body, I faced the leader of the pack and raised the flashlight up into a defensive position. The coyote gave me another growl, his eyes locked on mine. Things may not end well, but I was going to go down fighting.

The vibrating phone in my pocket startled me and I almost called out in alarm. Keeping my eyes locked on the beast yards in front of me, I fished out the phone and answered it in speaker mode. "Abbey?" It was my father's welcome voice.

"Dad, I don't have much time. What do you know about coyotes?"

I was convinced my father could hear the stress in my voice. To his credit, he only hesitated for the briefest of moments. "They travel and hunt in packs, they are cunning and adaptable, which explains their population growth, even as their natural habitat diminishes."

"Dad, I have a pack standing right in front of me." I watched as the lead coyote moved closer and I saw his breath in the cool night air.

"Hold on, I'm on the internet." His voice calm and steady, it helped me to remain the same. "Don't run from a coyote. They'll be all over you in a heartbeat."

"Okay..."

"Here we go. You're going to need to haze them."

"Haze them?"

"You need to remind them that they should be afraid of humans."

I watched the pack close up ranks behind the alpha who had never broken eye contact with me. He took another step, and I knew his next move would be to come at me. "They don't look any too afraid of me."

"You have my Maglite flashlight. It has a strobe. Turn off the flashlight and then give it three quick clicks."

I followed his directions, and the strobing began. "Okay, we have strobe."

"Great. Now stand tall, wave your arms and shout at the coyotes. And you should run at them."

Wait, what?

My rational mind raised a gigantic red flag, but I had to trust my father. Channeling Savannah as she came running out of her goal screaming at the other team's attacking player, I shrieked and ran at the lead coyote, waving the strobing flashlight.

It worked. They ran and regrouped at the edge of the forest. "It worked," I panted. "They ran."

"Are they out of sight?" my father asked.

"No, they are standing near the edge of the woods."

"Then you need to do it again."

Seriously?

"They have to leave the area entirely."

With a strong encore performance, I ran at them like a girl possessed. I was louder and more frantic than the first time. In a moment, the coyotes scattered into the forest.

"Done. They're gone." My adrenaline rush left me feeling shaky. There was the distinct possibility I could vomit.

"Holy crap!" Turner said, obviously on the speaker with my father. "You scared me, too. I may have wet myself a little."

I couldn't help but laugh as relief washed over me. "That was incredible, I've never seen anything like that before. Thought I was a goner..."

I stopped mid-sentence as I saw a pair of clowns holding sentry position on either side of the building. Beyond the dead clowns, there was no sign of life. Judging by the rundown condition of the building —and I was giving rundown buildings a bad name by comparing them to the World War II era standing scrap heap—no one had used the place for decades.

Still. The clowns were in place, which showed me the building was being used for some dark purpose. And I had a good idea by who.

The rear door was securely padlocked, and I noted the lock's newness. However, the metal panel next to the door wasn't nearly so secure and I was able to pull it out enough to crawl my way into the building. As the panel creaked back into place behind me, I immediately knew several things. One, I'd been there before. My waking dream during the road trip in the truck stop's bathroom had brought me to this building. There were few coincidences in my world.

Two, that meant Christina and Bri were in there somewhere. I heard them when I was exploring, so I knew I was in the right place. Which brought me to a third thought. The possessed evil clown I saw merging with that dark monster was Rellik. And guaranteed, he was here too.

We've all seen the movie cliché with the girl entering the killer's home. As she starts prowling around, the killer returns home, and the girl is forced to hide. No way was I lucky enough to have him off running around picking up a pizza or his dry cleaning. No, he would be here and I would confront him. I knew coming face to face with that clown would be extremely dangerous. There was more going on with Rellik than mental illness. Judging by my rest stop vision, I may well be facing down a demonically possessed psychotic clown.

My life was anything but a cliché.

Fortunately, there was a plan. The plan—as discussed with my father—was to communicate with the clowns that had reached out to me and ask where Christina and Bri were being held. Once we knew for sure where my friends were, we'd call in the sheriff to arrest Rellik. My father wanted me nowhere near the rogue clown. My issue with the plan was it left too much to chance and opened up the possibility that Rellik could get away, or worse—kill my friends or come after us again.

That was why I had my own plan.

SUDDEN DEATH RUSSIAN ROULETTE

THE PLACE WAS A MESS, EVEN WORSE THAN MY BEDROOM ON ITS worst day.

With debris everywhere, I moved cautiously down the dark corridor. I've never been the most coordinated person. I knew on a scale of clumsiness, I was way over towards walking disaster despite my budding soccer skills. It would be bad to call attention to myself, or worse, fall and injure myself. So, it was one foot carefully placed in front of the other.

Thankfully, when I turned the corner, there were hanging bulbs lighting the way. I was curious about where the electricity came from in the dilapidated building as I doubted it was connected to the energy grid. Hesitating at a T intersection, my gut sent me to the left, and I entered an even more rundown section of the building.

The building was much as I'd experienced earlier: damp, dilapidated and deserted. Dead quiet. That was, except for the shuffling sound. And it was getting louder with each shivering moment.

Oh, crap. Someone's coming.

Holding my breath, I flattened myself against the wall, willing myself to be one with the shadows. The horrifyingly loud sound of a nearby engine starting up almost gave me a heart attack. I put a hand over my mouth to keep silent—not that I could be heard over the generator's roar. The generator explained the electricity, anyway. Wasn't it usually a cat that jumped out at the heroine, and not some *so-loud-that-I-almost-peed-in-my-pants* generator?

Again, no clichés for me.

As I stood in place up against a wall, a figure passed by and moved into the light. It was Rellik. This time I recognized him, as his clown makeup was closer to how I saw him the first time. Even still, there was an angry haphazardness to it that made him look even more menacing than before.

I'd imagine it was like when you examine a painting, say a Monet. The brush strokes told a story of someone with an inner calmness that Monet achieved in his later life. Another artist's painting might not have any smooth lines, and had a jagged feel that led you to believe the artist was angry. Now, take that same artist and fill him up with enough meth to kill a rhino and you get an idea of what Rellik's face looked like.

With the image of his face still haunting me, Rellik continued down the corridor, not picking up on my presence. There was nothing else to do but follow him, so I stayed discreetly behind him until he turned a corner. But, when I peeked around the edge, he wasn't there.

Stepping out from the relative safety of the corner was about the riskiest move I could make, but I needed to know where Rellik was. With the generator loud enough to wake the dead, any sound I made was masked, but the reverse was also true. I wouldn't be able to hear his approach, either.

My imagination ran rampant as I pictured Rellik stepping out in front of me, a large knife in his hand, fresh blood dripping from the blade. I shook my head and tried to get the image from my mind as I ran down to the next corner. I ventured a peek around the wall.

Halfway down, Rellik leaned against the wall. Even though his face was turned away from me, I could tell he was talking to himself as I saw his chin bobbing up and down. Unfortunately, with the generator behind me, I couldn't make out what he was saying. As he talked, his hand slid along the wall, in an almost loving manner. It was like that moment in a musical when the character stops and begins to sing about a great love. Except Rellik would never be in a musical because he would pervert the concept of love into something dark and terrifying. No Broadway for this killer clown.

Without warning, the generator motor hissed to a stop and my ability to hear was restored. Rellik spoke, and the sound of his voice was light and sing-songy—which did nothing to take away the horror of his words.

"It seems that Christina no longer wants to chat with us. Such a petulant young lady. I may have to punish you...for her... stubbornness." Rellik drew out the last part of the sentence. His face had a smile that would be very much at home on a ravenous hyena.

Memories of my waking nightmare of being trapped in a wall with my tormenter lurking outside flooded my mind. I realized at that moment that Rellik was speaking not to himself, but to Bri.

Christina and Bri were here, entombed in the wall.

"I hope you're not getting bored with our conversation, my dear," he said as he picked up a 2x4 board. He slammed it into the wall with such force, a piece of the wall splintered off. Even though it was only a shriek, I recognized Bri's voice immediately.

After experiencing the terror of being trapped inside the wall for only a few moments, I couldn't even imagine what my friends were going through being in there for days. They'd never be the same after enduring his madness in those claustrophobic conditions.

I was going to kill that damn clown if it was the last thing I ever did.

"I've been polishing the act for my big comeback," he said, leaning close to the wall, "And, I've been sharpening my knife. Sharpening it so it goes in nice and easy." Rellik's voice was getting softer, and I found myself leaning around the corner to hear him.

"I'll tease you with the blade, let you feel its power and its bite. But don't worry, you'll get the point soon enough." Laughing at his own pun got me angrier.

Rellik pushed away from the wall and I ducked back behind the corner. Moving down the corridor as quickly as I could, I needed to find a place to make my call. Spotting a slightly open door, I squeezed through. Inside, I slid to the floor and pulled out my phone. My father answered right away. "Babe..."

"Daddy, he's here." I spoke in hushed tones, not wanting to draw any unwanted attention from the nearby psychotic clown with the large knife.

"Wait, you weren't supposed to get anywhere near the bad clown. Just information, remember?" My father caught himself and asked, "Are you safe?" The concern and fear evident in his voice.

"I'm okay, I'm hiding." I didn't want to say too much. "And Dad, Bri is here. I heard her."

"What about Christina?" he asked.

"I don't know. Rellik said Christina won't talk to him anymore. I suspect it's because she *can't* talk anymore."

I heard him take a deep breath. "Hang on, this will be over soon. I'm calling the police."

"Good. Where are you now?" I asked.

"We're by the edge of the clearing. Google Earth shows a metallic building on the other side of the meadow."

A thought flashed through my mind. "The coyotes."

"I've thought of that. There's two of us and we both have baseball bats. We'll be fine."

I looked out the door, afraid of what Rellik might do. "Dad, he's talking about using his knife on Bri."

"I'm calling 911 as soon as I hang up."

"We don't have that much time." I was terrified that we'd be too late. I had to get her out of here. "Dad, I need a diversion. You need to draw him away from Bri."

"We're up to the task. Give us a minute to get in place."

I wasn't convinced I had a minute. "Please hurry."

I popped my head around the corner and Rellik was still there. Only now, he had an enormous knife in his hand. He studied the blade with an expression of adoration. Running a finger ever-so-slowly along the blade, he said, "Let's play a game, shall we? I've always believed games to be a great diversion from the tediousness of our lives. You know, something to take our minds away from the struggles and fears we all carry."

Standing square to the wall, Rellik held the blade directly in front of his eyes. "I'm convinced that this game's exceedingly high stakes may be why the game has endured over the centuries. It has its origins in early Russia, you know."

I was getting a bad feeling about things as I watched him tense up.

"The game has had many names over the years. Azartnaya Igra. Ruletka. But you would be most familiar with its common name, Russian Roulette."

Without warning, Rellik drove the point through the wood panel as if it were a soggy piece of bread. I heard a gasp of terror, but not one of pain.

"Oh, did I miss?" He pulled the blade out with a horrible creak from the splintered plank. "No worries, I don't mind playing our game awhile longer. But we do need to find a winner. No tie games allowed. My favorite part is how the game always ends with sudden death."

He paused for a second as if listening to someone. I found myself leaning out from the corner to hear, all the while praying he wouldn't glance in my direction. From what I could tell, Bri had said something that caused Rellik to bark out a laugh.

"Technically this isn't Russian Roulette if we're not both playing? I will not be joining the game, I'm happy to report. We'll have to rename our little game, then. How about the game where the high school girl gets the point in the end? Too long of a name? Maybe Rellik's Roulette would be better."

Where was my diversion? Bri couldn't stall him much longer, but leave it to her to try to outwit him with logic. She was brilliant, quite possibly the most intelligent person I knew, but she wasn't street smart. Most of us learned early on that there was no reasoning with crazy.

I heard the beginning of her muffled reply, but it was cut short by Rellik's sudden puncture of the blade into the wall. Driven to the hilt, Rellik left the knife and danced around the space in front of the wall. "Ooh, I love this game." He leaned in to examine the knife and said, "You are one lucky girl."

With a loud creak, he effortlessly pulled the knife from the wall. "The one thing about luck, however, is it always runs out."

C'mon Dad, I could really use that diversion about now. And on cue, there was a loud thumping from the opposite side of the building. It sounded suspiciously like a baseball bat pounding against a metal building.

"Hold on a moment," he said, cocking his head. "We may have another player joining us." Rellik stomped past as I held my breath and willed him to keep going.

I raced around the corner and pressed myself into the wall behind a door. Rellik was in a hurry and was quickly gone. After counting to ten to make sure he had left, I had one thought on my mind. Rescue.

The thumping started up again in the distance. Then silence. *Keep him guessing, guys.*

I raced to the spot where Rellik used his knife on the wall, but I was worried I'd be exposed out in the corridor. Looking further down the hallway, there was a door that opened to a large space that shared the wall my friends were entombed in. I paused inside the doorway, thinking I could attack the wall from behind without being seen by Rellik—should he return.

There was another thump and the damn generator kicked on again, but thankfully not nearly so loud where I was. Stepping up to the back side of the wall, I searched for where Bri might be located. Wood splinters protruded from the wall in several spots. This must be where the knife was driven through the wall. I put my hand on the rough wood plank, leaning in close.

"Bri, can you hear me," I hissed. Listening, there was no voice, no scratching, no pounding. The generator was the only noise I heard. "Bri, it's Abbey. I'm here to get you out of this place."

And then I heard the most amazing sound ever. "Abbey? For real?" It was Bri's aching croak of a voice.

I slid over, my hand pressed against the wall. I couldn't help it, but tears flowed down my cheeks. "It's me. For real. Help is on the way, but I need to get you out of there."

I looked around for a crowbar to pry the boards away, but all I found was a chainsaw and several shovels. Using the chainsaw was an option I quickly rejected. I couldn't discount the noise factor bringing back Rellik, and honestly, I'd be worried about slicing Bri in half. Instead, I grabbed a flat spade and pushed the edge of the blade into the widest seam. On my knees, I put my full weight into it. The shovel's blade splintered the wood plank, leaving the rusty nail in place. Sliding the spade further down the plank, I pushed against the handle with both arms and the nail came out with the board, clattering to the floor.

I was immediately struck by the pungent smell of human waste. It wasn't a good smell at all. "You might need a long bath when you get home," I said.

"I'm not apologizing," Bri said. "Just get me out." Her voice was clearer with the board removed. Targeting the next board up, I jammed the blade in. It was no match for my sheer determination, and I had the board off in a moment. I found myself looking at Bri's ankles and I gave them a reassuring pat as I moved to the next plank. Before long, I was looking at her knees. "You'll be out soon," I told her.

And working like a madwoman, I furiously used the spade to free my friend. I was soon up to her belly button. I knew from my waking dream that the space was so incredibly tight, there wasn't room for her to fall down. The wall had pressed in on me from all sides. Pretty much a claustrophobic's worst nightmare.

With the board at Bri's chest height pulled off and added to the pile, she collapsed into my arms. "I can't believe you're here. I didn't think anyone was coming for me." Bri broke down into heaving sobs.

"Where's Christina?" I asked, brushing Bri's matted hair back from her eyes. A large bruise on her cheek hinted at the treatment she'd received from Rellik. I was going to kill that clown.

"She's next to me," Bri said as she pointed to the adjoining section.

"Hang on," I got to my feet, shovel in hand. "I'm not leaving her in there."

Beginning with a board around where I thought her head might be, I put everything into it, muscling the plank loose from its nail bonds. It clattered to the floor as the generator went silent again. The way Christina's vacant eyes stared at me, I knew she was nearly gone.

The moment I felt a change in the room's energy, I knew someone had joined us. It could be my father and Turner, but I doubted it. I spun around with shovel raised.

Standing inside the doorway, staring at me with an evil lust emanating from his dark eyes, was Rellik. His face was painted with a demonic visage, no friendly clown face to delight the kids. But it was more than the makeup; it was the terrifying intensity of the mad clown underneath that made him such a scary clown. And of course, the long blade clenched in his hand added to the scariness.

Rellik took a step forward.

I took a step back.

Bri slid against the wall behind me. The room had one door, only one way out. And that was through Rellik. But I knew it would come to this, and I was fine with it. His eyes never left mine, and then he spoke. "I've been waiting for this moment since I first saw you. The way you were cowering in the shadows, there was something in your fear that was so delicious. I knew then I needed you." He had an accent that I couldn't quite place, somewhere in eastern Europe I'd guess. He took another step towards me as my fingers tightened on the shovel.

"Imagine my delight when I find you've come to me." He ran a finger along the blade as he stared at me. The blade must have sliced his finger as several drops of blood run down the flat of the blade. He didn't seem to notice or care. "And we're going to have so much fun together. That is, after I finish with your friend."

Bri whimpered behind me.

"Hold on just a moment, Mr. badass clown," I said in the fiercest voice I could muster. This time it was me taking a step toward Rellik. "My friends have an issue with your behavior. Very inappropriate behavior for a clown."

For the first time, there was a chink in Rellik's confident manner. Brick, Lenny and a dozen of their closest friends surrounded him— and they didn't look happy. I don't know if Rellik could see them or feel their presence, but his body language had changed. Rellik stiffened up and dropped his arms to his sides, the knife no longer threatening.

Taking another step forward, I looked to press my advantage. Rellik doubled over and his body spasmed. I found myself taking a step back as I imagined Rellik might vomit all over me. The thing was, the reality was far worse than my imagination.

The dark thing from my road trip vision rose out of Rellik. Its gnarled claws and elongated body reminded me of a bat with its sinew and muscle visible under leathery skin. The creature's horrifying mouth cracked open and let out a terrible screech. Turning to the assembled clowns, Rellik raised his arms like a conductor of a hellish orchestra. He paused and looked up to the heavens, a smile on his face.

But the clowns weren't going to give up without a fight. They linked arms, appearing to gather strength from each other. It was the beginning of an epic battle between good and evil.

Screw this. I'd had enough. From the beginning, my plan differed from the one I made with my father. In mine, Rellik wouldn't have the opportunity to get away. He wouldn't have the opportunity to hurt anyone else. And he wouldn't have the opportunity to live out his miserable life in a cushy prison or psychiatric hospital. In my plan, Rellik died right here on the dirty concrete floor.

"Hey, Killer," I called as I stepped forward and kicked him in the knee, bringing his eyes back down to earth.

If he was startled to see Kelly's father's gun in my hand, he didn't show it. I'd brought it along hidden in my jacket with the plan to end him once and for all. I refused to waste any more time on that piece of filth. "Go to hell," I suggested as I raised the pistol.

"Abbey," Bri said from my side. "You can't do that." Her voice cracked.

I wanted to pull the trigger so bad, but her words had a hold on my soul and I wavered, finger on the trigger. I kept my eyes locked on the killer clown.

"Abbey, this isn't you. You can't let him—and what he did—stain you. Don't let his darkness consume you." Bri's voice gained strength as she spoke. "This is not the way."

My hand was anything but steady, the pistol shaking all over the place, but even so, Rellik was close enough for a killing shot. "He needs to be stopped, Bri. He was going to hurt you and Christina. He's going to kill us all if we don't stop him."

Bri moved closer, putting a calming hand on my shoulder. "If you pull that trigger, you don't know what it will do to you. You may never be the same." Her hand moved down my arm as she spoke. "Me, I'm already going to the dark side; I'm planning to go to law school to be an attorney. Give me the gun." I surrendered the weapon to her.

My whole body shook. "But we can't let him win. Darkness can't defeat the light. Not in my world," I said as I wept, my voice sounding hollow.

Emboldened by the sudden lack of an immediate threat, Rellik took a step forward. "Abbey, look around. This isn't your world." He sneered and barked out laughter, as he threw his hands dramatically up in the air. The hellish bat thing towering over him. "You're in my world. And I always win here, even with all your help."

Things weren't looking so good at the moment. The assembled clowns appeared to shrink back, like maybe Rellik was going to be too much for them. I hoped my father and Turner would arrive with the sheriff soon.

Rellik's eyes glinted with perverse glee and he took another step. The knife looked impossibly large in his hand.

"STOP!" Bri's shout carried the authority of a thousand policemen—or one angry school lunch lady.

Time slowed as the scene unfolded in front of me.

Rellik stared at her with his mouth open. The briefest of pauses, before he let out a blood-curdling scream and lunged.

I went to grab Bri and pull her from harm's way, but Bri was already in motion. She brought up the pistol and took aim, each pull of the trigger sounding like a cannon in the room.

The bullets tore at Rellik's flesh, ripping holes through his midsection. He stumbled back to the doorway as he tried vainly to grab the frame.

His body betrayed him, and he slid down to the floor in a lifeless heap.

The large bat creature stared at us for a long moment. Its open mouth had that fresh *I've-been-sucker-punched* look. It made me happy to see it lose its foothold in our world as it screeched before getting pulled downward. Its body looked exactly like syrup succumbing to the gravity of a kitchen drain.

Looking at Bri in shock, I took the gun from her limp hand. Relinquishing the weapon seemed to sap her energy, and she promptly sat down on the floor.

I prodded Rellik with my toe—prod may not be a strong enough word—to make sure he really was gone. Satisfied, I dropped the gun, finished, tired, spent.

Bri huddled on the floor, arms wrapped around her legs as she violently shook. She stared at me, but didn't need to say anything, as her thoughts were understood.

"Let's get out of this dump," I said, grabbing her hand and pulling her up. Her legs threatened to give out, and I wrapped an arm around her waist.

A soul-tearing scream startled me, and I swung us around. The scene in front of me was not what I expected, and my mouth hung open as I stared. A transparent version of Rellik was on his hands and knees as his lifeless body lay behind him. The clowns surrounded his ghostly form, moving menacingly closer. Brick broke out with a loud belly laugh as he pointed at Rellik, laughing so hard he doubled over. It didn't take long for Lenny and the others to join in. You may think it was mean spirited (no pun intended) laughter at Rellik's expense, but it wasn't. It was laughter of relief, laughter of joy and laughter of shared pain and redemption. It was the laughter of clowns.

Rellik, for his part, looked around in confusion. Gone was the tortured expression that spoke volumes of the hatred and madness existing below the surface. Replacing it, oddly enough, was a smile.

Time wasn't the only thing that healed all wounds, apparently. Death must be given its fair credit as well. I was astounded to see Rellik join his colleagues in laughter as he got to his feet with a helping hand from Lenny.

Light filled the room. I wasn't sure where it came from, but the brightness increased by the nanosecond as the darkness rapidly receded. The quality of the light was unusual in its warmth and omnipresence. Every shadow had been chased from the room.

I glanced over at Bri and she looked back with a wide smile and tears that flowed down her cheeks. The tears left streaks of pink as they washed away the filth of her captivity.

The number of clowns grew, the room filled with them now. They pressed in, surrounding the original dozen, as they added to the laughter. It was infectious and I couldn't help but join in.

"The Power of Love" from Huey Lewis came to me. The song was featured in one of my all-time favorite movies from the eighties, "Back to the Future." These clowns were about joy and happiness, laughter and comradery. All this came from love, the amazing power of love.

Beams of light rained down from above, their origin a mystery, as I couldn't tell where the beams came from. They were just there. It was hypnotic as the beams rippled in and out of existence. There was almost a feeling of being underwater with the sun beams filtering through the water. As each beam—each a uniquely different color from the others—appeared and disappeared, a clown was taken with it. It was as if the light was bringing each of the clowns home, one by one.

The crowd of clowns rapidly diminished as the fantastic light show continued. Soon, we were down to the original twelve clowns, plus one. The plus one loomed over Brick and Lenny, with a hand on each of their shoulders. The new clown was Stilts, who must have fallen victim to the Iowa tornado. Enveloped in an azure beam of light, he smiled and gave me a thumbs up, winking out of existence from our world.

A light beam vacillated between indigo and crimson washed over Rellik as he looked up to the heavens. Unlike the others, he didn't wink out of existence. Instead, Rellik nodded as if he were having a conversation with someone. The final nod was one of resignation as the light winked out. Rellik's gaze slowly drifted down and paused at Bri. He mouthed the words, "I'm sorry," before his eyes continued their downward journey.

The room remained filled with light, except for where Rellik stood.

It began with a shadow crossing his face, as blackness spread over his rigid figure. It was as if an oily black liquid covered his features, melting him. The way his features softened and drooped reminded me of the time I once put my Barbie in the microwave. The similarities were eerie.

Talons rose from below and pulled at him, dragging him to some dark place underneath it all. Within several horrifying seconds, Rellik was gone. His crumpled body was all that was left of him in our world.

The original twelve clowns remained, their laughter gone. They looked to me, and with a nod, put their hands together in a Namaste gesture, each giving a slight bow. The room brightened as simultaneous light beams enveloped each of the clowns. In a wink, they were gone, leaving me in a state of wonder.

Hearing a creak behind me, I spun around and heard a groan coming from Christina. Her eyes blinked as they struggled to regain footing in reality. After what she'd been through, it was a miracle she was even alive—let alone wanting to face consciousness. Thank you, God.

At that moment, a handful of sheriff's deputies came around the corner, guns leading the way. Several stopped at Rellik's body, while others stepped over him, sweeping into the room. I held up my hands and shrugged. I had zero idea what to say to them that would make any sense whatsoever.

"Clear," one of them called. They rushed over to pry the boards from Christina's prison. After a moment, she was freed and in the arms of a deputy. She looked dazed and confused.

My father, followed by Turner, came around the corner.

"Dad," I cried, relief washing over me. My emotions, pushed down for so long, fought their way to the surface and I broke down. My sobs echoed around the room as the deputies tried to find somewhere else to look, but I didn't care. I think I deserved that moment. Sometimes being the spooky girl could take a lot out of you.

THE FINAL CHAPTER

WITH ALL THE PUBLICITY FOLLOWING CHRISTINA AND BRI'S rescue, my greatest fear was losing my new friends. Growing up with ghostly visitors had led to a life of being on the outside looking in. Having friends had been difficult, if not impossible. I'd lost more friends than I cared to think about when they learned how unusual I really was. This time, it was different. My friends rallied around me.

We'd met as a team one last time to clean out our lockers. One by one, we entered the musty-smelling locker room after a greeting by Coach Johnson at the doorway. She'd surprised me when she said that even though she knew I had been new to soccer, she liked my confidence and had decided to give me a try. Up until then, I thought I had her fooled.

My mind was blown.

I'd been the first one there, and after throwing my cleats, sports bras, practice shirts and shorts, as well as my especially ripe socks into a gym bag, I couldn't bring myself to leave. The team experience was something I hadn't expected. I'd grown to love my teammates, and there was a palpable sense of loss that I wouldn't be seeing them every day.

The entry of Kelly and Lexi broke up my melancholy and had me on my feet. We embraced, no one willing to disengage, comfortable in our friendship that kept awkwardness far away. The tears flowed, but they came from relief and a happy place.

Soon, we were joined by Mary, Fran, Savannah, Greta, Paige, Julia, Lyndsay, Jaz, Sophie, Haily, and Zecky and there was laughter all around. We talked about anything and everything without ever mentioning a single clown. I was happy.

Lyndsay told a story about the time her summer coach tripped and fell over the first aid kit while trying to catch a ball that had been kicked to the sidelines. From then on, she said, the entire team was asking him, "Hey coach, remember that time you fell?" Everyone was laughing when Bri came around the corner. The room grew eerily silent as we all stared at her, unsure what to say after her ordeal.

She glanced around, before raising her palms. "C'mon, guys. This is a happy occasion. Give me some love."

The somberness vanished, and everyone shouted her name and hugged her like they never wanted to let go. Little Bri was mobbed. It was crazy, sweet and beautiful.

Someone turned on music, and surprisingly, it was Cyndi Lauper's "Girls Just Want to Have Fun," one of my favorite party songs. I remember reading about Lauper saying it was truly an anthem for women around the world and had a sustaining message that women are powerful human beings. I couldn't agree more. And you could dance to it.

When the moment happened, it caught me by surprise. Bri got everyone to settle down after the song ended, and she turned to face the group. "I have something I need to say." She dabbed at her eyes.

The entire team quieted, which considering our players, was quite the feat.

Bri tried several times to speak, but her words got caught in her throat. But we, her teammates, had her back.

"You have this, Bri."

"Take your time."

"We're here for you, Bri."

"C'mon girl. Preach it."

At this, Bri smiled. It was a tender, brave smile that melted my heart. She glanced around the room and spoke.

"Thank you so much. I couldn't imagine life without you all. You are my joy, my strength, my everything." She paused to wipe her eyes. She wasn't the only one.

"But I wouldn't be here right now if it wasn't for Abbey."

She took a deep breath, and of course everyone turned to look at me. I kept my focus on Bri.

"Abbey found me, and at great peril to herself, rescued me. She stood up to that...that..." her voice trailed off with a tremble.

"Rellik, the bad clown," I said. Speaking his name took away whatever power he still held over us. "Rellik is gone. Forever."

"About that," Kelly said. "Apparently, one of you shot Rellik with my father's gun. Would you ladies care to tell us which of you pulled the trigger?"

Bri looked at me. I looked at her.

We shook our heads.

"I didn't think so," Kelly said. "Which is quite all right. I wouldn't take credit either, no matter how many victims he's had."

"It's not about credit or blame," I said. "It was about stopping him before he hurt anyone else."

"Amen to that," Coach Johnson said. She'd joined us while we were talking. "I've got to run, I have an appointment with the athletic director to discuss a larger budget for our next season. But you all take care and be safe. And Abbey," she said. I glanced over, surprised to hear my name. "Being new, you probably don't know that every year I give out team awards. This was a strange and shortened season; they're not all like this. So this season I'm only giving one, the MVP award. As I mulled over the candidates, there are so many of you that are worthy of the award. But the tipping point came when I factored in that you rescued both Bri and Christina. Abbey, you are the team's most valuable player. Congratulations."

No idea what to say, I just stood there, numbly shaking my coach's hand.

My teammates knew what to do, and they mobbed me with hugs and love. I loved it. Never in a million years would I have predicted this would have happened, especially thinking back to the embarrassing start when I was left on the ground while Kelly scored. It goes to show how much you can accomplish when you don't give up.

After Coach Johnson left, we stayed. No one wanted to leave.

Bri spoke up. "There's one more thing we need to talk about. As most of you know, Abbey has some unusual abilities where ghosts are concerned. Without those abilities, I'd be dead. I'd like to propose that as her teammates and as her friends, we vow to keep her paranormal abilities a secret. That's what friends do: we look out for each other."

"We got you, ghost girl."

"Your secret is safe with us."

"Ghostie, we got your back."

Like that, from every one of my teammates. Every. One. Of. Them.

Bri looked around the group, her expression turned serious. "If you accept this vow of secrecy, put your hand in." She put her hand on my shoulder.

There was no hesitation as all of my teammates placed their hands on me.

"Good, we're agreed. This is our promise, our secret—and our Abbey. No matter how abnormal she may be."

That broke up the entire room, me included.

I sat alone in the darkness, calm and relaxed. And I waited. Not for long though, he'd come. He had to.

I was back at Pine Ridge after hours again. I sighed as I glanced around the stairwell. It felt like it was becoming a habit for me—a habit I needed to break.

The last week was a whirlwind. Bri was unharmed and spent just a day in the hospital. Christina was still at St. John's, but looked to be recovering nicely. She was severely dehydrated, and after the doctors started giving her intravenous fluids, she perked up considerably.

When our entire team went to visit after cleaning out our gym lockers, I saw glimmers of the joyful Christina I knew, though she still had a haunted look when discussing what happened to her. Would that ever go away?

There was a lot of confusion when the police found a gun and a very dead clown.

I'd told the officers that I was the one who used the gun. I hadn't wanted Bri to jeopardize her chances of getting into law school, and afterwards she quietly pulled me aside and profusely thanked me for keeping her out of the spotlight. Fortunately, the police didn't give me much of a hard time for killing Rellik. Maybe it was because he'd kidnapped and imprisoned several girls and was found with a knife in his grubby hand. When they asked how we found Rellik's hideout, I explained that we'd spotted him near school and had followed him. A spokesman for the Minnesota Bureau of Criminal Apprehension said Rellik was believed to be responsible for a series of murdered high school girls in upstate New York. There were also similar killings in Kansas and in a small town in Michigan outside of Detroit. He said there was little doubt we all would have been murdered as well.

My father wasn't as accepting, however. He grilled me relentlessly about sneaking the pistol out of the house. He seemed especially concerned about my intent even after telling him I brought the pistol along as a *just-in-case-everything-went-wrong* preparation. I reminded my father that he often lectured me about the value of being prepared for whatever life threw at me. I told him because I was the only one that could get the clown's help and save my friends, I hadn't wanted him to say no. But since I knew there was considerably more risk than I wanted to admit, I needed to come prepared. After finishing my explanation, he studied me for a long time. I wasn't convinced he believed me, but he let it go.

After the news broke, it was a complete media circus—if you'll excuse the expression. The national media descended on our small community, with me being in the center. Apparently, having a fourteen-year-old girl shoot and kill a crazed serial killer clown didn't happen very often. I was invited to appear on Good Morning America, the Today Show, as well as several of the late-night talk shows. I politely declined every single one of them.

Afterwards, Turner and I were closer than ever, and that was a good thing. He accepted me for who I am, as strange as that may be. And that was all the security I could ask for. Paula Abdul's eighties song, "Forever your girl" danced its way through my thoughts, and I smiled.

I felt the chill before I heard his voice.

"Abbey."

Peter sat next to me. A moment ago, he hadn't been there, and now he just was.

"Hello, Peter." He pushed his dirty blonde hair away from his eyes. "Or should I say, great Uncle Peter?" I got his eyes staring into mine as he nodded.

"We're family," he said with a smile. I smiled in return.

"Do you recognize where we are?" I asked. He looked around the stairwell and shrugged.

I held his gaze, but he wasn't giving me anything that clued me in on what he thought.

"This is the north wing, the same stairwell where you..." I looked him in the eyes. "Peter, this is where you died."

He looked down at his clenched hands. "I don't remember anything about that."

I wasn't buying his story. Alive or dead, there were always "tells" when someone was lying. First, he wouldn't look me in the eye, and second, his clenched hands conveyed his emotional turmoil. He wasn't being honest with me—or himself.

"Peter," I said.

He didn't reply, but ask anyone, I am stubborn. I closed my eyes and pictured making contact with Peter. "Peter," I said softly.

Focusing my mind and energy on Peter's hand, I placed mine over his, willing myself to make physical contact. His cool hand was clammy to the touch, but it was there, and I squeezed it. I opened my eyes and repeated, "Peter."

He looked up at me.

"Peter," I began. "An earthbound spirit is a human spirit that hasn't properly passed over. They haven't gone on to the next level or into the light, heaven, whatever you choose to call it. They remain behind, here on earth, and are responsible for many ghost sightings and haunted places. Peter, you are an earthbound spirit."

He nodded.

"Once our bodies die, we are still there. Our spirits last forever, and our spirit is what makes us who we are. That spirit can become trapped in a certain area—or structure. Like a school."

Peter held my gaze, but he still wrung his hands beneath mine. I knew why he was stuck at our school, and it was time he knew as well.

"Suicide can trap a spirit here and prevent them from moving on. These spirits are lost from all the others. Their misery, pain and torment can be a strong emotional anchor to this realm. They may also fear judgment and refuse to enter the light for their fear of Hell."

His eyes narrowed as his dark eyes pierced mine.

"Peter, I'm not judging you for killing yourself, but you need to own up to it. The first step in any recovery is to admit what you have done."

"I..." His eyes told the story of a tortured soul. He looked down and nodded. He whispered, "I felt so hopeless. So utterly hopeless. And no one understood."

I nodded. "We've come a long way in our understanding of depression. It's way more common than you might think. It may not seem like it at the time, but the feeling of hopelessness won't last. It's a minor blip on the road of life. Life is a series of peaks and valleys. A year down the road, most of us would be looking back down at that valley and wondering what the big deal was."

Peter glanced around the stairwell. "So, I'm trapped forever? Doomed here for eternity because I took my own life?"

I shook my head. "You are only trapped in your mind. You shouldn't be afraid to move on. Forget your fear of judgment. There are far better things ahead for you. The light will bring you sensational peace, love, happiness and comfort. And you'll reunite with your loved ones who are waiting for you to join them."

"The light..." Peter's face had a new expression that he hadn't shown before. It was hope.

In my zone now, I squeezed his hand and felt a warmth that I hadn't felt from him before. Getting to my feet, I pulled him up. I looked into his eyes. "Peter, the light is here for you. This light is love and forgiveness. Do you see it?"

Peter's face beamed, a broad smile livening up his face. Tears rolled down his cheeks. "It's beautiful." His voice choked with emotion.

I don't know how I could see it too, but I could. An impossibly bright light shone with beams streaming outward. The light was warm and accepting. Four figures waited at the edge of the light. Two adult figures and two smaller ones, both girls.

"Your family is here to bring you across. They miss you very much."

"Father, Mother," he said. "Elise. Jen." His body was trembling.

I let go of his hand. "Go. Go to the light. Go to your family." My face felt the warmth of the light, and I couldn't help but cry. The feeling was indescribable as he took a tentative step toward the light. With a glance over his shoulder, he smiled at me and I saw the joy on his face. His peace washed over me as well. "I love you, Peter. I'll see you again."

No longer holding back, Peter raced toward the light. In a heartbeat, he embraced his family. Happily reunited, they were pulled into the brightness, moving from our world into the next.

The Cure's "Just like Heaven" picked that moment to come to mind. The eighties were always going to be my soundtrack and its music would always help me understand the craziness that was my life. I hoped Peter would find his happiness in his new, improved home.

The light gone, I was left standing alone in the dark stairwell. No worries, though. Seeing what was waiting for us changed a person. How could it not? Even though goosebumps covered my arms, a warm feeling soaked deep into my soul. I smiled as I headed down the stairs toward home. The school would be empty for hours before the sleep deprived herd returned to socialize, learn and carry on with life. Happily, I could finally get back to a normal life—such as it was.

I jumped down the last three steps and laughed. I was never going to be normal, and I was okay with that. Being the ghost girl was a good thing. A very good thing.

ACKNOWLEDGMENTS

I can't imagine the pressure that award show winners are under to remember everyone to thank, be interesting and say it all coherently. And to do it all without a keyboard in front of you. Madness.

There are times that characters virtually write themselves—making my life easier. But in this case, my character Abbey wanted to write the acknowledgements:

Hiya, Abbey here. First, a big congratulations on finishing this book. Now go post a review. Allan swears it's not an ego thing, but it's important in getting this book noticed and finding a wider audience. I'll wait here until you're back.

Thank you for that honest review and hope you spelled my name right. On to the thanks yous.

It may sound self-serving, but I really need to thank the real-life Abbey for being born. I wouldn't be here without you.

A shoutout to the U17 Mahtomedi girls that my team was based on: Greta Berger, Sabrina DuMond, Haily Fechter, Jasmine Herne, Mary Beth Huyer, Ryan Imsdahl, Kelly Kirkland Nelson, Lexis Lowell, Sahvannah Markovich, Julia McKay, Lyndsay Praml, Jessica Sparrow, Sophie Strandquist, Christina Teufert, Fran Weess, and Paige Welsh. You guys rock.

I know Allan really wanted to thank everyone at Immortal Works Press. This small, but scrappy publisher puts out some amazing literary works. And this book. Specifically, he mentioned his editor, John M. Olsen for getting all those words into the right places. Staci Olsen for taking a chance on Allan in the first place, as well as her legendary layout skills. Creative Manager, Ashley Literski for her, well, creative managing (and brilliant cover design). Chief Editor

Holli Anderson for being chief. And Publisher Jason King for sending over that million dollar contract in the first place. I'm happy to report that Allan is dressing better these days.

Allan's family is important to him and he wants everyone to know that novels don't just happen. Having a family of loved ones behind him, supporting and listening (and humoring him), is the secret to his success. Thank you, Jen, as well as Abbey, Andrew, Ben, Cade, Dan and Suzanna. Also, thanks to his mother Eleanor and brother Mark.

Other people he'd like to thank (honestly, this guy won't stop talking) include the coaching family and players of the St. Croix Soccer Club. Local bookstores near him such as Lake Country Booksellers in White Bear Lake and Valley Booksellers in Stillwater. Author John Sandford and his Prey series for motivating Allan to write in the first place. His fellow Immortal Works authors. And the friends who inspire many of this book's characters.

Okay, he's done.

I have just one important thank you of my own: Thanks to all the ghosts. That shit is real.

Abbey (for Allan)

ABOUT THE AUTHOR

Author Allan Evans has been finding writing success of late. His debut novel, Abnormally Abbey (the first book in this series) published in fall of 2020. A short story, Silent Night, was in the Haunted Yuletide anthology (December 2020) and a serial killer thriller set in the Twin Cities, Killer Blonde, published in 2021.

Son of famed Twin Cities jazz musician Doc Evans, Evans has been writing advertising and marketing for nearly two decades. A soccer coach, you can often find him on the field teaching kids about soccer and life. Evans lives the Twin Cities.